I0598798

Death's Talisman

Book Two of the
Lady of Death

J.F. Posthumus

Credits:
Death's Talisman was written by J. F. Posthumus
Cover art by J. F. Posthumus

Death's Talisman by: J. F. Posthumus, 1st edition, New Mythology Press 2019
Death's Talisman by J. F. Posthumus, 2nd edition, Three Ravens Publishing 2020
Trade Paperback ISBN: 978-1-951768-13-3

To the Dragon, the Incubus, the Imp, and the drow terror twins—the Ifrit and Werewolf. May the world survive you all.

Acknowledgements

Thanks to everyone who made this possible

Chapter One

A tiny crack appeared in the shell of the egg. The fissure skittered down the shell in a ragged line. The egg, storm-cloud gray with swirls of silvery blue, looked like an eerie sky, the thin break resembling a lightning bolt. The air in the room, and the entire house, grew thick with anticipation and Magick.

Anyone with the slightest amount of Magickal ability knew there was power in life and death. As a necromancer with centuries of knowledge and a considerable amount of skill, I had first-hand experience with the power of death. I was keenly aware that the longer-lived and energetic the creature or being, the greater the power. It was something scholars throughout the ages had argued against, but that made it no less true.

Like many beings, I had an ex to thank for my current situation. Nick had been a minor dabbler in the Art, but mostly he used whatever he could to benefit his lust for attention, mortal power, and wealth. After Nick had been stripped of his Magick, I was informed that most of his income had been accumulated through his illegal business of buying or capturing rare Magickal creatures and selling them to the highest bidder. A hatching dragon egg had bound itself to me when I rescued it from that fate.

It seemed my penchant for rescuing helpless creatures had finally decided to bite me. Not literally. Not yet. Not only did I have no clue how to care for a newly hatched dragon, I had an ancient, grumpy, and extremely dominant undead one encased in a skull. I'd been beyond nervous and anxious when I revealed the egg to Maekyl, my undead dragon, but my fear had been for naught.

Maekyl was protective of the unborn, instructing me in the best methods for caring for the egg and the eventual hatchling. He even told me where to find the proper spells for capturing the Magick the hatching would create.

Waste not, want not.

The same, however, did not apply to my relationship with my current lover. Fergus Sterling was overprotective and determined to keep me from furthering my necromantic studies. Or, for that matter, any Magickal study of which he didn't approve. For the next eight or so months, I wouldn't be casting any necromantic spells, but that didn't mean I couldn't peruse the best tomes and further my Magickal knowledge in other areas. Sterling, however, being one of the Ancient Powers, didn't agree. He insisted that doing little to no Magick would be in the best interests of the unborn child. We had had no lack of arguments, which had amused the hell out of Maekyl and caused an increase in my blood pressure and a shortening of my temper.

At least the arrogant lout wasn't around to prevent me from casting the spell to safely capture the excess Magick generated by the hatching of the dragon egg.

I sat on the sofa, watching the color of the egg shift and swirl as the dragon inside slowly worked its way free. The skull containing Maekyl, captured by my father centuries before I was born, faced the hatching egg. The skull's eye sockets glittered with eagerness and anticipation.

Kharzsa, the nabrasu cub gifted to me by the owners of the Fellhaven tavern, was stretched out on the sofa behind me, tails twitching. Maekyl had been giddy when I acquired a nabrasu to eat negative energy and release positive. The female cub had quickly settled in and made herself at home. Kharzsa was a breed found in a savannah-like area of another realm. Her cheetah coloring allowed her to blend into her surroundings, and her foxlike ears gave her above-average hearing. Maekyl's insight on the creatures made me wonder how he knew so much about them. So far, I had resisted the urge to ask.

"Catherine?" a voice called from the upper levels of my house.

The glowing light in the empty sockets of the skull shifted from the hatching egg to me. No laughter danced within their depths. Not this time.

"It figures he would show up at this moment. He isn't going to be happy," Maekyl said, stating the obvious.

Shrugging, I gave the hatching egg my undivided attention. "Too bad for him. He's not my keeper, and I've broken no laws."

Maekyl chortled. "You've never had a keeper, child. It is common knowledge the job would be too hazardous for even the most foolish to undertake."

I tried glowering at Maekyl. Really. But considering the truth of his words and my snort of laughter, I failed.

The steps on the stairs echoed around the quiet basement where Maekyl, Kharzsa, and I were seated. It was the safest place for the egg to hatch, and it happened to be where I did all my Magick. The lower level had been built by dwarves and would withstand anything short of a volcano. The workers had built it as payment after I'd helped them remove a few nasty undead creatures from their tunnels. They had been extremely apologetic about not being able to ensure the basement's survival against an erupting volcano, even though such requirements were outside their skill set.

Standing, I turned to face Sterling as he descended the stairs. He was handsome, and his movements were smooth and elegant. His brown hair was immaculately groomed, and there wasn't a piece of clothing that didn't fall perfectly over a body that could have graced the cover of a men's fitness magazine. He was perfect from head to toe.

His brown eyes typically twinkled and danced with mischief and mirth. Though, it seemed lately, that laughter had given way to solemn broodiness. I missed the laughter and sly smiles we shared after he hired me to find the legendary Eye of Amon a mere six weeks ago.

Perhaps it had to do with the fact that I was pregnant with his child? As far as I knew, every child he had ever fathered was dead, either by his hand or someone else's.

His face was unreadable as he paused at the bottom of the staircase. He inhaled deeply before meeting my eyes and holding them.

"What are you doing?" he asked in a far-too-quiet voice.

Delightful. He was in a mood again.

I turned away from him and settled back on the sofa. If I had considered him an enemy, or even a nebulous ally, I would never have done that. So, I let him see my back. Lover, behold my powerplay.

"Watching my egg hatch," I replied in a casual tone. If I allowed my temper to flare, there would be another argument. Kharzsa purred behind me, and I reached up to scratch her behind her ears.

There was a definite pause, and the tension in the room fell significantly. My little pet was doing her job, taking in negative energy and producing positive. Glancing over my shoulder toward Sterling, I noticed a stunned expression flash across his features before a look of curiosity replaced it.

Turning back to the egg, I watched as more cracks broke the surface and a tiny hole appeared. Maekyl scooted forward eagerly, his attention on nothing but the egg.

"My apologies," Sterling said as he neared the sofa. "I thought—"

"You thought I was doing some spell that a woman in my 'delicate condition' shouldn't be doing." I finished for him. "How could a woman of any power possibly do Magick of any sort while pregnant? It isn't as though I'm half Fae or anything."

From the corner of my eye, I caught Sterling flinching, and I hid the satisfied smile that threatened to form.

He sighed. "Have I been that bad?" he asked before pressing a kiss upon my head.

Maekyl snorted. "Worse, actually." He paused, then added in a faux-thoughtful tone, "Then again, this is the first time someone with considerable power has been mother to any child of your blood. Perhaps you're simply afraid, as most human males are when their women are in such 'delicate' conditions. It's a lack of knowledge about how to behave, or some nonsense akin to it."

Sterling glowered at the skull. Maekyl, not about to give him any satisfaction, returned to ignoring everything but the egg.

Holding his gaze on Maekyl, Sterling said, "Don't forget we have a dinner date at Fellhaven at seven tonight."

"I'm not sure I should leave if it hasn't hatched by then," I said slowly.

"Don't worry, Cat," Maekyl said cheerfully. "It's only two in the afternoon. The little darling will hatch soon." He pivoted his vessel to face me, his gaze studying me intently. "Can't you tell by the Magick in the air?"

I blinked a few times at the skull before drawing a breath and testing the Magick in the room. As soon as I did, it began enveloping me in a heady embrace. It was considerably different from, yet similar to, death Magick. I was surprised that I read this Magick as easily as I did that caused by death.

Each time I killed in a ceremony, the Magick built up to an apex, then swirled down around me, allowing me to form it into whatever I desired. This Magick was doing the same, if not slower, though the power was greater than any a mortal creature had ever created.

There had only been one time previously when Magick had been this strong. I turned to look at the counter where a large crystal pulsed with the Magick it held captive. Hopefully, it would be large enough.

"I can tell now," I said, turning back to the skull. "Brings back some interesting memories."

Maekyl chuckled. "I'm sure. Don't worry. It will be enough."

"What will be enough?" Sterling demanded.

Maekyl and I ignored him. If I answered, yet another argument would ensue.

The Magick was growing, and the egg was starting to shake. I moved the egg to the sofa so it wouldn't roll onto the floor. Maekyl slid across the coffee table so he could see better.

Sterling sighed, moved around the sofa, and perched on the arm of a chair. His gaze, however, was not on the egg. It remained fixed on me, and I wasn't certain I wanted to know what he was thinking.

The tiny hole grew larger, and the pale white of an egg tooth, the little beak used to break through shells, appeared for a brief moment before vanishing. It was replaced by a round, gleaming eye that peered through the hole. The eye closed, opened, then closed again as the shell stopped quivering.

This pause wasn't unexpected. Hatching was difficult for any creature, whether it was a bird or reptile, or the oddball mammal. There are two types of mammals that lay eggs. The echidnas and the platypus. Odd fact, even trolls won't eat echidna eggs. Ah, the things your mind kicks up when you're pregnant.

I wouldn't start worrying until Maekyl began fretting. He was, after all, wiser in all things dragon than me.

The Magick in the air thickened and became palpable, even before the egg began shivering and shaking again. I found myself leaning forward, my eyes glued to the egg. There was a part of me that wanted to revel in the Magick that was filling the room. It was tantalizing and pure, unlike anything I'd experienced. At least not of this magnitude. That, however, was going to have to take a backseat to the egg. It now had large cracks in the shell and the jagged hole was growing larger.

A hand slid into mine, and I glanced down and found Sterling holding my hand. He gave it a quick squeeze before letting go. Smiling, I turned back to the egg and the imminent hatchling.

There was no question when the baby finished breaking through the shell, officially 'hatching;' the power in the room hit a crescendo. It filled me with a warmth and headiness that made me wonder if that was what inebriation was like.

A large portion of the shell broke away, revealing the shimmering scales of the tiny drake.

Tiny, being a comparative word, since it was the size of a six-month old cat. The little hatchling squeaked once before the egg fell on its side. The drake squawked indignantly, and the power of the room created a swirl of hot air, causing my hair to sway in the resulting breeze.

Sparks danced in the air and there was a hint of ozone, akin to what one would smell after a lightning strike. I wasn't certain if it was from the Magick created by the hatching or if the little dragon had something to do with it.

I heard a sizzling sound, and the shell cracked and fell from around the hatchling. The little dragon lifted its silvery head, gave a sleepy smile, and promptly curled up on the sofa amidst the broken shell pieces.

The Magick went from feeling like a force of nature to a warm blanket drifting down to lay warmly against my skin. I glanced at Sterling, who was staring at the dragon. I couldn't decipher the expression on his face, but the origin of the aura around Maekyl was obvious. The undead dragon was beaming as though he were a proud father. Impossible, all things considered, but that did nothing to stop the glee dancing in the ornate skull's glowing orbs.

I picked up a piece of the shell. The silvery blue shifted colors as the light played against the surface. It was far thicker than I imagined and felt somewhere between leather and a bird eggshell, though there was no give to the surface.

As the Magick faded from the room, Sterling reached over to help clean up the broken shell. Or, he would have helped if the newly hatched dragon hadn't woken up and snapped at his hand. Sterling jerked back, and Maekyl's teeth clacked together in a mockery of laughter.

"Best let Cat take care of that," Maekyl said with a smirk. "Even hatchlings are protective, and the little ones have a nasty bite. Just a moment; forget I said that. Carry on."

Sterling narrowed his gaze at the tiny baby, which looked up at him with blue eyes that glittered with tiny sparks of silver. It yawned widely, stood on wobbly legs, and floundered toward my leg. Curling back up into a tight little ball of scales, its tail tucked around its nose and filmy wings curled inward, it appeared to fall asleep.

I looked over at my lover, and chuckled. "You two are going to have to come to an agreement."

"Tell that to the hatchling," Sterling muttered.

The dragon snorted, opened a single eye for a brief moment, then closed it again with another snort. Apparently, she had other ideas.

Chapter Two

Fellhaven Tavern was a favored eatery for anyone and everyone in the Magickal community. Located in Waynesboro, Virginia, it was owned and operated by a husband and wife duo. The wife happened to be an elf, knowledgeable in the arcane. As far as couples went, they were an unlikely pair, yet the perfect couple. They loved each other dearly, had several children, and probably had epic arguments. They were also incredible businesspeople who kept Fellhaven open and thriving while many other bars and eateries faltered and failed.

Personally, I loved the place. They boasted a stage, and live bands played frequently. Karaoke was only for those who could actually hold a tune. Otherwise, being booed off stage was the best you could hope for since the only thing forbidden inside on those nights was conventional weaponry. Food, chairs, glasses, makeshift missiles created by nearby objects? They'd all been hurled at that stage. I'd been there for a couple of their karaoke nights. I may also have been a part of the mischief and mayhem on those occasions.

Tonight, though, I was nervous and uneasy. Sterling had invited the Speaker of the Council and an old family friend, Dyrmith, to dine with us at Fellhaven. I didn't mind Dyrmith, who happened to be a dragon, since he was a frequent visitor at my mother's court. Hopefully, he wouldn't chide me for not visiting my mother, a fairy queen with her own kingdom in the fae realm.

The Speaker was an ancient elf, as well as the voice of the Council, the group which oversaw All-Things-Magickal. She spoke the decrees and judgements the Council made, the laws decided, and the verdict of anything the Council ruled upon. She was not, in fact, the head of the council. From my understanding, the members all had an equal say and voted amongst themselves in a democratic way.

I doubted the dinner was simply a meeting of the minds amid delicious food and drink. So, when we entered Fellhaven and were escorted to one of the private dining rooms, I wasn't disappointed to find the table set and the elf and dragon already talking quietly to each other. Our hostess left us after we were seated, promising a server would be there momentarily to take our orders for our preferred beverages, and when we were ready, our meals.

Our arrival disturbed the room's atmosphere, as evidenced by the complete silence at our table that stretched longer than my patience allowed.

After the server took our orders, I broke the silence. "What is this about?"

Dyrmith smiled slyly as he lifted a glass of water to his lips. Over the rim, he asked, "Have you spoken to your parents recently?"

That was a dangerous question. I prefer to keep my private life private. However, my parents were also members of the Council, so maybe the question was innocuous. Doubtful, but one could always hope.

"I talked to Dad last week. He called to ask how I was doing and whether I was planning on visiting Mom during the Winter Solstice," I replied.

"Your mother mentioned you haven't visited her recently," the Speaker stated. A single, perfect brow rose in question. "It seems the last time she saw you was during the judgement against Nicolai Wright."

"So, this is an intervention?" I asked, lacing my hands together in front of me. "My mother requested you speak to me about my visiting her?"

The Speaker smirked as Dyrmith chuckled. Sterling looked studiously at the dining ware before him. I suspected he had more to do with the current question than anyone else.

"I see." There was no way I could be angry at the Speaker or Dyrmith. Sterling, however, was another story. He could have mentioned this before now. "There are extenuating circumstances which have kept me from visiting Mom."

"We know," the Speaker and Dyrmith said simultaneously. They looked at each other and shared similar smiles.

"We are aware of what has transpired," Dyrmith said, the smile on his lips meeting his eyes. "The Speaker, Sterling, and I have not informed your parents. That is for you to do. Your mother, however, is rather insistent you come visit."

That didn't sound good. When Mother became imperious, she did drastic things. "How insistent?" I asked cautiously.

"She hasn't sent a formal decree," Dyrmith retorted with a chuckle, "though I suspect that has more to do with someone mentioning the thinning of the veils between the realms."

The dragon winked at me.

"Thank you, Dyrmith," I said with a sigh of relief. I owed him one. I paused before latching onto a more important fact. "What about the veils thinning?"

"They have been growing weaker between the realms. It's allowing all sorts of things to cross over from the regions of Heaven, Hell, and the other realms." Sadness marred the Speaker's voice as she answered my question. "It would actually be a good time to visit your mother's realm, all things considered, dear."

My gaze slid from her to Sterling. For some reason, he hadn't seen fit to mention any of this to me. I wasn't certain if it was because he was being overly protective or if there was some other reason.

"But those aren't the reasons we requested this dinner," the Speaker stated, her voice becoming more proper and formal. I turned my attention back to her and noticed she was sitting straighter. "Have you given thought to our request?"

I blinked a few times, trying to remember what request she was referring to, then it dawned on me. The request about my becoming a member of the Council.

"I'm still considering it." Before any of them could speak, I added, "It's an honor to be put on retainer by the Council as a Retriever and Appraiser, but I'm not entirely certain I want to be beholden to the Council. It might cause conflicts with my other work."

Dyrmith smirked as the Speaker waved a hand dismissively. "There is no reason for you to be part of the mortals' world. Even associating with blooders and werewolves is below your station."

I drew a breath and let it out slowly, trying to keep a lid on my temper. Not once had my parents ever tried to tell me who I could or couldn't associate with, and they had more right than anyone else to do so.

Sterling placed his hand over mine and squeezed my fingers. I glanced at him sharply.

"Catherine has always been her own person, ruled by no one but herself," he said smoothly. Lifting his glass of water to his lips, he added, "It is for her to choose whether she wishes to be in our employ."

As he took a sip from his glass, I stared at him for a few moments. His comment was something I hadn't expected. Such consideration, blended with understanding, reminded me of the first week of our relationship. Truthfully, it reminded me of almost every moment we'd had together, prior to the discovery that I was pregnant with his child.

The affection in his eyes was too much, and I looked away from him. It was far safer to turn my attention to the room than to continue staring at him with a lovelorn expression on my face. Thankfully, the framed artwork on the wall drew my attention.

Today's selection consisted of photographs of the local skyline and cityscapes taken in the fall and spring. I suspected they were taken by the owners of Fellhaven, or perhaps one of their friends. Mark and Jen were ardent supporters of local artists and businesses.

My companions sat in tense silence. A server brought a couple of baskets of breadsticks,

"Have you considered other career paths, Catherine?" Dyrmith asked easily as he broke off a piece of breadstick. Dipping it into the flavored oil on the table, he smiled at me with twinkling eyes. "The business of a necromancer has dwindled over the centuries. The belief in Magick has dwindled, and with it, the profession of a witch. Surely you have considered the possibility that your current position, and job, will vanish in time."

"Everything dies, eventually," I said, meeting his gaze. "But there is also life. Where one thing dies, something else begins. Eventually, I will be required to rule my mother's realm. Until then, I prefer to embrace my skills and offer my services to the Magickal community."

"And your association with mundanes?" There was no mistaking the derision in the Speaker's voice as she questioned me.

"I will keep my position until I tire of it," I replied, smiling slightly. "I will also keep in contact with mundanes."

Her reply was interrupted by the door as it banged open. Just inside the frame stood Nic Wright, my ex-boyfriend. His eyes were wild as he stormed into the room, his gaze sweeping over everyone until it landed on me.

"Whore!" he yelled, his eyes bright, his expression crazed. "Lying bitch!"

I tipped my head to the side, not bothered by the slur. I'd been called far worse in my centuries of life.

Nic looked horrible, but I had little time to consider his sallow, sunken eyes and horrendous weight loss before he whipped out a large semi-automatic pistol and leveled it at me.

He waved the gun wildly as he yelled, "Go to hell, you whoring bitch!"

With those words, gunfire echoed throughout the room. A few screams blended with the shots. I threw up my hands, desperately hoping to form a shield to prevent my death or injury.

I heard the unmistakable sound of something splattering against the walls and furniture. I couldn't see anything around me, but then I realized the blackness was that my eyes were closed. I felt Magick filling the room, pressing against me. Some was from what had caused Nic to be splattered against everything. The rest was from the deaths that had occurred in the last minute or two.

The death-born Magick swirled around me, caressing my skin with a lover's touch. Dark and seductive, I wished I could collect it in my hands and feed it into a crystal or some other item. There was something faintly familiar about it, but I couldn't figure out what, so I let it go.

I looked at the still form of the elf who had once been the Speaker of the Council, and I drew a breath, then let it out slowly. I turned my gaze to Dyrmith, who was staring at me.

Oddly, there wasn't a lot of screaming or crying or shouting. In fact, the room was strangely silent. Tearing my eyes away from the dragon, I saw the solemn eyes of the other patrons staring at me.

Death was an old friend. I'd not only seen murder; I had dealt it. This, though, was unsettling. Decades had passed since so many people had stared at me after someone had been killed. When I'd committed murder, guilt and confusion didn't well up in me. Probably because I acted with intent, or didn't care about the departed, but I digress.

Creepy didn't begin to cover this situation.

Chapter Three

After several seconds of silence and complete stillness, there was a flurry of activity. The other patrons departed their tables to converge on ours or vanish out the door. A couple went to the splatter that was—or rather had been—Nickolai Wright.

I was back to contemplating the best method for capturing the uncontained Magick that was quickly dwindling when Jen swept into the room like a pissed off hurricane. Mark was just behind her, not looking any happier than his wife. I had to hide my smile at how smoothly they moved together.

They paused briefly before they converged on the table and the splatter.

"Move."

It was the only word Mark spoke, but every person who hadn't been part of my table backed up until they were several feet away from the proprietors and the table with the now-dead Speaker. Jen didn't bother checking the Speaker's pulse.

"Sterling, can she be resurrected?" Jen asked without pause.

It was Dyrmith who responded. "No, Lady. The Speaker was one of the oldest beings, and by her own decree, she cannot be brought back, even if we all gathered our power and tried."

"Damn." There was nothing but regret in her voice. "Next of kin?"

Sterling snorted. Jen met his glower with a deceptively bland expression. She lifted a single brow slowly.

"Someone is going to need to claim the body. Who should one contact to inquire about such a thing?" she asked.

"This is not the time for such remarks," Sterling growled.

A smirk pulled at Jen's lips as she looked around the body. I couldn't help but chuckle. When Sterling glowered at me, I smiled sweetly.

"It's a valid question," I stated before turning to Jen. "What are you looking for?"

"The casings," she stated before taking a step back. In the next breath, her hands began moving in an intricate dance of spell weaving that wasn't familiar. It made me wonder where she learned the Craft. And from whom.

As she drew the Magick to her and shaped it, Mark moved away from the mess that had been my ex-boyfriend and began conferring with Dyrmith. Everyone else had converged in the farthest corner and were talking quietly amongst themselves.

The completion of the spell brought forth the spent shell casings and the bullets that were not embedded in a corpse.

"It appears that trying to resurrect the Speaker would have been fruitless, even if she had not already seen to it," Sterling stated, grabbing the floating, jet-black items from the air. He held them up, inches from my face. I narrowed my eyes at the jerk as he continued, "Obsidian. Only one being can create obsidian weapons. The same being who would dream of dealing with worthless beings such as he." Sterling jerked his head toward the goo. "And you thought he was an ally."

"Impossible." The word came out sharp and biting. I wasn't in a forgiving mood, nor was I in the mood to allow anyone to tell me who could or couldn't be my associates or friends. Or allies. "Magick does not work on true obsidian weapons."

Sterling's features grew darker, and an unseen wind ruffled his hair. If we'd been outside, I suspected dark clouds would be billowing and threatening a downpour of rain, hail, thunder and lightning. Perhaps a meteor or twelve.

"How would you know that?" he managed to ask between barely parted lips. I could hear his teeth grinding.

Sterling, I might add, is uber powerful. I had debates with my undead dragon leiche about who could possibly be more powerful than Sterling. So far, the list only included one other being, and he didn't even live in my realm. That being, an Elvin warlord necromancer of incredible power, authority, and wealth, also happened to be the being who had cornered the obsidian weaponry market. Not just in selling them, but in crafting them as well. In fact, they weren't created in my realm. Xantos Zaurahel, the dark elf warlord and necromancer, oversaw their creation in his realm.

As such, they weren't common. Anyone who wanted one of the weapons had to go through Xantos to obtain it or take it from someone who owned one. From what Maekyl told me, it was easier to steal from hungry dragons than Xantos or anyone who had an obsidian weapon. I didn't doubt Maekyl.

"You do remember that Xantos gifted me a pair of obsidian scythes?" I said, turning my flighty attention back to the problem at hand.

Sterling growled, which I took as an affirmative.

"If I didn't test every form of Magick I could against the substance, extensively and to the best of my abilities, I wouldn't be a good Magick user. I can definitely say, for certain and without doubt, that Magick does not work against an obsidian weapon. Magick dies upon contact, and the skin of anyone with even a slight propensity towards Magick will burn upon contact with true obsidian weaponry."

Sterling's hair became more ruffled, and I was starting to wonder how dark the outside sky was going to get if he didn't calm down.

"You...I thought you agreed not to do any...great Magick while you are—" he began.

I heard a loud crack that sounded like a lightning striking. Sterling stopped looming over me long enough to turn his head toward the sound. I took the opportunity to take a step back.

"Now that I have your attention," Jen stated reasonably, "please calm down and shut up."

Sterling's face grew darker, and between blinks, Jen drew her obsidian dagger and lightly began tapping it against her palm. I tipped my head to one side, curious as to how the obsidian wasn't adversely affecting Jen since she could cast Magick.

Jen gave him a not-so-pleasant smile. "I would not be pleased if I had to give you a physical demonstration of the unique properties of one of these weapons."

Mark stepped behind and to the side of his wife. "You aren't jealous of the old man, are you, Sterling?" Mark asked, a smirk pulling at his lips. "If you aren't prepared to accept Catherine as she is, and accept the fact that Xantos, for all his faults and annoyances, is someone anyone with a brain would want to learn from, you might as well break off whatever you have with her."

The lightbulb finally clicked on. That was what he was so pissed about! Sterling didn't like Xantos, so he didn't want me around him. Xantos was unpredictable and dangerous, as well as a powerful force. That I found the dark elf appealing on every level probably didn't help.

"I'll bet you've been allowing him to visit his old nemesis, too," Jen mused thoughtfully. I shrugged. She and Mark chuckled. "Yeah, I figured. Since he's been visiting us more, I knew there had to be an ulterior motive, and that dragon skull of yours is almost as infamous as you are, Cat."

Sterling's expression froze. He closed his eyes and took a deep breath before letting it out slowly. The wind slowed, then ceased. I shot Mark and Jen a thankful smile.

"My apologies for allowing my temper to overcome my judgement," Sterling said in his usual, suave voice. He opened his eyes and looked at the owners, who were watching him with amused expressions. "I had not realized Xantos was such a frequent…guest."

Wrapping an arm around Jen, Mark pulled her back against him and kissed the top of her head. "It's understandable. Jen was just as bad, if not worse."

"Was not," Jen muttered, though the amusement in her eyes spoke volumes.

With a laugh, Mark released his wife and fished a phone out of his pocket. "I'll call Raz and let him know what happened. I doubt he'll want an official investigation, all things considered, but I'd rather not have to face his temper, on top of this mess."

Jen rolled her eyes. The dagger vanished, and she moved toward the audience in the corner. I was fairly certain Sterling had forgotten about them.

Sterling chuckled and shook his head slightly, as though trying to clear the cobwebs from his thoughts. He met my gaze and said, "I am sorry, Cat. I don't trust Xantos. He rarely, if ever, does anything benevolent without an ulterior motive. I…am concerned and worried about why he has taken such a keen interest in you and a renewed one in Maekyl."

"Apology accepted," I replied with a smile. "Don't worry. I feel the same way about him, but that doesn't mean I don't want to learn whatever he wants to teach."

I was about to add something witty, but the little dragon hatchling I thought we'd left at home picked that moment to pop its head out of my purse and flounder its way to my shoulder. The purse had been under the table, and I suspected the hatchling had snuck inside before we left home.

Apparently, the young one had other ideas. It didn't seem to want to forgive Sterling, because it hissed at him and little sparks danced down its spine and along its wings. If it hadn't been so cute, I might have considered it threatening.

Jen and Mark looked up from what they were doing, then glanced at each other. Jen giggled. Mark shrugged and placed the phone he had been talking on against his chest.

"Okay, we serve her kind, as well. Someone tell the kitchen staff to bring a plate of raw meat."

Chapter Four

The dragon hatchling, which I had decided I would name Arylla, sat in the middle of a nearby table. She was happily chomping through the raw buffalo, deer, chicken, and gods knew what else Fellhaven's kitchen staff had brought out. Jen, having finished with the crowd and damage control, took a seat at the table and cooed at the hatchling. The little one had no objection to Jen stroking her scales while she ate.

Raziel, better known as the Angel of Mysteries, stood beside the table where we had been seated at. His immaculate appearance was marred by the scowl on his face. Sterling and Mark were talking with him. I had already given my statement to Raz's assistant detectives, and I was sitting with Dyrmith. Watching the hatchling eat, and Jen's obvious delight at being so close to the little critter, was a welcome distraction.

"They won't be putting this one on the police records," Dyrmith observed. "At least, not the whole story."

"How do you know that? Because the victim was the Speaker?" I asked.

"Because of the staff Raz brought with him. They are working with better equipment than any citizen police force currently uses." The dragon nodded at the sleek tablets I hadn't paid much attention to. Both of the detectives that had come with Raz were rapidly typing on them.

"Those are military grade or better," added Dyrmith.

"So, there won't be any filing with the human, uh, mundane police force?"

"There will be a homicide report, with a person using an overpowered handgun or assault rifle to explain the amount of damage," Dyrmith said, obviously not pleased with the scenario. "They care much more for their agendas and fragile trappings of order than for justice or truth."

I took a longer look and opened my senses to the two detectives. Both were dark skinned. One was of African heritage and the other was, I thought, Spanish or Hispanic. They were human looking and in mediocre states of fitness.

My inner sight and heightened sense of smell found two dents in their armor. The suits were rather plain, except they were not of cotton or any other human-made cloth. They were of the chameleon material woven by high elves that shifted to suit the wish of the wearer. And beneath the heavily applied cologne, the faint smell of jasmine, lavender, and a not-quite-from-Earth fragrance lingered.

"The detectives are angels," I whispered aloud in realization. "Angels in disguise. Are they local?"

Dyrmith chuckled.

"They travel all over the state with Raz," he explained. "They appear as officers or detectives for whatever jurisdiction they are in."

"That's a nice setup." I paused, frowning. "I thought Raz was with the Staunton P.D."

Dyrmith smiled slyly, and I noticed his eyes were shining with approval. "It appears some were incorrect in believing you were ignorant of everything occurring around you." He kept his voice whisper-soft as he continued speaking. "Raziel is officially a part of that department, though only he knows why. I have suspicions, but they aren't important at the moment. As an angel with knowledge of the Magickal community, he travels around the state investigating anything that is of a Magickal nature. His 'team' is comprised, largely, of angels."

"I didn't isolate myself," I stated in a hushed, but firm, voice. "Not completely." Dyrmith chuckled, and I grinned cheekily. "It's still a pretty sweet setup."

"Indeed." Dyrmith gave me his complete attention, and his voice grew softer and graver, if that was possible. "You do realize that, with the Speaker's death, it is now far more important for you to accept a seat upon the Council? Maybe even replace the Speaker? It is, perhaps, the easiest job, if not the most visible one."

There was something in his eyes that gave me pause. I wondered if there was something he wasn't telling me, then I realized there was always going to be something he wasn't telling me. He was a dragon, after all. They didn't like to part with anything, especially secrets.

"When do you need a response?" I asked, not entirely certain I wanted a job that put me in the bull's eye for every being who was pissed off at the Council. Though, all things considered, I was probably one of the few people who had a legacy of fear following her around that could do it.

Dyrmith turned his attention to Mark, Sterling, and Raz. "Soon." He didn't look at me as he spoke again. "Catherine, you are absolutely certain that Xantos had nothing to do with what has transpired?"

"Yes," I said without thought. Then I paused and sighed. "I'll ask him to meet with me, and I'll see what he thinks about all of this."

"Please do that." The dragon drew me away a little further, until our soft voices wouldn't be overheard by anyone. He leveled his gaze on me, and I was suddenly worried. "I am not saying this to rush your decision, but perhaps it would be wise for you to visit your mother for a couple of weeks. A fortnight, if you prefer the old term. Think, for a moment, about what has transpired and who was involved."

I took a breath and did as he requested, more because he was acting as a mentor rather than a parental figure. Considering he had occasionally tutored me while I was in my mother's realm, it wasn't a new experience.

As the implications dawned on me, I couldn't stop my eyes from widening, and it took me a moment to snap my jaw shut.

"Nick was stripped of his power by Sterling at the Council's decree. There is no way he could have imbued any Magick into those bullets." I met Dyrmith's steady gaze. "Someone set him up to kill me." I paused, my eyes turning to the trio of men. "Do you think they've figured it out already?"

"I'm certain Sterling and Mark suspect that very thing. Jen can be just as insightful. I do not know about the, ahem, illustrious angel."

"Well. Shit." I sighed. "I was really hoping I could put off telling Mom a while longer. She is not going to be happy."

Dyrmith patted my shoulder. There was great mirth in his voice when he spoke again. "Don't worry, dear. She won't kill you."

That was what I was afraid of.

Once Raziel finished talking, he and his assistants vacated the restaurant. They were quite grouchy. Sterling had also vanished from the room, and everyone who had been there when the disaster struck had decided they, too, had better places to be. Or, at least, they decided to eat somewhere other than the large room we were in. Jen had reluctantly returned to her duties as hostess and co-proprietor. That left me, Dyrmith, and the hatchling to eat in silence.

Sterling returned as dessert was brought in, a chocolate confection featuring a perfectly-baked cake, frosting, ice cream, and fudge. The dessert brought delight and heavenly smells. Sterling seemed to exude concern and worry with every breath and step he took.

Dyrmith rose gracefully from his chair. "Now that you have returned, I will let you two enjoy dessert without me." Leaning down, he kissed my cheek, nodded at Sterling, and departed.

Sterling sank into the chair and stared at the chocolate-on-chocolate-on-chocolate dessert, uncertain whether he wanted to eat some.

"You almost died," he finally said. He wasn't looking at me, and his voice was barely audible. "Catherine, I'm not saying this to start another argument. I think it might be best if you visited your mother until we, that is Raz and I, can figure out who is trying to kill you."

Looking at the chocolate, I decided the best thing to do was eat it. I lifted the fork to my mouth and savored the gooeyness as I chewed. I carefully refilled the fork with more cake, fudge, and ice cream as I finished the mouthful of yumminess.

When I remained silent and didn't appear to be a volcano on the edge of eruption, he continued speaking in that same quiet, soothing voice. "Your mother has complete control over her realm. She's a fairy queen, and her word is law. She kept you safe growing up. I know she can do it again."

There was hope edging his last sentence, and I realized he was truly concerned about me. I also realized he was hopeful that my mother could still protect me and our unborn child. Either that, or he wasn't certain what sort of welcome I would receive.

"We have had a lot of arguments lately, haven't we?" I asked. "Perhaps we should talk about those, then work our way toward my staying with Mom for a while."

Surprisingly, Sterling nodded and took a small bite of cake. Taking it as a sign of agreement, I continued. "I presume you believe I will do something stupid, like overuse Magick? Or even do Magick that would harm our child?"

That was just too weird to say. Probably because I still didn't think I was ready to be a mother. Then, again, who is?

"Yes," Sterling said with a sigh. "You must admit, you do have a propensity for doing rash, one might even say foolish, things. Your history certainly points toward someone who doesn't mind taking risks, regardless of what the possible outcomes might be."

I choked on the bite of cake I'd been eating. I took a sip of soda to help clear my throat. "You wouldn't possibly be talking about that mess with the Eye of Amon? Or my inviting Xantos over to parlay with Maekyl? Or even my wayward youth when I earned the title of Lady of Death and spawned all the tales?"

"Oh, no, Lady," Sterling replied with a smile, his dark eyes twinkling. "I could not possibly be thinking about any of that. I was absolutely referring to you storming off to rescue those poor Magickal creatures, and how you ended up with that darling little cloud dragon, now draped around your neck."

Reaching up, I rubbed Arylla under her chin. She purred and yawned, then returned to purring in her sleep.

"I've always been a sucker for critters," I said dismissively, not bothering to hide the laughter in my voice. It was my turn to sigh. "I concede your point, though please note that I have done nothing to jeopardize my unborn child. May I also point out that both Maekyl and Xantos have been behaving during Xantos' visits? And Maekyl has also been rather protective of me and the formerly-unhatched egg."

Sterling smiled wanly. "Please, Catherine. It has been a very, very long time since I have sired an offspring. The last time…" he trailed off and did something I'd never seen him do before—he shrugged. "I only had one child that grew into adulthood, and he died from natural causes. He did not have a Magickal talent. At all. Every other child, with even a slight gift of Magick, died by my hand or another's for foolish reasons."

That wasn't a surprise. Maekyl had explained about Sterling's former children, without using names or saying a lot. It was mostly "they all died, most of them by him." It wasn't an uncommon story. My mother had a similar story about her children. So far, I was the only one who had survived into adulthood and had lived longer than a century.

When I stopped to consider how my mother behaved toward me, I realized that Sterling may have been over-reacting, but he had an understandable reason. Mom had been overly protective toward me while I grew up in her realm. That had played into why I ended up causing a literal reign of terror during my glory days as the Lady of Death. The fact that I hadn't yet contemplated how best to protect the world from a child that could easily be worse than I was meant I hadn't yet come to terms with the situation.

"You do realize she may want to keep me there forever and a day?" I asked. Sterling snorted, and I shrugged as I took another bite. I let him think about that as I chewed and swallowed. "I don't think she will be too happy with you, either."

Sterling smiled slightly. "I have known your mother for a long time. I doubt she will be that unreasonable."

He obviously didn't know Mom very well if he thought that. But, hey, that was his problem.

"Okay. I'll go visit my mother while you and Raz try to figure things out. But I am not staying there for a long time." Sometimes it was easier to give in. I didn't always do it gracefully, but I was willing to compromise. "I'll go right after I discuss this with Xantos."

The expression on Sterling's face was priceless, and I wanted to laugh. Instead, I concentrated on eating my dessert.

Sometimes I could be an evil person.

Chapter Five

There are two problems when you have to go through a middleman to contact someone powerful.

The first problem is not being able to arrange meetings in what one would consider a suitable place at a suitable time. The other is that Xantos loves throwing beings off balance. Add in an undead black dragon, trapped in a skull, who I rarely take anywhere, and you have the perfect recipe for mischief and embarrassment.

In my case, it was walking into my living room three days after Sterling liquidated Nick to find Xantos Zaurahel, necromancer and warlord, sitting on my recently acquired antique rocking chair as though it were a throne. He was obviously awaiting my appearance, though he didn't give any indication whatsoever about how long he had been sitting there waiting.

Since Maekyl hadn't woken me, I had to presume he was in on whatever Xantos had planned.

Thankfully, this was not an occasion where I was walking about my home in the nude. I was wearing a long nightgown that hugged my figure and a plush, black, fleece robe, tied at the waist with a matching belt. I stopped long enough to blink a few times to make sure I wasn't imagining the ebony-skinned, silver-haired elf.

"Would you like coffee or tea?" I finally asked, deciding Xantos wasn't a figment of my imagination, created by an exhausted brain.

"Elderberry tea would be delightful. You can prepare it while you explain why you had me summoned," Xantos replied in a silken voice that was far too polite and smooth.

I snapped my fingers and gave a faux-regretful shake of my head. "Drats. I knew there was something I forget to pick up from the store."

Xantos waved dismissively, then gestured toward my living room window. On the sill sat an unfamiliar, large, clay pot. A well-tended plant was growing out of the soil, sprouting a plethora of large leaves. It was obvious the plant wasn't from this realm, especially since it bore little resemblance to the elderberry plants that grew on this planet. This elderberry plant was not your normal elderberry shrub. Not even a small, well-trimmed one. It resembled the type of herb you would find in the grocery store produce section. There were no berries and no blooming flowers.

"It's best when harvested fresh," he explained with a smirk.

Biting back a laugh, I tried glowering at him before crossing the room and carefully harvesting the leaves for his tea. Thankfully, the task gave me time to remove the grin from my face so he wouldn't be able to see how much I enjoyed our verbal volleying.

After picking enough leaves, I headed to the kitchen, where I proceeded to make fresh tea for Xantos and me. My mind wandered on what might happen to a member of his staff who erred on such a task. Never before had I been so thankful I knew how to make a proper cup of tea.

"I'm waiting," Xantos prompted.

He could wait a little longer. I remained silent as I finished making the tea and gathered sugar, cream, and spoons onto a tray, along with the teapot and two cups.

Returning to the living room, I levitated the tray and knocked twice on the French provincial coffee table that had been made around 1910. It had floral designs carved into the walnut wood.

"Wakey, wakey, Ahndray," I said, lowering the tray onto the table.

As the table came 'alive,' I sank into the corner of my sofa. The table had been a gift to me from my father. It had originally been a joke between us, probably due to repeated viewings of Disney's Beauty and the Beast.

I poured two cups of tea, added plenty of sugar to mine, and stirred it with a spoon as I leaned back against the cushions. The table trotted over to Xantos and settled into place. The table moved so smoothly, not a drop splashed or spilled. Smiling pleasantly, I took a sip, curled my legs under me, drew a breath, and spoke. "I requested that Maekyl ask for an audience on my behalf due to an incident that occurred several days ago. Did he tell you what happened, or do I need to bore you with the details?"

"Even if he did, I would prefer to hear your account of the event," Xantos countered.

"I was dining with Sterling, Dyrmith, and the Speaker of the Council when Nick came barging in, waving a gun. Do I need to explain what a gun is to you?"

Xantos favored me with a neutral expression and a single word, "No."

"He killed the Speaker, then Sterling liquidated him." I paused and took a sip of my tea. It had a dark, strong, bitter flavor reminiscent of a good coffee with a floral aftertaste. The perfect drink for a pleasant morning conversation about killing people. "The bullets and casings were Magiked to look like obsidian. Nick could not have done it because he was stripped of Magick a couple of months ago."

It takes a great deal to wrinkle Xantos's cool demeanor. My eyes and ears took note of how his teeth ground together just the slightest bit at my words.

"Whoever Nickolai, the miserable worm, was working with wanted to implicate me. At least," he reflected, "they wanted your old man and his party of ambitious pawns to feel as though I could be implicated."

"That did seem to be the thought of the night," I agreed. "That is, until I pointed out that Magick does not affect obsidian. It didn't hurt that Jen backed up my statement." I paused before sighing. "It really is a pity I can't do necromancy. I'm still nebulous about whether or not I should thank you for deactivating my infertility ring."

Xantos smiled before saying, "Time will tell. Now, since you obviously don't consider me a suspect, and I care so very little for the blessings of the self-declared Council, why are we here?"

Meeting Xantos's gaze evenly, I returned the smile. "I would like your thoughts on what happened. I value your opinion, and it isn't as though I can summon Nick's spirit and question it."

"To begin with, you're quite wrong," Xantos said in a droll tone. He took his cup of tea in both hands. "Speaking to the dead and summoning the spirits for information fall into a lovely neutral area and won't affect unborn offspring. And minor uses of necromancy, in this realm, won't put your little dumpling in danger."

Startled, I laughed. I suspected he was being a smartass and wasn't being affectionate with the phrase, but it was funny. There was no doubt in my mind that Maekyl was listening to this conversation and laughing too. Now he would probably refer to my unborn as a 'dumpling' until it was born. And maybe after, too.

"I was taught, incorrectly it would seem, that necromancy was bad for a pregnant woman. That the black Magick used would, to put it rather mildly, be harmful to the unborn," I replied, not bothering to hide my confusion.

He took a long sip of his tea before replying. "In some realms, that would be true. Here, however, Magick's power has faded far too much for there to be a genuine cause for concern. At least on a minor scale." Xantos smiled around the cup as he added, "Unfortunately, doing something delightfully worthy of your namesake, such as raising an undead army? That would almost certainly cause some ill effect."

"It's been years since I did anything as exciting as that," I murmured before taking a sip of my tea. "Since there is no harm to be had, care to join me while I question Nick's remains?"

Nodding, he curled his lips into a genuine smile, one that met his eyes. "Absolutely."

Chapter Six

O ne of the misconceptions people have about Magick is that they believe a circle is required for almost everything. In all honesty, it's only needed for summoning living creatures. Demons and angels require a bit more than a circle, but they're incredibly powerful beings.

Sitting in my living room, sipping tea, with an ancient and powerful necromancer who made me look like a silly schoolgirl? I might have been somewhat self-conscious about what I was going to do. But, hey, why not? I trusted Xantos to not do anything that would harm me or my unborn. He had far better methods for doing that.

I didn't bother placing my cup on the animated French coffee table before the summoning. Instead, I held it as I lounged on my sofa, speaking the proper words. I decided to forgo fancy gestures. As Xantos had done earlier to make the elderberry plant appear on my windowsill, I gestured briefly with my free hand.

Seconds ticked by as the spirit of Nicolai Wright formed in the center of my living room. Appropriately enough, since he had always wanted to be the center of attention, he formed directly in front of my large-screen television. I took another sip of my tea, adding just enough Magick to warm it to my preferred temperature.

"What?" the apparition blurted. He spun around, frantically looking all over the room to try and get oriented. He spotted me, then paused to look at himself.

"This is just great! I'm dead, aren't I? And you've summoned me! It's never enough for you, is it, Cat?" Nick's astral form was, at least in his belief, screaming at me.

I had cast a buffering charm in the room so nothing would be too loud, let alone alarm my neighbors. Xantos was smiling, and I knew I was doing the same. Nick wasn't going to talk about what we were interested in until he finished rambling. Thus, we smiled and waited.

"It's not enough that you take everything from me!" Nick's ghost went on. "Every day it gnawed at me constantly. I know you loved that!" The spirit jabbed a translucent finger at me. "So much, every day, until nothing but hate and revenge woke me in the mornings!"

"Poor, wayward lad, who couldn't sleep until noon anymore," Xantos teased. His voice held just the right amount of parental condescendence to really set Nick off.

Nick started stomping around the living room. Or rather, he tried to. His feet didn't make a sound when they hit the floor. He did sink through the floor a little further with each attempt, and that got me snickering.

"Sure! Go ahead! It's all funny to you!" Nick wailed while trying to remain petulant. "But I finally got motivated to do something about it! I planned to kill you. And you spoiled that for me too! You are so selfish! Killed me on top of it! What a bitch!"

"Nope! That wasn't me," I replied cheerfully. "That was Sterling. Sadly, he wasn't fast enough to prevent the Speaker's death. At least, you were a lousy shot and hit her instead of me."

"The Speaker had it coming! You all had it coming!" he screeched.

"Where did you get the weapon and ammunition?" Xantos cut in. "The false obsidian has been found out, little toad, so your plot has failed in almost every way. A pathetic end to a wasted and petulant existence."

"You didn't summon me," Nick gleefully replied. "I don't have to tell you anything."

Before I could repeat the question and make Nick answer, Xantos shot his left hand out and pointed at Nick's ghost. Immediately, a small portal opened, and two minor demons flew out of it. They latched onto Nick's astral form and began, to my surprise, to munch on Nick's feet. There was no blood, but chunks of both feet began disappearing into the seemingly hungry maws of the demons. Nick shrieked as if he were alive and being eaten by sharks.

"Enjoy your last minutes of existence, in any form, while my little friends consume you. Or, tell me any truth I request. It's your choice," Xantos's said, his voice a contented purr. He reminded me of a pleased feline eating a mouse.

"Every answer you want! I swear it!" Nick screamed.

Xantos nodded, and the demons backed away exactly twelve inches. There were definite chunks, bordered by little tooth marks, missing from what had been Nick's feet. If he had been living, there would have been a lot of blood. Since he was already dead, it just looked eerie.

"The gun was loaned to me, under the condition that I fire every one of the special bullets when I went after Cat." Nick's voice was raw with hate and some version of pain. I didn't understand how he could feel pain, since his nervous system was gone, but whatever. He continued. "Didn't matter if I put them all in Cat or killed any of the Council members. To me, it was a win-win situation."

"The weapon was loaned to you?" I interjected. "You were expected to give it back? How did you know there would be Council members present when you came after me?"

"Yeah, I was supposed to give it back when it was all over. Didn't matter to me. As long as I got to pay you back, I was up for whatever conditions the priestess laid out."

"Priestess?" Xantos and I asked together.

"That's what she calls herself. Her email is highelfpriestess667@gmail.com," Nick explained with a dismissive tone. "For all I knew, she was an old, sweaty, fat guy who catfished those who didn't give him favors. Never met in person or video chatted."

He began to pace, except that he was missing half of each foot and was hovering six inches above the ground. Neither Xantos nor I said anything. The demons floated behind him like bodyguards or wranglers.

"I spent months researching how to kill a witch from a safe distance. Unfortunately, there really isn't such a thing as a safe distance from a powerful witch. Everything requires you to be close enough to see the target," Nick's spirit grumbled.

"Because you couldn't use Magick," I said. "You could only use a limited Magickal object, just like the mundanes of the world."

If a non-Magickal being attempted to use a Magickal object that drew energy from its user, the object wouldn't work, or it barely functioned. However, objects could be imbued with a limited amount of Magickal energy that could be released by anyone. Put simply, if you weren't a warlock or witch, or Magickally inclined, you couldn't wave a wand or any other true Magick object and get results.

"You have to rub it in, even after I'm dead, don't you?" Nick grumbled.

"Cease your whimpering and continue the explanations," Xantos said. His voice and posture clearly indicated he had no more patience.

"Fine, fine, I'll explain," Nick whined.

He hunched over, and for a moment, I almost felt like telling Xantos to sic the demons on him again. Nick was annoying whether alive or dead. He was plenty annoying when he was arrogant and angry, even more so when he was cowed.

"The priestess sent the gun and bullets to me after we talked for a month. She sought me out because of the answers I was looking for. I wanted you dead, the council dead. She asked me if I really wanted to get revenge, or if I just wanted my ability to use Magick again," Nick explained.

"You talked online for a month?" I guessed aloud.

"Yes, first through emails and then messenger. She became my confidant; she said she was making sure I really wanted revenge instead of just having an excuse to be angry."

"Fools are easily led no matter what realm and measure," Xantos declared.

Nick went on as if Xantos hadn't spoken.

"She, or whatever the priestess is, knew the Council fools would be meeting with you soon." Nick had resumed his version of pacing while he spoke. Half of his shins were beneath the level of the floor. "They were going to ask you to be one of the members. When the gun arrived, there was a note with the time and place of your meeting so I would have the opportunity to finally get my revenge."

He stopped, almost knee deep in the floor, and pointed at me. His words came out shrill and accusing. "You couldn't even let me have my revenge! Why couldn't you die and let me have some happiness?"

Xantos cut in while the ghost continued to accuse and whine. "We have no further use of him, correct?"

Shrugging, I took a long sip of tea, savoring the unusual taste. The bitterness dropped with the heat of the water, so it now tasted fruitier. It was an odd beverage, but I enjoyed it.

"I highly doubt anyone can get any more useful knowledge from him," I stated with a dismissive air.

Holding his left hand up, Xantos said, "Eat the head first, I've tired of his mewling."

With that, Xantos closed his hand into a fist.

The demons obeyed.

Chapter Seven

Once the 'clean up' was done, I finished my tea and turned to Xantos.

"This adds a whole new level of mess to things," I observed. "I can think of a few possibilities. There's a mole, a spy, or a leak in the Council, and they want to overthrow it. Someone wants me dead, aside from Nick. Or news of my pregnancy has hit the proverbial grapevine, and someone isn't thrilled with the idea of my having Sterling's offspring."

"Those are not the only possibilities," Xantos replied. "However, regardless of what motives and beings are in play, you need to be somewhere safe. A secret place, if possible. A location that allows you to use Magick more freely, since added protection and defense are going to be required."

"Is that a subtle suggestion that I come stay with you?" I half teased.

"I refuse to be subtle, ever," he countered. "No, I would not want you to stay in my realm until this situation is resolved. And that is not a slight against you."

"Why wouldn't you?" I asked, trying to keep the sulking out of my voice and mood.

"You could use Magick, any Magick, as you please, but a whole different parade of concerns would be at your back," Xantos answered immediately. "You are from a different realm, and just as this one dims your power, mine would expand it beyond your comprehension."

"Why? Magick thrives in your realm, same as it does in my mother's. Shouldn't it be the same rules and physics?" I was genuinely interested in the answer. Sterling had actively avoided any conversation along this line.

"It's not the same Magick, Cat." His voice was not condescending, but it was firm. "I've spent considerable time watching the self-proclaimed scientists of this world. Perhaps it's a trapping of the human race or conditioned into whoever lives here, but too many ignore the simplest truths. What works in one place does not necessarily work in another, or in the same way. Soil is different all over the world, so no seed, in its pure and natural form, grows the same way everywhere. Energy is more complex than seeds and more subjective to its place of origin. Magick is the manipulation of energy."

I studied the ancient dark elf for a few moments, allowing my brain to mull over his words.

"I've only been to this realm and my mother's. Magick in her realm is stronger, but it is different in how it's used. Most who live there are true Magickal beings." I paused, trying to find the right words. "This is a topic I can rarely get anyone to talk about, so if my questions sound childish and ignorant, that is the reason. Is Magick common in your world? Not in the way my mother's is Magickal, but in some other way?"

"Magick grows from almost everything in my realm, but it does not hold it all together," Xantos said carefully. He leaned forward as he spoke. "That's the biggest difference between these realms. Magick is produced here, but it is the difference between a small brush and what are called redwood trees in this realm and world."

"Then I suppose it's a good thing I'm going to visit my mother's realm for a while," I stated. After I smiled slyly at him, I added, "Do you have any theories about how Nick's mysterious, self-proclaimed priestess made bullets appear to be obsidian?"

"It would take a good deal of energy and concentration, but a simple spell. Any opaque quartz from this world would suffice. Once broken and ground into the desired shape, most competent users could polymorph it, giving it the black, glassy appearance of obsidian. As I mentioned, it would take a lot of time, focus and energy to make it such, but it would not be difficult. The quartz would store some measure of spell energy. Non-users or those only able to touch Magick could easily be fooled." Xantos smirked. "If someone wanted to truly make one of those chemically-dependent weapons into the slayer of Magickal beings, the inner barrel would be made of obsidian. Not the bullets."

"That wasn't the case. The barrel wouldn't have been destroyed when Nick was turned into a large blob of goo," I replied. "And the bullets appeared to be obsidian to all of us. Jen was able to summon them to her, should that be an important detail to you."

"I suppose the cloudy agate in this realm would hold enough energy to fool almost anyone without a direct investigation or sensing of its properties. The non-users know enough about machines to make one that would carve the bullet shape out of that material," he retorted.

Tapping a finger on the arm of the sofa, I made a noncommittal sound. I then stood and walked over to Xantos, my left hand in a fist. Lifting a brow, I turned my hand and opened it before the elf. In my palm was a bullet, complete with the casing.

"Really? Are you certain?" I asked, taking care to keep insolence out of my voice.

Xantos frowned and plucked the shell out of my hand in a gesture so quick I almost missed it.

Closing his long fingers around the object, Xantos whispered, "Ipsum revelare."

Energy immediately gathered around his fist. Every color of the rainbow sprang from between his fingers. He remained that way for a considerable time, perhaps a full minute. When he opened his hand, the shell was unchanged. The bullet, however, was grey and bore no resemblance to any quartz or glass I had ever seen.

"This was formed from slate," Xantos said, his voice lower and colder than usual. "In terms of raw power, I could do this, as could your mother. Sterling? No. He and others would require help."

He sat back and flicked the shell toward me. I caught it easily but kept my gaze on him. He ground his teeth but paused long enough to speak further. "This is the work of a demigod, or someone with unlimited access to a talisman with the power to change objects on a molecular level. The Magick reminds me of a talisman that was created to turn mundane objects into the most powerful weapons possible. It was not created by me but did exist some centuries ago in this realm. I had not heard of its coming back into use. Further investigation will be necessary."

Bolting upright from his seat, Xantos walked past me, speaking rapidly. "Go to your mother's realm. I will contact you when I have learned something. Thank you for the tea."

Before I could respond, he walked through a seamless tear in reality and was gone, leaving his words to haunt me.

A talisman that could turn anything into a super weapon. Oh. Fuck. Me.

Standing, I headed for the stairs, weaving spells as I moved. Before I reached the door, my rooms were cleaning themselves, dishes were being washed and put away, and other household chores were being completed.

"Maekyl, I need you to find Trix," I said without preamble. "I know you were listening to us. If the talisman was recovered and restored, would it be as it was before?"

A shadow dragon, Trix had been an ally during my Lady of Death era. Maekyl swore her actual name was Taierix, but I'd never attempted to summon her using it. Since Maekyl had crushed on her hard, and the feelings were mutual—as far as I could tell—I suspected he would be the best being to find my old friend and companion. I needed her to answer some important questions.

"Absolutely. Some fluctuation in its power is probable, of course." Maekyl sounded chipper, damn him. "Depending on who reassembled the talisman and what energy was used to restore it, it could be less effective. Since it wasn't you, it cannot operate at peak efficiency."

"Damn it," I muttered. There were too many variables, and few of them were good in my opinion. "I thought it was destroyed. I would have heard if any of the pieces had been discovered or if it had been restored."

"Yes, that is troublesome," Maekyl replied, although there was the slightest bit of mockery in his voice.

"What do you know about this?" I asked, trying to not growl.

The talisman was not a figment of anyone's imagination. It had been created centuries earlier and had done exactly as Xantos described. It had been broken into pieces, and those pieces dispersed to various parts of the world. I may have had a large hand in its destruction. At least, I thought I had destroyed it.

Apparently, I had simply broken it into parts that could be put back together.

Maekyl's glow grew brighter. "I, Lady? Nothing." When I remained silent, my glower darkening, his voice grew sullen as he continued, "Fine. I felt the presence of something powerful. I believed it was another artifact being created or used. There are a few in this world, after all. I remained silent because there was nothing I knew that would interest you."

"What have you heard?" I demanded.

The teeth of the dragon skull ground together. "There have been the usual rumblings of those interested in your ever-growing power. Some are wondering whether you will be returning to your previous reign, which was glorious, I might add." He sighed dreamily. "The power, the followers. The majesty you embodied."

Rolling my eyes, I tried to remain calm. "Maekyl."

"There are many who have spent their lives searching for the talisman. Xantos is one of those beings. It was a thing of great power."

"It was also a thing of great terror," I added.

"No, Lady," Maekyl chided. "That wasn't the talisman. That was you. The talisman merely added an extra layer of terror to your already-considerable reputation."

"Details, details," I said, dismissively. "Stop trying to change the subject. Has the talisman been restored?"

Maekyl smiled slyly. Or at least as slyly as a skull can manage. "There is only one way to be absolutely certain."

"No."

He sighed dramatically. "Then there is no way to know without seeing it or waiting for more attacks with identical weapons. Even in your delicate condition, you will be able to discover the truth of their origin and whether they are from that particular artifact."

"That was not the answer I was looking for," I grumbled.

"It's the only answer to your unyielding choices," he retorted. "Are you still going to your mommy's?"

"For a short visit, yes," I rejoined. There was one thing, though, just in case he was right. "Maekyl, I am giving you permission to defend and protect my home without restrictions while I am gone and until this is done. You know my rules. You know who I welcome within these walls. Allow no thief. Allow none with malicious intent."

Delight danced in the skull's eyes. "Your wish, my Lady, is my command to obey."

Chapter Eight

"I don't think I'm ready for this," I said a couple of hours later.

Dad, sitting across from me, looked up from his plate of baked prosciutto-wrapped dates. His eyes were wide, and one eyebrow was cocked. He had invited me to dinner at his favorite Italian restaurant, mentioning my godfather would also be joining us, and I was more than happy to accept.

It had taken my father barely a minute to realize his little girl was pregnant. I'd never been so thankful to have him as a father.

"To select your entree, eat your appetizer, be joined at the dinner table by a vampire, or something else?" he asked before plucking one of the appetizers from his plate and popping it into his mouth.

I looked at the three Polenta Bolognese cups on my plate, warm and ready to be consumed.

"Ha ha, very funny," I retorted before picking up one of the appetizers and nibbling at it. At least I didn't feel as though I were going to have a panic attack. "You know exactly what I mean, Dad. Mom is going to want his head on a platter. And I'll be lucky if she lets me return without an entourage."

"Not so many years ago, she would have tried to keep you from returning at all," he reminded me. "At least she's cut a few apron strings."

"She did threaten that when I was dating Nick," I said with a grin. Popping the cup into my mouth, I chewed for a while, enjoying the savory flavors. Swallowing, I took a sip of my soda. "Do you think it's possible she'll just be happy? I know it's going to be impossible to keep her from finding out."

"Eventually, she will be happy," Dad relented. "But you know she's got to go through all the stages first: Denial, anger, bargaining..."

"It's the anger and bargaining I'm worried about," I admitted.

My mother was not someone to trifle with or anger. Every member of her court could attest to that, no matter if they are alive or dead. I, as her only surviving child, was her heir. The claimed heir, since inheriting a fae queen's realm didn't necessarily mean I had to be the eldest daughter. As long as the heir was blood-related, she could decree anyone to be her heir.

Since I was the claimed heir of her realm, I had considerable power on the fae-side of the Veils. When I entered that world, my power grew. In my mother's realm, my word was overpowered only by hers and my father's. Typically, a queen didn't give such power to any she took as a lover or spouse, but Mom had broken tradition. Their love was pure and true, even if they didn't live together and had other lovers on occasion.

As immortal beings, it wasn't unheard of to take time away from each other. What was unusual was that they loved each other as much today as they had centuries ago. I always suspected it was because Dad never backed down from Mom, despite her position and power. Not that I'd ever say that anywhere either of them could hear me.

"You can handle whatever she does." Dad broke into my thoughts. "My biggest concern is your use of spellcraft while you're there, like a gambler who won a jackpot but hasn't left Vegas yet."

"I won't be that bad," I began, but trailed off, giggling at my father's disbelieving stare.

One brow was raised, and his lips were pressed together and twisted into something between a grimace and a frown.

"Okay, I know I've been bad before. What if I promise to keep my use of Magick to a minimum? I won't burn everything in sight or anyone who makes me mad." I paused before adding impishly, "I'll bring my lovely scythes and use them, instead."

"That's so much more reassuring," Dad said, jokingly. "Now, please, decide on your entree before they bring our guest's steak tartare, and he arrives."

"I thought that might appease you, Dear Father," I quipped. "I think I'll go with the Chicken Françoise with a side salad."

My father nodded. He picked up the small, electronic tablet used to order and tapped in my request. He probably ordered Tagliolini ai Porcinior or something similarly heavy for himself, I thought. At least I wouldn't spend the meal smelling truffles. They are divine, but I'm not partial to their unique scent.

After savoring a second appetizer, I asked, "What do you think about this mess I've gotten myself into?"

"I'm fine with you having a child," Dad said with mild amusement. "Your choice of partner is unexpected, at least to me. As for the attempted murder, I should have obliterated Nickolai the first time he came calling for you."

"I won't argue that. I might have complained some then, but not now." My brain finally registered what Dad had said, and my jaw dropped. "Who told you about Nick's attempt? And what's the likelihood Mom doesn't know about either thing yet?"

If Mom knew, I was doomed.

"I haven't told her," Dad assured me. "Although it would be folly to expect her not to have heard something about the attempt. The Speaker was an old friend of your mother's, after all."

"Well, that's something," I grumbled. "I guess word of the Speaker's death would have spread pretty quickly."

"As well as some of the circumstances surrounding such an event," he rejoined. "One of your mother's trusted spies in this realm frequents Fellhaven daily. She was there that night."

I stared at my father for a few moments. Damn it. I needed to recreate my own network of spies and mercenaries if I was going to return to any position of power, especially if it had anything to do with the Council.

"Are you going to be at Mom's when I go visit?" I asked, a plan starting to form.

"I can be."

"I would feel a lot better if you were," I said in complete honesty. "Um... do you think it would be okay with Mom if you brought Jade along? I'd feel a lot safer if she was at my side, especially since it's been a long time since I've been at Mom's for a lengthy stay."

"Very well. If it will comfort you, I shall. Jade is certainly welcome to be at my side." Dad's eyes twinkled. "Such a woman at my side might even make your mother jealous. She's so much fun when she's jealous."

Laughing, I held up my hands. "I really don't want to know, Dad! But thank you for bringing Jade."

I was certain Jade would help me. She had been instrumental in developing my network the first time. All things considered; I didn't think she would object to helping create another network of spies. Maekyl was a given. There wasn't much of anything he wouldn't do if it helped me become a power again. He still had hopes I'd take over the world. He didn't care if I succeeded. But the level of chaos and carnage that would accompany any attempt would be his bread and wine.

"You are plotting something," Dad interjected. He wasn't asking a question.

"When am I not?" I replied. Upon seeing his darkening expression, I giggled. "Okay, fine. Yes, I am, but it isn't anything that will break any laws. At least, not any of ours. I don't even bother trying to keep up with all the mundane laws."

Whatever reply he might have been preparing was lost with the arrival of our food and my godfather, whom I have always known as "Uncle Tony."

Tony Moretti knew my dad during their childhood, and their friendship hadn't wavered even after he'd been turned. I had only known Tony as a vampire. Though not a blood relative, 'Uncle Tony' was a dear friend and my godfather. He was also an über powerful being who could terrify anyone, even the boogeyman.

He looked frightening to most people, especially in the dark. His features were sharp, pronounced, and lean. If his ears had been pointed, he could have been mistaken for an elf. Instead their rounded tips suggested a human heritage. His scars gave him the appearance of someone who had survived the most horrible things the world offered, many times over, and still walked out of the debris on his own feet.

Piercing blue eyes studied me as his thin lips, set beneath a Jewish nose, formed a smile. Everything about him suggested he'd make the perfect villain, though anyone who got to know him realized that even though he was a predator, he could be the most caring person you'd ever meet.

I respected him, and I typically amused him, so I had no clue what would make him angry. I wasn't entirely certain I wanted to know, either.

Leaning over, Tony gave me a hug, before taking a seat between Dad and me. He wasn't wearing his usual shadow-Magick-imbued leather duster, but that was the only thing that was different about him.

"Hello, Uncle Tony," I said happily. "It's good to see you again."

"It's good to see you, as well, my dear," he replied as a waitress appeared from seemingly nowhere with a drink in hand. It appeared to be a Bloody Mary, but anything was possible in this tavern. "Are you faring well?"

"So far, the only difficulty I've encountered is panicking about the visit to my mother," I replied honestly.

Tony smiled slyly. "I'm certain Viviane will be delighted to see you and will want you to stay for a while, though I suspect it will be longer than you desire."

Shrugging, I took a sip of my drink. "I guess it's to be expected, all things considered."

"Yes, about that—" Tony began, but stopped when my father held up his hand. He looked at my father. "Really, Simon, if she's going to Viv's side of the Veil, certain things should be addressed. She's survived this long, despite the mischief during her wild, wayward youth. She can withstand what needs to be told."

"I have no interest in debating that," my father replied. "How should we proceed?"

"The direct approach has always been my favorite," Tony said. He took a long sip of his drink while looking at my dad.

"Fine," Dad grumbled. "You start."

"There is a faction within your mother's realm that does not believe you should inherit the throne," Tony said. My father grunted, and Tony smiled at him. "I will let Simon fill in the details."

"My blood brother, the podsnappery," Dad said with some irritation.

"You're upset about this whole situation. It will work out, and you'll take the egg in the end. As will Cat."

"As much as I love to see you two falling into Victorian habits, can one of you explain why I suddenly have so many enemies in Mom's court?"

"It's not so suddenly, really," said Tony.

"It's not so much enemies as a growing faction of people who want to see something or someone new ruling the realm," Dad explained, before Tony could go on. "They are of the opinion that you will not only repeat the decisions made by your mother that they disagree with, but that you will make worse ones because you have spent so little time there."

"You no longer know the land or its people," Tony said with a chuckle. "It's the same old political scam—get those who are afraid off their duffs and up in arms."

Dad shrugged in half-hearted agreement. "You may or may not be bothered by them while you are at Court.

But they do exist and have grown in numbers and noise over the years."

"It isn't as though I need to worry about claiming the throne any time soon, like in the next century or two," I retorted. Though they did have a point, which I was willing to concede. "I'll need to spend more time there, anyway, after the babe is born. The child will need to know her grandmother, after all. Which brings up something else," Turning my attention to my godfather, I continued, "I've allowed many things to lapse during my self-imposed exile, such as my spy network."

"Something of interest finally sparks the conversation!" Tony said eagerly.

"My daughter's well-being isn't of interest?" Dad snapped.

"You weren't paying attention when she earned her lovely moniker. I was. Her well-being is something I am far more confident in than you are," corrected Tony.

"I believe he and Mom were trying hard to ignore my antics during that time," I teased. "Would you be able to help me reform my network, Uncle Tony? I know Jade would assist, if I asked, but I don't have anyone to oversee it. Until Maekyl can locate Trix, I don't know anyone I can trust who also knows how to setup and run a network. Aside from you, of course."

"I shall make it my utmost priority," my godfather declared proudly. "Give me a fortnight, and I will hand you the keys to the information kingdom."

"Thank you, Uncle Tony," I replied warmly. I tipped my head to the side as a thought occurred, and I couldn't help but ask, "You aren't asking who Trix is. Do you know her? Or know of her?"

"The shadow dragon who originated the true art of spying? Your ally during those most formidable years? Yes," Tony said in good humor, "I know of her. She does not care much for my kind."

That made me laugh. "I noticed that." Glancing at my father, who had a decidedly sour expression on his face, I changed the topic. "I suspect the faction you mentioned isn't the only thing you wished to speak to me about."

"Too much to go over at a single meal," replied Tony. The server arrived at our table with our food.

"Father?" I prompted. "Is there anything else of import I should know?"

"Should it ever come up, Sterling and your mother have always had a platonic relationship," Dad said dismissively. He smiled at our server and spoke to him in Italian.

Tony leaned over and whispered to me, "No matter how heated the two of them got, it was always above table."

Our plates were laid before us, while extra servers arrived to refill glasses and pass out napkins. Tony wasted no time digging into his steak.

Chapter Nine

There is not a lot that terrifies me. Spiders? Nope, they go squish. Snakes? Not my thing, but they're great for certain spells. Facing down an old god from myth? Uh-uh.

My parents, however, could make me curl up in a fetal ball while hiding in a corner under my bed. My mother's temper is epic, especially in her realm. Suspecting she wouldn't be thrilled to learn she was going to be a grandmother, I stared at the door that opened into her realm in absolute terror.

"Nope, I've changed my mind. I'm going to barricade myself in my basement and never come out," I said, turning to walk away.

Sterling grabbed me and turned me back toward the door. "It will be okay, Catherine."

Damn it. He had to use that tone of voice, didn't he? My little cloud dragon, who had decided that, as her mother, I was not leaving without her, had taken to pretending she was a scarf. Curled around my neck, she pressed against me and purred.

It was so lovely to have both of them on the same side of something.

Maekyl's voice cut clearly through my thoughts. "You could visit Xantos."

That was the perfect encouragement. There was no way in hell, any hell, I would visit Xantos without going to see my mother first. And the rat bastard knew it.

I reached out and turned the doorknob. His cackling laughter didn't stop until I shut the door behind us.

***

A faerie realm is not unlike my own world. At least, my mother's realm was a great deal like a fantasy version of Earth. The colors were brighter and far more vivid, and the sounds were clear, with a warmth that could not be found anywhere else. Believe me, I tried finding it elsewhere and came up lacking.

The castle my mother lived in was made from marble and stone. Polished to a deep shine, there wasn't a speck of dust to be found anywhere. Since I was my mother's heir, I could control what opened where in her realm, so the door had opened into my chambers. My living quarters were opulent and vast. I entered the small gathering room where I could entertain guests, if I so chose. Normally, I didn't bother. The gathering room had a door that led into my spacious main chamber. From there, you could go to my bedchamber, lavatory, den, small library, dressing room, and the huge tub that I loved. The warm springs that fed the cast iron tub might help ease the aches that accompanied my pregnancy.

Having dressed in proper garb prior to leaving, I headed straight for the vanity. My mother would have sensed my arrival, and likely Sterling's, since the entire castle and realm were connected to her. Regardless, or perhaps because of that, I took the time to grab a tiara and some appropriate jewelry.

I didn't think anyone would make the mistake of not recognizing me as the princess, but it was impossible to tell how many new courtiers had appeared in the time I'd been gone. So, after making certain the tiara wouldn't fall off, I drew a breath and stared at my reflection in the mirror for a few moments.

I'd wrapped my black hair artfully around the silver tiara. My eyes were the same brown they'd always been, my face angular, my figure svelte. Not quite six feet, I was a perfect blend of my almost-human father and my fairy mother. Since Dad was a powerful wizard, I couldn't call him completely human, as most humans were mundanes without a speck of Magick in them.

Confusing, I know. The flighty thoughts did keep me from running home, though. Drawing a deep breath, I straightened non-existent wrinkles in the opulent, near-gossamer gown that fell in soft folds around me.

I turned to Sterling.

"Shall we?" I asked.

Once he nodded in agreement, I slid my gaze over his more traditional wizard robes and headed for the door. We didn't stop until we approached the Grand Hall where my mother held Court.

A footman held open the door as we approached, and I silenced the crier before he could announce my arrival to everyone in the room. One guard stiffened, but after taking a single look at me, relaxed and resumed his former position.

Many of the people in the room did double-takes when they saw us. I wasn't certain if they were staring at the dragon around my neck, Sterling who was escorting me rather possessively and wearing non-mundane garb, or the weapons that rested at each of my hips. Or, perhaps, they were staring because it was my first time home in many months.

Okay, it was more like a year.

The fae courtiers milling about parted before us when we moved toward the dais that held my parents' thrones. I was on edge and felt my pulse race. I didn't expect a bad welcome, but I didn't know how Mom was going to take the news of my pregnancy.

Mother looked beautiful. Her hair, so dark it had purple and blue highlights, was coiled elegantly around her head. Her silver diadem sparkled with amber and sapphire jewels, in complementary contrast to her hair. Gold embroidery shimmered along the skirt, bodice, and cuffs of her sleeves, giving weight to her otherwise filmy gown. Even so, every bit of frippery she wore brought out the dark blue material. The color of the gown matched my mother's eyes, which narrowed slightly as they swept over me from head to toe.

"Welcome home, my daughter," Mom said as she stood.

Without pausing, I walked up the stairs until I, too, stood a good five feet above everyone below us.

She embraced me, before holding me at arm's length.

"It's good to see you again, safe and in one piece," she said quietly so no one else could hear. Turning to the room, she spoke in a louder voice. "As my daughter's arrival is a wonderful surprise, I will be taking a reprieve from Court this eve."

Without another word, my hand firmly grasped in hers, she led me down the dais and out of the room. My father, I noticed, paused to murmur something to one of the guards before falling into step behind us with Sterling at his side.

No one spoke until we stood inside my parents' favorite den. We'd often spent evenings here during my childhood, sitting and reading or playing chess. Or talking. Or a variety of other things when Mother didn't have to, or want to, tend to Courtly duties.

This was also where we had gotten into many family arguments, which may have been why she brought us here. Some things never changed. That tiny comfort was what kept me from running away.

"Explain," Mother said. Her voice and gaze were hot and unyielding.

"It's rather simple, Mom. I'm pregnant. Sterling is the father. And I wanted to tell you before your spies did," I replied, keeping my expression somber and my gaze steady.

As my mother opened her mouth to speak, Dad gently suggested, "Breathe."

She stopped, closed her eyes, and inhaled sharply. After a pause, the queen of the realm exhaled slowly. "Simplifying the situation does not present the answers I expect."

"What answers do you want?" I fired back. "I can't answer questions that aren't asked."

From the fire in my mother's eyes, I suspected this was going to be an argument the bards were going to sing about.

"Explain how your infertility ring failed or why you didn't bother to utilize it," Mother said slowly, in the way that meant she was trying to keep her temper.

"Oh, that," I said, as I searched for the best way to explain it without the volcano erupting. Such didn't seem possible, but at least, she couldn't place all the blame on me or Sterling. "Xantos deactivated the ring. I didn't realize he had, and I don't know why he did. You'd have to ask him."

"Xantos," Mother hissed. She snapped her left arm out and made a slashing gesture with her hand. A tear opened in mid-air, stretching until it was roughly the size of a door. Within, I could see a dark hallway. "I will pull him off that ghastly excuse for a throne he sits on and drag him here to answer for this."

"Before you do that," Dad interjected, "shouldn't we allow preparations to be made? Tickets, vendors, and every single healer in the realm to be at the ready?"

"Calling out a veritable demigod, even one as loathsome as he, might not be the best approach to this situation," Sterling offered politely.

"Your opinion was not asked for," Mother coldly replied. She stared at the doorway but did not move. I had seen that look before; she was weighing the wisdom of the two men against her knowledge and will. More than likely, I stopped breathing while waiting to see which she would choose.

"Mom, we didn't exactly sit down and discuss birth control," I added cautiously. "We probably should have, and we probably should have realized the ring was no longer bespelled. Isn't it all a moot point now? From my understanding, Xantos does odd, I suppose, pranks, to people he likes?"

A small part of me was greatly intrigued by the idea of what he did to those he didn't like. But I was also a strange woman with unusual tastes.

"Xantos is a professional shit disturber," Dad bluntly observed. "You've got his notice, but as for liking you... that remains to be seen."

"It is his habit to cause chaos wherever he can," Sterling explained. "He particularly enjoys making people pay for their lack of observation or notice of things that have become commonplace."

There was no way I was going to mention that Xantos had discussed it with me when he removed the spell from the ring. Some things needed to remain unspoken. Besides, I liked the interfering jerk.

"Mom, if I'm not angry, why are you? I'm the one who's pregnant," I said, attempting to draw her attention back to what seemed to be her biggest complaint.

"I am not angry about your pregnancy as much as I am about whom you have sired a child with," she said calmly. A bit too calmly. I realized she was about to go nuclear a second before she turned on Sterling.

"Is this the thanks I get for suggesting Catherine aid you in the retrieval of the Eye of Amon? Which, I might add, nearly got both of you killed. You are not a god, nor were you sired by one! You said you would pull her from her reclusive ways! If I had known your method was to bed her, I would never have agreed to such folly!"

"Mom—" I began, but the fire in her eyes and her stiff posture stopped me. She held out a hand to silence me.

"She is not merely my little princess; she is my heir. My heart. My daughter. Damn it, Myrddin! Catherine is the one who brings me joy and gives me pride! My only child who survived! Something I thought you, of all people, could understand!" Mother paused for a breath, and all I could do was stare at her like a gaping fish, complete with wide, unblinking eyes and open mouth. "What do you call her?"

If her previous words hadn't left my world spinning, her final question nearly stopped my heart. The hands on my shoulders belonged to my father. I'd know their grip anywhere. It was a comfort, but my mother had moved until she and Sterling were facing off, almost nose-to-nose. Desperate to distract myself from the drama before me, I attempted to focus on the odd word my mother had all but spat at Sterling. The name

Myrddin was slightly familiar, but all I could remember was that it was a Welsh name I'd heard in passing a handful of times.

Sterling opened and closed his mouth a few times. Finally, he managed to stutter, "I call her 'Cat?'"

He sounded as though he were trying to learn a language but couldn't pronounce the words correctly. It might have been funny, except that my mother was thoroughly pissed off and obviously expected a different answer.

Mother's other hand slashed out toward the tear she had made. The scene inside changed to the interior of a room I had never seen. Antiques filled the room, in a way that made me wonder if it was a home or a museum. Since I'd never been to Sterling's home, I suspected that's what I was seeing. Mother's eyes crackled with Magick as she spoke to Sterling.

"You are unwelcome in my realm until further notice! Any attempt to communicate with my daughter will mean banishment until the end of my days!"

Before Sterling could respond, he was hurled by an unseen, but certainly not unfelt, force into the open tear. The rip in time and space sealed behind him with no sound.

"Mother!" I all but screeched, finally able to speak again. "If he's not going to be here, neither am I!"

"No," Mother said firmly. "You will remain here until further notice. If he cannot admit, at least to himself, what you truly mean to him, he does not deserve you."

"Vivian," my father said, "I'm not going to argue with you. However, this situation requires a lot of thought and discussion."

"I should never have trusted him after the incident with the damned sword and those two idiot kids!" Mother spat. "He will get a talking to, rest assured of that! I removed him from my sight until I can talk to him without rending his flesh from his bones in the same breath!"

"You are upsetting our daughter and doing so without improving this predicament." Dad's tone was becoming less gentlemanly with each word. I could feel energy flowing off of him in waves.

"Can my child's first impression of her grandmother not include you two arguing and yelling?" I asked firmly.

"Yes, darlings," a silky voice intoned from the opposite end of the room. "Don't fight in front of the children."

We spun toward the source of the sound. My mother was already pulling her arm back to cast a spell at Xantos.

"You don't open a doorway into my lair without my notice, Queen," the dark elf proclaimed. "I don't care if you want to attempt a banishment. I need not step foot into your realm to lay waste to it."

My eyes darted back and forth between the casually leaning Xantos and the poised-to-strike Queen Mother. Dad stepped up, hands out.

"It is a domestic issue that has grown hot, Xantos. Your interference caused it, and we have no need of more," Dad said calmly.

"So good to know my work is recognized, if not appreciated," Xantos replied in a somewhat cheerful tone. "And whatever this is, it's not all my doing. But I've made it clear that opening my doors is folly. Thus, I shall be off...for now."

As Xantos vanished, my mother lowered her arm and muttered loud enough for us to hear, "His doors? Arrogant ass."

Chapter Ten

My parents escorted me to my chambers in silence. I suspected they were either arguing silently with each other or themselves. Either way, I was thankful for the quiet. It allowed me time to muddle through what had just happened.

I opened the door to my chambers and saw Jade reclining in one of the opulent chairs. She looked up from the book she'd been reading before setting it aside and standing.

"Went that well?" She asked with the tiniest of smiles. To my parents, she bowed. "Your highnesses."

"Bah. None of that here, Alhiri," Mom said, holding her hands out to Jade as she strode into the room. "You are family."

Jade embraced my mother, before turning to my father and giving him a hug, as well.

"Do you wish for me to leave?" Jade asked.

"No need," Dad replied. "Cat would throw a fit or tell you everything, anyway."

Jade snickered. I shrugged. There was no point in denying it.

"Catherine," my mother finally said, her tone far different from the one she'd used a few minutes earlier. Concern filled her face as she spoke. "Surely you are aware that every child Sterling has sired is dead. Only one died of old age, but he had no Magickal connection. He was also the only one that did not father a child."

I glanced at my father, and he nodded, adding, "Every child has died in battle or by Sterling's hand. The last child attempted a complete coup of the Council. Killed nearly every member. It was a battle of epic proportions."

My mother picked up when my father stopped talking. "The question we have, and the one everyone else will be asking, is what Sterling is going to do."

"He's had plenty of opportunities to do anything he wants to the baby or me. Oddly enough, the baby isn't a source of contention between us," I declared. Not that I was going to mention that we had argued often about what spells I should and shouldn't be doing. That was between Sterling and me. "And considering you kidnapped Dad and held him prisoner, I don't think you should be telling me how to conduct my love life."

Jade coughed. Dad cleared his throat. I prepared for the incoming explosion from my mother.

Mother's eyes narrowed. She clenched her fists, and her nostrils flared as she pulled in deep breaths.

Nope. She was not happy with that quip.

"No door will be opened by you or anyone else within my kingdom. Not until I decide otherwise. Your escort, while you are here, will include those of my choosing, as well as Alhiri." She snorted. "She is the only one you will ever trust to watch your back."

Without another word, Mother turned and stalked away. She didn't get the chance to blow the doors open, because someone opened them before she got there. The woman standing in the doorway didn't curtsey for a few heartbeats, and I wondered if she'd be the first victim of my mother's temper.

Alas, it wasn't to be, because the blonde curtsied low, bowing her head as she stared at my mother's feet. Mother snarled silently before storming past the woman. I thought it a shame when I realized she was someone I recognized from my childhood, and she was most decidedly not someone I'd call a close friend. A frenemy, perhaps, but not someone I'd trust with a secret.

Blondie came into my chambers as though she belonged there. That is, until she noticed that my father, Jade, and I weren't smiling or in welcoming moods. She paused, then curtsied low, her demeanor changing to one of servitude.

"Miriria Lathos," I said in a cool tone. Not in the mood to play Courtly politics, I asked, "What do you want?"

Looking up with a slight smirk on her lips, she replied, "I am to be your liaison, of sorts, while you here."

"What she really means, Catherine, is she cajoled her way into the position of babysitter while you're here. You'll be stuck with her even if you dismiss the rest of your entourage," a male voice quipped from outside my room. The owner of the voice stepped into my doorway and leaned against the frame; arms crossed. "Not here an hour, and you've already created a sensational stir."

Cildur Laedragryl grinned as I stared at him in shock. He was about my height, with golden blonde hair that fell in barely-there waves to his shoulders, dark blue eyes, and dimples that added to his boyish features. He wore Courtly garb, a mid-thigh-length, dark emerald tunic with silver Celtic-style embroidery, silver breeches that were skintight, and black, mid-shin leather boots.

We had grown up together, but the last time I'd visited my mother, he had not been able to come to Court, due to the responsibilities of running his parents' estates. The son of a baron, his duties came before all else. I understood and respected that. Duties were part of our life, even if they did intrude upon fun.

"Oh, I'm sorry," he continued in a voice that was anything but apologetic. "Should I show my fealty to you, Princess?" He smirked as he walked toward my father and me. Pausing an arm's length away, he bowed extravagantly. "My King! How wonderful it is to be within your awe-inspiring presence!"

"Don't make me send you to the dungeons," my father said. "If I leave you here, will you and Jade keep my daughter out of trouble?" He paused before adding, "Or at least keep her out of any trouble that will draw Viv's attention?"

Standing straight, Cildur met my father's gaze, a mischievous smile curving his lips. "I am certain we can prevent any death or major destruction from occurring this night, Your Highness."

"See that you do," my father said. Turning, he gave me a brief hug and kiss on the cheek before shaking Jade's hand. "I'll take my leave of you." His attention shifted to Miriria. "When my daughter dismisses you, you will leave. Despite my wife's overblown sense of motherly protectiveness, Catherine is not a prisoner and is entitled to her privacy."

As was not uncommon, Miriria interjected, "Worry not, Your Highness. I will keep track of her and report any worrisome activity."

Without saying a word, Father departed my suite, leaving me with two of my most beloved friends and a frenemy. I waited until the door closed completely behind Dad before glancing first at Cildur, then at Jade.

"One would require a tongue to wag, I believe," I stated, as I rubbed Arylla under her chin.

"I do believe so, yes," Jade replied, thoughtfully.

"A bit early to begin the torture, isn't it?" Cildur asked. He held a hand out to Arylla, who sniffed his fingers before rooting into them so he could rub her head. "I thought you typically waited until after dinner to torture and maim those who annoy you."

"Exceptions can be made," I retorted.

"I wasn't aware the Lady of Death followed any particular guidelines or rules," Miriria cheerfully interjected. "You've always seemed to follow your impulses."

I exchanged an amused look with Cildur. Jade snorted.

Shrugging, I said, "I was rarely impulsive, and as the humans are wont to say, there was a method to my madness."

"It's going to be so educational to finally get to converse with you about the rich history you left behind," Miriria replied. She was seemingly unphased by anything I had said or implied.

"Yes, I'm sure it will." Though I attempted to sound pleasant and enthusiastic about the prospect of extended conversation with Miriria, my voice came out pained and thick with sarcasm. Cildur snorted and tried to cover his humor by coughing loudly.

"I'm here. So, for now, she is watched," Cildur finally said. "Thank you, Lady."

Miriria frowned for the briefest moment, then composed her smile and enthusiasm.

"Of course, Your Lordship. Ring when you are ready to leave or retire for the evening."

Cildur nodded. Miriria left the room. The instant the door clicked shut, I inhaled sharply and exhaled through my gritted teeth.

"She has grown more annoying over the years," I growled. There were many reasons I avoided Court and most of my mother's people. "Who's up for raiding the kitchen?"

Chapter Eleven

Several hours later, after our so-called 'raid,' we sat in my lounge enjoying delicious food and the best wine I could grab when no one was looking. Though the 'raid' had mainly consisted of not getting in the way of the chefs as they made our favorite finger foods and snacks, the theft of the wine was fairly substantial. My mother's wines were coveted by a great many in her realm and the surrounding kingdoms.

Our bottles for the night were exceptional vintages that paired wonderfully with our trays of food.

"You are determined to anger your mother until she places you in the dungeons," Cildur stated casually, laughter twinkling in his eyes.

Jade laughed. "Except that isn't about to happen, since our beloved princess is loved by her parents."

Sharing a laugh, we clinked our glasses together and raised them in a silent toast before taking a drink. It was a ritual we had shared from a young age. Though the first theft of wine had not happened until our teen years, stealing from the kitchens had begun the moment we could plan any sort of mischief.

After several moments of silence, Cildur nibbled at a pastry, his eyes growing serious. "I believe it's time to address a few things, my dear cousin. Perhaps a good starting point would be why your mother has forbidden you to leave her domain."

"Well, that's rather simple," I replied, trying to sound far more nonchalant than I felt. "I'm actually surprised that pit of vipers Mother calls her Court hasn't told the entire world."

Jade snickered, and Cildur laughed. He held the puff pastry daintily in his fingers as he said, "Out with it, cousin!"

"I'm pregnant," I said with a shrug.

Jade laughed. "That isn't all of it. Since she doesn't want to tell you, I will. She's pregnant with Sterling's child. Her mother is rather pissed. I suspect she thinks he crossed a line."

"More like a vast canyon," Cildur said in awe. "Congratulations, my dear."

His eyes traveled to the glass of wine in my hand. "Don't humans frown on that?"

"I know, I know; I'm half human. But everyone knows fae wine is nothing like human wine, and I haven't had more than one glass tonight. Besides, I'm more fae than human."

Cildur shrugged. "Every fae drinks wine while pregnant, and no child is ever born with the defects that plague humans. Even when the child is half-human, it doesn't affect them." He paused, a smirk forming on his lips. "So. You and Sterling? You always did like older, truly dangerous types."

"Yes, Sterling and I. Mother is angry that he hasn't professed his undying love for me or sworn to keep me from harm or some other foolish thing," I grumbled as I searched for a chocolate-filled pastry. Finding one, I bit into it, savoring the bittersweet filling. Several euphoric moments of chewing later, I concluded my thoughts. "For that matter, I don't know exactly how I feel about him."

"You're obviously attracted to him," Jade said as she nibbled on a slice of candied fruit. "And you weren't wrong in challenging your mother. She lusted for your father and kidnapped him. Love came later."

"A lot later," Cildur agreed. "My parents say their courtship was filled with arguments and fights. They would often spar with swords and Magick. Your mother, I believe, fell in love with your father because he didn't bow before her, nor did he allow her to dominate him. At least, that's my impression from the bard's songs I've heard and poems I've read, not to mention what my parents have told me."

"I'm not so sure Mom agrees," I said ruefully. "I honestly don't think Sterling would hurt me or our baby." Gods, did that seem strange to say! "He seems to be more concerned that something will happen, and I'll get hurt or overdo things or use the wrong Magick."

"You mean dark Magick," Cildur said. "The kind you're really good at."

"Yes, that," I said in agreement, laughter in my voice. "I'm not entirely certain he really understands or acknowledges my necromancy or realizes how much it's a part of me."

"It isn't just necromancy," Jade interjected. "Necromancy is the more infamous Magick. You've also leaned toward other gray and black Magicks that humans should never do while pregnant. And during my younger days, anyone who did black Magick while pregnant ended up birthing a child that was twisted and evil. Black Magick corrupted the unborn." She shrugged and took a sip of her wine before continuing. "Magick has changed a great deal since the Victorian age."

"That's going to be a stocking point between you and Sterling, I fear," Cildur admitted.

"Sticking point," corrected Jade.

"I would rather speak in High Elf, but Cat is probably too out of practice to hold a conversation. And yours, Jade, always sounds like you're drunk and swearing," Cildur said.

"I hate the language of High Elves," Jade grumbled. "It sounds like beings trying to lure infants to sleep."

"For the record, I am not out of practice," I interjected. "We can converse in High Elf later. Mom didn't give Sterling a chance to talk to me, let alone answer her questions. Now he's banished from the place I'm stuck. If either of you have any suggestions about how I can escape, please let me know."

"You can always come to my father's kingdom as a regaled guest. My family would love to see you," suggested Cildur.

Apparently being pregnant even screwed with a half-fae's hormones. My eyes grew way too misty. Arylla must have sensed my change of emotions because she wound herself tighter around my neck and began purring. Loudly.

"That is the sweetest offer I've had in a long time, I think," I admitted. "But, if the rumors are true, I need to return to the human realm. Soon."

Cildur straightened in his chair. "I heard that someone tried to kill you. A former lover, according to the rumors. But I thought he tried to kill you using mundane weaponry."

"Not exactly," Jade said smoothly. "The weapon used was a human one, made of iron and metal. The bullet was shaped and Magicked to make it look like it was made of obsidian." She paused. "You do know what guns and bullets are, yes?" Cildur nodded. Jade grinned her approval and said, "Right. Despite all appearances, the bullet was not obsidian. There are scant few things that could be used to accomplish that feat."

"And one is the Talisman of Death," Cildur gasped. "By the gods, Catherine! You want to return to the mortal realm to search for that thing? I know you used it during your days of reigning glory, but the Talisman isn't something to trifle with!"

"Cildur, I cannot in good conscience allow anyone else to lay claim to that talisman. I was led to believe it had been destroyed," I said, trying to figure out how not to tell him the entire truth about the talisman. He would be obligated to inform my parents, if I told him everything, and I needed to be able to leave. Preferably within this century. "I tried destroying the talisman, Cildur, so I feel a good deal of responsibility for it."

"I suppose that old skull of yours is demanding you retrieve it?" Cildur grumbled as he shifted in his chair. "There are so many rumors about that damned talisman. I suspect the one about it being made by Merlin's daughter and ultimately ending up in Maekyl's considerable hoard is the closest to the truth, especially since you once used it."

"Merlin's daughter?" I asked, hoping to shift suspicion of its origin away from me and Maekyl.

"Morgana," Jade and Cildur said together before laughing.

"The sordid truth of that entire tale is that Morgana and Arthur were actually Merlin's children," Cildur stated, still chuckling. "You'd have to ask your mother if Uthur Pendragon knew who their father truly was, though."

"Perhaps I will stay here for a while," I said playfully. "It seems I have a lot of history to learn."

Cildur held his glass up in a salute to me. Jade and I lifted ours to him before we took sips.

Despite the circumstances, it really was nice to be home again.

Chapter Twelve

The life of a royal isn't merely a life of luxury. Actual work was involved. Most of it was political. All of it required a poker face that could withstand anything. I was fairly certain the resting bitch face had been created by fae nobility, most certainly the royals. My mother had a face that didn't break, unless she was in a private room with family. Then she didn't bother hiding her emotions. My father's poker face was almost as good.

Having a good poker face was almost a prerequisite for anyone with Magickal blood or inclinations. Not everyone managed to master the art of concealing their thoughts and emotions, though.

Personally, I'd discovered that having the perfect poker face, or resting bitch face, was good for some things and some people, but not for everything. Sometimes, showing emotion was exactly what was needed.

That knowledge might have contributed to people cowering when I was obviously pissed off, especially during my more infamous days. Even now, people didn't like it when I was angry. At least, that was true in the mortal realm. Considering my parents decided my trial of age while I was stuck in Mom's realm would be to obtain a truce between the low giants and the waterfolk, it was going to be interesting to see if my reputation held weight, now.

Dressed in a teal gown with dark blue trim that somehow seemed to float around me, I tried to keep from wondering what was going on in the human realm. Someone, somewhere, was using a talisman they had no right to control or possess.

In fact, I suspected they weren't in complete control of it. Magickal things often altered over time. Since the item had been broken and reassembled, I knew it had changed. When something powerful changes, the result usually isn't for the better. I knew how the talisman had been made and that it wasn't entirely whole. One piece was still hidden, and I planned on keeping it that way. At least for now.

Forcing my mind back to the task at hand, I entered my mother's illustrious and elegant office. This was her official office, where nobles met to negotiate treaties, plan strategies, talk with peers, and gain advice. Official complaints and rulings were handled in the throne room.

Since my task was to broker a treaty my mother had not been able to negotiate in the past few years, I suspected this was meant to be a task to keep me busy. Either my mother hoped my patience had grown over the years, or my father had decided to let me handle the problem my way. I suspected, strongly, it was the latter.

My suspicions were further confirmed when the ambassadors sent to argue over the treaty stalked into the office a few moments after I'd taken a seat behind Mother's enormous desk. Behind each ambassador trailed a contingent of cohorts.

None of them looked happy or enthusiastic. That was fine, because I wasn't too happy about having to deal with squabbling, petulant fae who refused to come to an agreement.

"I thought we would be meeting with Her Majesty," the leader of the low giants grumbled.

Low giants were tribal people who typically stood between six and eight feet tall. Hill giants, like Jade, who was currently positioned behind and to the right of me, were typically taller—their average height was between eight and ten feet. Jade was really short for a hill giant since she was around six feet tall.

The low giant, the leader of this group, was seven feet tall with straight brown hair and a rather flat face. His nose had been broken a few times, judging by the twists and lumps.

Krundruk of the Clan Bitterlok stared at me with black eyes, and he barely contained a snarl. If he was hoping to intimidate me with his height and obvious disapproval, he was in for a grand disappointment.

Or perhaps it was because Jade stood in the position normally held by an advisor, except she was armed and armored. The short cloak she wore was blood red and charcoal gray, my personal colors. The brooch clasping it shut bore the same symbol that every heir was given. A silver stripe running down the front right side of the cloak indicated her position as the head of my personal guards.

Typically, I would have two guards, one on each side. The fact that she stood alone, behind me on my right, suggested one of three things—I was a fool, I had faith that she could handle anyone in the room with ease, or I was far more powerful and confident than most fae princesses. Or maybe it was a combination of the three.

"Let's see what she has to offer," said Baerar, ambassador of the water folk. There was a sly gleam in his eyes that I had seen many times during my Lady of Death days.

This was shaping up to be far more interesting than I'd originally thought. With luck, I might find the event enjoyable. My hopes were squashed slightly when the door opened and Miriria swept in, trailing the smell of lilies behind her. Instead of watching my Court-ordered spoilsport, I watched the ambassadors turn toward her and gaze appreciatively.

Baerar noticed me watching him and smirked as Miri walked over and stood at my left shoulder. Turning slightly, I glared at her, and she quickly took two steps back. Not the distance I preferred, but it was better than having her within striking distance. We would definitely have a discussion after this meeting ended.

"Now that there won't be any more interruptions," I began, "why don't we discuss the terms of the truce you two will be signing."

"Isn't that presumptuous, milady?" Krundruk asked, his body stiffening.

I drew a breath and leaned back in my chair as I looked at him. My posture was nothing but regal and my tone cool.

"You and your counterpart have spent the last several years bickering like children. Both of you have been wasting the queen's valuable time over something that should have been agreed upon in a relatively short time." I paused for a few heartbeats. Long enough for the room to grow silent. "I am not my mother. I do not suffer fools of any race. If you do not come to an agreement, I will destroy everything you hold dear, then resume negotiations with your replacements. Eventually, I am certain I will encounter some who will see that negotiating a truce is in their best interests."

"Milady," Miri murmured, "I don't believe—"

Jade moved slightly, and I heard my so-called-handmaiden inhale sharply, her sentence broken before she could finish. Some things didn't require a signal from me. Silencing annoying, wannabe advisors was one of them.

Krundruk snorted. "You do not have the power or authority to do that." I lifted my brows in silent challenge. He lifted his chin and leaned forward. "You are not brazen enough to do something so foolhardy."

Sighing dramatically, I looked down at the desk. It was so much fun when someone challenged me. Clasping my hands together loosely, I began weaving a spell.

Without warning, I stood, sweeping my arms out in a grand gesture. Magick poured forth and flooded the area around the low giants. The ambassador's entourage began choking and clawing at their throats and chests. Their eyes bulged, and their tongues lolled from their mouths. Grotesque grimaces contorted their faces as they collapsed to the floor.

Krundruk spun around before jumping back toward my desk. As the last of his people took their final breath, he turned back around, his hands clenched into fists. It was a pity they weren't allowed weapons. I would have enjoyed a brief sparring match with the arrogant lout. But, alas, ambassadors did not carry weapons in my mother's castle. In fact, only guards were supposed to be armed. I never followed that rule, either.

He slammed his hands down on the top of my desk, leaning forward as he growled at me. "You will pay for this!"

I heard Jade take a step forward, but I held Krundruk's gaze. I knew better than to remove my eyes from the enemy. And, I hadn't finished the spell. It was a two-parter. The first part killed his entourage. The second part was now coming to fruition.

His entourage rose from their death sprawls, their eyes fogged over by death, their faces slack. They lunged forward, grabbing the ambassador by the arms and neck. Unlike humans, low giants did not void everything in their bladders or stomachs upon death, which meant their clothing was still clean. A shame, since that often added to the horror.

Krundruk yelped, kicked, and jerked, but his undead foes were too strong. They began dragging him slowly backward toward the door as he yelled and shrieked.

"When you die," I warned him, "you will become my servant, and you will have no say in the matter. Decide now if you prefer that over a peace treaty."

"Agreed! I'll do as you request!" he shrieked, as he kicked and tried to twist free from the undead. "Please, Your Highness!"

I gestured slightly, and my servants dropped him to the floor. He picked himself up slowly, eyeing them cautiously. They remained standing, eerily and unnaturally still. He returned to my desk, quiet and reserved, fear shining in his eyes and evident on his face.

"Any objections, Baerar?" I asked politely.

"No, Princess," he replied smoothly.

"Good," I said. I reached into a drawer and pulled out copies of the treaty drawn up by my mother's best wordsmiths and presented a copy to each of them. I'd made a few adjustments to the original which didn't favor either side. "Read these, then sign them."

"Yes, Your Highness," both men said together. Reaching forward, they took the agreements and began reading them in silence.

Chapter Thirteen

The moment the two ambassadors and their living entourage departed the office, I turned upon Miriria.

Before I could say anything, she shrieked like a fangirl and squealed, "That was amazing! I cannot believe I got to witness the Lady of Death in action!" She inhaled before speaking again. "I've heard the tales and legends and, of course, I saw you as a young girl before you left to make your name in the mortal realm, but I never thought I'd get to see you actually do something! Everyone always wondered if the legends were true, but after seeing you, here, I don't believe anything was exaggerated! Not at all!"

I glanced at Jade and saw her rolling her eyes, though there was amusement in them, and she was smirking.

"I can always knock her out if she starts groveling," Jade muttered.

I snorted as Miri glowered at Jade. She tossed her head, then turned back to me.

"I honestly doubt Their Highnesses will approve of your methods, though," Miri said, adopting her previous imperious bearing.

Shrugging, I said, "Then Mother shouldn't have told me to handle this affair in any way I saw fit." At Miri's startled expression, I smiled. It wasn't a pleasant smile.

"Apparently you weren't aware of that," Jade observed.

Thankfully, the door opened before either Miri or I could respond. Cildur glanced at my undead minions standing like statues to the side of the door and chuckled. Shaking his head, he said, "Now I understand why your mother is a bit unhappy and wishes to see you." He turned toward my appointed fangirl-handmaiden. "Your presence is not required."

Miriria sniffed and tossed her head again. Perhaps that was her signature maneuver. "My duty is to accompany the princess, so I'll wait for her outside."

Cildur frowned but didn't argue. I exchanged shrugs with Jade. Since I couldn't completely countermand my mother's direct order, I'd have to find other ways of dealing with the irritating woman.

"Lead the way, my friend," I said cheerfully. "My minions can follow behind us."

Cildur snorted but didn't comment. He silently offered me his arm, and I accepted it with a grin. Jade fell in behind us, forcing Miri to stay behind her. I had to give the handmaiden credit; she did try to take a position behind me. Unfortunately for her, Jade was too quick. Between the armor and the Magickal items Jade wore, little could harm her. The weaponry Jade bore, however, would do a great deal of harm to others.

Behind the three of us, the undead, low giant entourage followed in silence. They had no weapons or Magick, but the undead didn't need it. I wanted them with me as a reminder of who I was, and what I was capable of doing. Nothing shy of mass destruction draws attention like a parade.

* * *

The trek to my parents was a short one. Cildur accompanied us to my mother's study, allowing Jade and me to enter before shutting the door behind us, leaving my minions outside the room with him and my handmaiden babysitter.

My father was hiding his laughter behind a glass of whiskey. Mother, however, was frowning darkly.

"I suppose expecting restraint from you would have been too much?" Mother bellowed. "This is the four hundred and forty sixth time you've ignored my no murder in the realm law!"

"Actually, it's the four hundred and forty seventh," Dad corrected her gleefully. "There was that time she murdered the dwarven prince and his nomadic band."

"That could be considered self-defense, which is allowed in the realm," countered Mother.

"No, the bassist was definitely running away," chided Father, smiling wider. "Just because she crushed him under the troll-sized violinist—"

"Hey, I wasn't aiming for the guy running away!" I yelled. I hadn't meant to be loud or to defend myself in their quarrel, so I went silent.

"I will not be deflected from the incident at hand by this old argument," Mother announced in her queenly there-shall-be-no-further-talking voice. Tossing the hem of her dress away from her feet, Mother began pacing. "Do not tell me that reanimating the ambassador's entourage means you didn't kill them. While it was clever to have them attack him to prove your point, you still slew, without just cause, almost a dozen people. You came home for protection. The gift of sanctuary does not include my having to protect everyone in my realm from you!"

"They signed the treaty," I said, trying not to smile. I don't think there was a time when she didn't scold me for my methods. This kind of argument usually happened no matter what the outcome. "It's not like I'm going to return to my glory days, Mother."

"The fact that you still call them your glory days is what concerns me the most!" she countered.

"They were rather enjoyable, Mother," I replied, trying not to give into laughter. Dad coughed, and I resisted the urge to wink at him. "Really, Mom. You're the one who decided I need to stay here for my protection."

"Why would I do that, I wonder?" Mother asked curtly. "Perhaps your penchant for making reckless decisions when danger is approaching?"

"It's not like Sterling hasn't kept me safe," I countered, my laughter ebbing away. "Mom, he barely lets me read any of my tomes or journals, let alone do any Magick he deems 'wrong,'"

"How sweet of him." Her tone was sour, and her expression was far from pleased. "If he wasn't protecting his own interests, I might consider it a noble gesture."

"What do you mean by that?" I demanded.

"Merlin has sired many children and considering how most of them have ended up? He's hoping to keep this one alive!" Mother said the words like a curse.

Dad groaned.

"Wait. What?" I asked, all anger and laughter vanishing. "Sterling is Merlin?" From the expression on my father's face, it appeared I was the only one in my family who didn't know Sterling was the legendary Merlin.

"And where did our daughter get her lack of subtlety?" Dad asked.

"Obviously, Sterling is Merlin!" Mother exclaimed. "He pretends to be ruled by the Council, but he actually runs it! How do you think he knows everything? Have your father and I ever openly shared information? Do you think the other Council members are more open?" She threw her head back and laughed. "You have the sparkles and colors of blinding infatuation in your eyes, haven't you? You don't have a clue."

Turning, I saw Jade looking at me evenly. She showed no sign of surprise or shock.

Turning back to my parents, I narrowed my gaze as another realization hit home. "Is that why you threatened me with the Council all those years ago? You said if the Council found out what I'd been doing, they'd want my head on a platter. That I'd be tried and found guilty, and I wouldn't like the punishment."

"We told you because it was true, no matter what form the leader of the Council wore at the time," Dad replied in a calm, even voice. "If the decision had been against you, you would have paid the penalty. You've always had a problem being held accountable by others. No less as a child."

At least, they didn't know everything I'd done back then. A small mercy, in my opinion.

"So, you kicked Merlin out of your realm because... why? Because he refused to declare his undying love for me? Or because he didn't give you the answers you wanted, Mom?" I retorted, still trying to grasp the news that I was having Merlin's child.

"Pretty much," Dad muttered.

Mom shot him a glare that implied he wouldn't be sleeping with her any time soon. Then she turned her gaze back toward me.

"You can focus on what you think is valid, my daughter, or you can listen and gain wisdom." Before continuing, she seemed to realize her temper had gotten the better of her, and she sighed. "Merlin stopped letting anyone see him as a figure of legend after two of his children, two of the few that survived to adulthood, nearly destroyed England and sent that world into a dark place for far too long. The realm you currently call yours is still paying the price for what happened."

"Arthur and Morgana," Dad elucidated somberly.

"His other children have had less infamous, but no less tragic, ends," Mother continued. "So, perhaps you now comprehend my lack of enthusiasm at your being burdened with his child?"

"It's only a burden if I allow it," I countered flatly. "Arthur and Morgana had a mortal mother. From everything I've heard, every child of his had a mortal mother. Or did someone from our community, with an equally strong bloodline, give birth to one of his children?"

"I haven't bothered to ask or investigate," Mother replied stiffly. "Since I became a member of the Council, I've spent far too much time dealing with the messes Merlin's offspring caused."

"I see." Turning to Dad, I asked, "Do you feel the same?"

"We share some concerns," Dad admitted. "But I usually prepare for the worst and see how things develop before jumping in."

Speech would not come. My brain refused to form words or even sarcasm. The silence hung in the air for a few heartbeats.

"You've just been given a lot to absorb and consider," Dad said. He turned to my mother as he added, "Why don't we let her return to her chambers to reflect and rest?"

Mother opened her mouth, then closed it. After a moment, she nodded, then turned away.

I strode from the room without ordering Miri to stay behind. Jade would do that for me. Cildur and Jade talked quietly, leaving me with my thoughts.

I really hated having the rug yanked out from under me.

Chapter Fourteen

Jade sat in a chair as I paced my room. I wasn't certain whether I was furious at my parents, Merlin, or life in general. Arylla was curled up in Jade's lap watching me.

"Why didn't you tell me?" I demanded.

Jade sighed and looked away. "It wasn't my place, Catherine." She turned her eyes back to me. "I also didn't realize you didn't know."

"No. I didn't know Sterling was Merlin," I snapped. "Mom always talked about how Merlin took her beneath his proverbial wing. How he had her give Arthur the sword of legend. No wonder she always spoke so... warmly about him."

"Yet she banished him from her realm when he crossed the line and knocked up her daughter," Jade said. "You do know why, right?"

I glowered at her. "Do tell, oh knowledgeable one."

Jade chuckled. "For one, neither of you have said anything about your feelings for each other. Your mother knows your penchant for having a male harem. What I don't think she realizes is you only choose those you can't dominate, and that list is becoming increasingly shorter. And Merlin has gone to extreme measures to keep any child of his from being born since one of his offspring was killed by a couple members of the Council during an attempted coup."

"Tell me something I don't know," I retorted.

"Very well," Jade replied. "You are the only child your mother has birthed that has lived to adulthood, let alone past a century. Every other child has died from war, assassination, illness, or by her hand. Your child is her sole grandchild. I don't believe she imagined you would have a child yet, let alone by the one person she trusted to end your self-imposed isolation."

"I guess he brought me out of isolation a great deal more than anyone, including me, expected," I said, my voice heavy with exasperation.

"That's part of why your mom is so furious with him," Jade explained patiently. "He crossed an invisible line by not only being your lover, but by getting you pregnant. It doesn't matter that it wasn't anything either of you did. She's your mother, so she's going to be unreasonable. Besides, you do have a habit of killing people who anger you."

"That's beside the point," I retorted loftily. "I don't kill everyone, only those who deserve it."

"As your parent, and the notoriously aggressive one at that," Jade continued, "she is always going to see you as a younger, less controlled version of herself."

"So?"

"So, she isn't going to trust you to make wise decisions," she replied. "Especially since you've made what she probably considers a colossal mistake."

"Great," I said with a sigh. "It's so nice to know my mother thinks my getting pregnant was a mistake."

"Pregnant by the one being she can't outright destroy," a muffled voice said.

I jumped, wondering where in the Hells Maekyl was hiding. I heard his voice again, still heavily muffled. "Well, one of the few, at least."

I realized, finally, why I was hearing him.

It only took a few moments to unpack the crystal dragon skull I'd tucked into the bag Xantos had given me. I had sent that bag, which was bigger on the inside than the outside, ahead with Jade and my father. It had originally held several gold bars and the boxes that contained the hand scythes Xantos gifted me, but it looked no bigger than a gift bag and weighed about the same. I had tucked my scythes and the crystal skull inside before sending it with my father.

The crystal skull was barely larger than my hand, and it was the only way Maekyl and I had to communicate while I was in my mother's realm. Father had given it to me when he gave me Maekyl, and I made certain I took it with me whenever I visited her. The eyes were glowing red, since Maekyl was using the skull to communicate with me.

"Nice to hear from you, Maekyl," I said, placing the skull on a table. "I think you hit the nail on the head with Mom. At least Dad isn't flipping out."

"I wish you'd take my little talisman for a stroll while you're there," he replied. "I do love the scenery in your mother's realm. But yes, had you been impregnated by a mere mortal, or even someone only halfway worthy, your mother would have been at ease. She could have vaporized them at will."

"Remind me to never date a mortal," I grumbled. "Please tell me you have some good news. Like a way to escape my mother's realm."

"Didn't take her long to confine you to her realm, did it? I suppose you didn't see that coming any more than you realized your lover's true identity," Maekyl commented.

"'Actually, I did suspect Mom would do something like this, but I didn't have much choice in the matter, did I?" I glowered at the flashing red eyes in the crystal skull. "Why did no one bother mentioning that Sterling is Merlin?"

"Perhaps everyone presumed you were intelligent enough to figure it out or that he would tell you." Maekyl paused before adding in what he probably meant as a thoughtful tone, "Why didn't he tell you?" Instead, it came across as sly and snarky.

Damn it. I couldn't argue with that logic, even if Maekyl was being an ass about it. "Perhaps he didn't think it was important. I'm sure he would have told me prior to my taking the position as Speaker of the Council."

The words sounded lame and pitiful as they left my mouth.

"I have no doubt," Maekyl said smoothly. "Considering the Speaker and he have a telepathic connection; it would be difficult for him to hide such a thing from you. In fact, every member on the Council knows Fergus Sterling's actual identity, even if they were clueless prior to assuming their position."

"Indeed?" I asked, realizing a few things would have to happen prior to my officially accepting the position, including establishing mental wards that would keep Merlin from stealing my thoughts when I didn't want him to. "I'll deal with that later. How are things going at home? Have you heard from Trix?"

"Actually, Trix is why I contacted you. I found her," Maekyl replied.

"Where was she? When will she be there?" I demanded.

Maekyl chuckled. "She was actually in the realm where Xantos lives, a charming place she called the Shades of Death."

"How long until she's home?"

Maekyl chuckled again. "Within the week. Possibly sooner. Don't worry, I'll tell her all the sordid details about what's happened since you ended your reign."

"It would have been a longer reign if my parents hadn't intruded," I grumbled half-heartedly.

"Maybe by five years," Maekyl commented. "Then Merlin would have come for you."

There was a long pause before I was able to make my tongue work again. "What?"

"He and your mother have been as close as siblings since Camelot. He is older than she, and he has always looked upon her as a little sister. Charming, really, when you think about it." I could almost see Maekyl smirking. "He heard tales about your capers and gave your parents ten years to end your reign. Since your mum has always been like a sister to him, he wanted to give her a chance to stop you."

"How generous," I muttered. Apparently, there were a good many secrets between us. It also explained why he was so determined that I not peruse the darkest of my tomes. "I need a way out of here, Maekyl. No one in my mother's realm will be able to help me. She's made certain of that."

"I will find some options," Maekyl replied in a confidant tone.

"Thanks, Maekyl," I said before turning to Jade. "Shall we take him for a walk before he arranges my departure?"

Chapter Fifteen

Having successfully angered my mother, again, I refrained from breaking any more rules for the rest of the day. Instead, I wandered through my mother's vast gardens, enjoying the pleasant weather and Jade's companionship. I was fairly certain that would not have been the case if Miri had trailed along with us, but there were ways of exiting my mother's castle without being seen. Fortunately, I knew most of them.

By the time the bells tolled, signaling the evening hour when all would gather to mingle before dinner, I had calmed down enough that I wouldn't give into the temptation to have my merry band of undead low giants dance and perform before the gathered courtiers, no matter how much I might enjoy it.

It didn't take Miriria long to find me or for others to join my quiet conversation with a few of my old childhood friends. During a lull in the conversation, one of Miri's flunkies spoke up.

"You are the mortal realm's 'Lady of Death?' My, my! You have been a subject of debate for ages!" The flunky's excitement practically glowed around her. I didn't want to have a conversation with this... person. But, she carried on. "The Queen forbids us to talk about it, but it's such a provocative title. Why not

'Queen of Death' or princess or some higher title? Did other beings rule above you? I think one of the old gods gave you the name, but everyone here has their own belief."

Jade interjected while I took deep breaths. The mantra "don't vaporize these idiots" clanged repeatedly in my head.

"The mortals of the realm coined the term," Jade explained, smiling and speaking as a teacher would to a group of children. "For them, 'Lady' refers to someone of grace, presence, and persona. She doesn't have to be a royal."

"She gracefully handed out death? Or delivered judgment for one of the old gods with a commanding and strong presence?" someone asked.

The mantra pounded louder in my head.

"No gods were involved," Jade continued in her tone of faux patience. "She did everything with—what is the mortal term? Ah, yes: Style."

There was a hushed sigh from the flunkies. Hells, Jade was making them fans of the stories. Soon, they'd be asking for autographs or pictures with me.

"Catherine amassed enough power and skill to thwart any attempt from mortals to defeat her," Cildur added. "Since they have little to no real knowledge of our people, everything she did had a grace they could barely fathom."

Oh, gods, he was laying it on thick. Maybe I should kill him? No, it would solve nothing.

He didn't stop there. In a calm, serene voice, he added, "Mortals are prone to worship our people simply on our natural beauty. Catherine was and is coveted by them for that, along with her strength and grace. She simply used to kill a lot of them regularly."

"Are mortals that annoying?" The first flunky that had spoken asked. Her eagerness was doubled. "Or were there that many attempts to challenge you? Or both?"

"Mortals can be very annoying," I began slowly. At least Mother wasn't here to spell my mouth shut. Or maybe it was a pity? "I didn't kill everyone who crossed my path, only those who deserved it." For the most part. "Or those who challenged my rule. The title was gifted to me when I attained my position of power. The truth isn't nearly as exciting as the legends."

"She is being modest, a trait she picked up from the mortals. Modesty is a trait many humans have, usually to their detriment," Jade said. She smiled wider as I glared at her. "A prince among mortals, called a sheik, first called her by that name. He was trying to impress and flatter her, expecting her to take mercy on him and his soldiers."

"It worked for him, in a way." Cildur laughed as he spoke. "The sheik was spared and, until he died, he cleaned chambers after your orgies, as I recall."

Well, dammit. Leave it to those two to interject enough truth into the story that I couldn't honestly deny what they were saying. I wondered if my teeth were in danger of breaking from grinding together.

"I did give the sheik a choice. He could work as a servant and attempt to redeem himself, or he could die," I said, hoping to end the conversation. "He chose to work as a servant and try to escape." My mouth betrayed me and added, "He wasn't good at escaping, though."

Giggles burst out of the flunkies.

"His cleaning skills did improve," Jade added. The giggling grew to roars of laughter.

"How did you procure a castle? Was it a gift or did you attack and claim it as your own?" someone asked as the laughter died down.

Miri gazed at me, her eyes glittering. "Indeed. Many of us grew up hearing the legends and stories. Even now, there aren't many who don't feel some fear when hearing your name. Surely it isn't unwarranted!"

My first impulse was to reply with a line from one of the mortal comedies I've seen. I forced my mouth to stay shut until the impulse passed.

Maybe I had spent too much time around mundanes?

This verbal barrage did shed some light on why my mother forbade any discussion about my reign. At least Maekyl wasn't here to spread word of his darling Lady of Death. The tales he'd tell would have them eating out of his non-existent hands, and they wouldn't be lies or exaggerations, which was the problem.

If I was going to embrace the truth of who I was, I guess I needed to start with my past. I'd eventually have to tell my child, so why not start with the adults?

"Fine, fine. You want the truth? I'll give you the truth," I said, trying to keep from snapping out the words.

Jade snickered, and I glowered at her again, which didn't faze her.

"The sheik heard the name used by some local peasants. They paid their tithe to me and, in return, I granted them protection. Actual protection. I also resolved the problems they brought before me, as my mother does with her subjects."

Cildur laughed. "I seem to remember that they quickly learned how to resolve their petty squabbles."

"Details. Details." I waved off his comments, despite the giggles around us. "The peasants gave me the title because of the way I claimed the castle. The claiming is what brought the sheik."

The anticipation could have been cut with a blade. Arylla trilled softly in my ear. Apparently, she was enjoying herself. I took a moment to reflect.

"No, that's not entirely accurate," I admitted. "The castle is what attracted the sheik. He thought it was abandoned. He was only wrong by a few centuries."

"And one being," Cildur added playfully.

"The castle is what lured me to the area. I heard about a wondrous palace built in the mountains of a land called Tuscany, with a room for every day of the mortal year," I recalled fondly.

"That would be three hundred and sixty-five," Jade informed the flunkies. "Days and rooms."

A hushed awe flowed over the group. That number was even impressive in my mother's realm, where we resided in a castle with two hundred rooms.

"I went to see this marvel of construction. As fate would have it, the noble who owned it was quite paranoid." The memory made me smile. "Even the peasants who lived outside the castle were wary of anyone approaching. I was riding a beautiful black stallion and wearing stunning clothing made in this realm, but all who saw me gazed at me with distrust in their eyes. When I arrived at the castle gates, the guards demanded my business. My request to see the splendor of the Spanish noble's home and to congratulate him on its beauty was met with hatred. I was accused of being a scout for a waiting hoard who wanted to claim the Castello for their ruler, a seductress who intended to ingratiate herself to their lord and live off his riches."

Shock and quiet giggles met this last statement. I nodded.

"Certainly, none of you would tolerate such insults, so you can understand my position," I said. "I slew the guards of the front watch with a gesture, save one. I spared him so he could report my presence to his ruler."

Some of the listeners shifted uncomfortably, but many did not. Miri was smiling and staring at me. I continued my narrative.

"The noble, carried by four servants, arrived with two score soldiers. I laughed at his arrogance and absurdity. This mortal male was no god. He wasn't even a proper ruler. Yet, he expected to be treated so lavishly? I wanted to strike him down for his ignorance and pride. Instead, I apologized for making an example of his hirelings, explaining that I wanted to make sure he did not mistake me for the common trash his guards had.

"As it turned out, the guards had gotten their attitudes from their employer." The memory of the confrontation still made my face burn, and I'm sure my eyes blazed while I continued. "He made several insulting remarks before I lashed out and killed the servants carrying him. When he crashed to the ground, I laughed and asked him if he still felt mighty. Scrambling away, he commanded his guards in an unsettled voice to destroy me." I knew my amusement was showing on my face, and there was laughter in my voice. "Instead of wiping them out with a single spell, I decided to have some fun. To make a show of the slaughter, as it were.

"One by one and two by two the guards fell at my hands. When everyone at the entrance and front of the castle was stilled, I fetched my hand scythes from the saddle. I went from room to room, ending every life, until I found the noble. He was cowering behind five guards who barely put up a struggle. Pointing a scythe that dripped the blood of those he had taken into his grand place, I offered him a choice: Surrender his home to me or perish like all before him."

Everyone was holding their breath, awaiting what came next. I really hadn't done myself any favors, but what else could I do?

"So, what did he choose?" someone broke the silence, eager anticipation in every word.

"He began babbling like a fool, spewing threats and declaring vengeance." I smirked at the memory. "He died, and his skull became the greeter at the main gates."

The gathered group of listeners, which appeared to be growing, chuckled.

"That can't be the only reason they called you Lady of Death," another voice said.

I couldn't see who it was, but the voice sounded familiar.

"Oh, no. Absolutely not," Jade said. The broad smile on her face showed how much she was enjoying herself. "She was renowned for reanimating the dead and having them do menial labor."

Cildur laughed, before adding, "She commanded many groups of undead to walk into a giant bonfire when she grew tired of the rotting corpses or their failures."

"Or who they were," Jade said. "She also had a throne crafted from the bones of her enemies by the remaining undead."

"Don't forget the horde of skulls she used to speak to those inside and outside the castle. I think that was my favorite." Cildur chuckled. "Many who went to the castle were terrified before they met the glamorous woman who ruled her land, making certain her peasants' lives were safe and relatively comfortable."

"Happy workers make for productive workers," I said loftily. "In that era, ensuring their safety ensured their loyalty to me, especially after the way they were treated by the lord I had slain."

Jade and Cildur exchanged grins. They might not have planned any of this, but they were certainly taking advantage of the opportunity to gloat about my reign in the mortal realm.

A few moments later, Cildur gave me a sidelong glance. "Being a good ruler is more than keeping people safe and content. You ruled with an iron fist that was just and fair. That your preferred method of corporal punishment was death encouraged the peasants to police themselves for 'trifling' matters." I glowered at him, which he laughed at before continuing. "There was no peasant within the surrounding lands who did not know of your infamous parties and orgies or the power you commanded with ease. You were a witch to be reckoned with in their eyes. Either that or a goddess."

"That was the opinion of most men who saw her," Jade muttered none-too-quietly. "That she had to be an ancient goddess returned to rule."

"What of the talisman?" the familiar voice asked.

This time, I saw who was speaking, and I recognized her.

Cloris was not someone I would have called a friend, let alone a 'fan.' There was a faction within my mother's kingdom who didn't believe I should be my mother's heir, partly because my father was human, but also because I was a necromancer who repeatedly broke the rules. Because I was the Princess Royal, they believed I should follow and uphold the rules, not break them at every turn. I had no proof, but I suspected the biggest grievance they had against me was that I didn't permanently live within my mother's realm.

How could an heir possibly know how to rule a realm, let alone know anything about the people in it, if she did not reside in the kingdom and shadow the queen's every move? I strongly suspected the group believed I should follow my mother into the privy just to learn the 'proper' way to use the toilet. Why Cloris was listening to the legend behind my "Lady of Death" title was beyond me.

"It came to me during my reign," I replied, keeping the explanation short and simplistic. "It was an invaluable item."

"Did you actually use a dull table knife to cut off someone's head?" someone asked. The question was echoed by several others.

Morbidity and a love of the macabre are not solely mortal human interests. The fae, I assure you, are even more interested in grisly tales.

"Oh, yes," Jade said solemnly. "The talisman was often used to turn mundane weapons into incredible items that defied the laws of nature and physics."

She and I exchanged knowing expressions. The talisman had been used for more than that, but none who knew the truth were going to describe everything that could be done with it.

I nodded and continued the tale. "It was after an evening meal. An orgy was planned for later that night. While I was busy tending to last minute details, one of the servants tried to attack me."

"The servant had been paid to do so," Jade interjected.

"Indeed. This occurred in the dining room where the feasts took place. Since I had just acquired the talisman, I was curious to see what I could do with it. I didn't have any other useful weapon at hand, so I said the proper words, and the knife became a deadly weapon. I conjured a shield, then beheaded the servant with a single stroke of the knife. Sadly, I was unable to capture the Magick of that particular death."

"There are many stories behind how you obtained the talisman," Cloris insisted. "What is the truth? How did you really acquire it?"

So, that was the real reason she was among the gathered fans. I studied the woman. Her golden hair was braided and wrapped into an elaborate coil around her head. Her peach halter gown was fitted to her slender body but did nothing for her complexion or her too-angular face. As with most of the gowns in my mother's world, the fabric was soft and seemed to float in the air.

"Where did you obtain the ring you wear that detects and neutralizes poison? Or the earrings that keep your mind protected from certain spells?" I countered. A sly smile curled my lips. "I could keep going."

Cloris's face flushed a vivid red, and she looked away quickly.

Several others chuckled, and I heard sporadic murmurs.

I took the opportunity to end the conversation. "I think that's enough, at least for now. If this continues, my mother is going to find out, and she is not going to be happy."

There was a collective sigh followed by quiet agreement from the eldest members of the group.

Slowly, everyone dispersed, and I was left with Jade, Cildur, and Miri.

I still wasn't certain who I wanted to flog the most, though I was leaning toward the unwanted groupie.

"What happened to the amulet?" Miri asked after everyone left.

I sighed and glowered at her. "It was destroyed. I'm certain you can find a bard or twelve who can regale you with exploits from my reigning days."

Thankfully, the bells chimed, signaling the evening feast. I swept past Miri and wove through the crowd until I was far away from the annoying groupie. Jade kept pace and Cildur, I suspected, wasn't far behind.

At least, for the evening feast, I'd be seated beside my father or mother. I wouldn't have to worry about entertaining a group of fans by recounting stories of my glorious, yet depressingly short, reign in the human realm.

Chapter Sixteen

The dinner had not been as much of an escape as I had hoped. Instead, the topics of discussion had been me, my health, and my mother's plan for my entire pregnancy while I was in her realm.

There was nothing more "enjoyable" than answering questions about when I was going to begin planning the nursery, what I was going to put in it, and what foods didn't agree with me. Throw in some good, old-fashioned ass-kissing from Miri and Cloris, and I was more than ready to retrieve my hand scythes and go on a murderous rampage.

I had rarely been so happy to retreat to my rooms. I was tempted to stay hidden in my suite for the remainder of my time here.

As I stood in the middle of my room debating what I wanted to do, I felt a shift in the air around me. A portal took form and grew until it was the size and relative shape of a door.

Blinking in dumbfounded shock, I stared at the portal as I recognized the Magick.

I heard an all-too-familiar voice through the opening. "Don't stand and dawdle, unless you'd prefer to remain in your mother's realm until she decides to release you?"

"No, that's quite all right," I said.

I had no time to pack. I grabbed my twin scythes and my bag of holding, into which I dropped Maekyl's crystal skull, and left everything else. Arylla was curled around my neck, her tiny claws clutching me tightly. Stepping through the portal, I departed my mother's realm and stepped into Xantos's domain. I didn't feel a moment's regret, even though I knew my mother was going to be thoroughly pissed at Xantos and me. I took a moment to orient myself.

I had no doubt I stood in his office, which was anything but small. The carpet was lush and thick, silencing my steps as I moved away from the portal that closed behind me and walked further into the room. The walls were not stone, as one would expect in a medieval society. They were a dark, rich wood that absorbed sound. Paintings of elves hung on one wall, while bookshelves lined the others. Weapons filled the spaces in between the art and book, and none appeared to be only for display. Glancing over my shoulder, I saw an enormous mirror that covered most of one wall and reflected the room back at me.

What captured my attention and kept it, though, was not the paintings, the contents of the bookshelves, the elegant desk, or the elf sitting behind it, but the Magick that filled the air. It was strong, heady, and when I looked at myself, I discovered it was spilling off me as I moved.

Holding my right hand up, I watched as glowing, glittering dust poured from my skin, vanishing before it touched the floor. It was Magick in its purest form.

Magick as I had never seen it, not even in my mother's realm. It reminded me of pixie dust as the mundanes presented it in the movies, trailing behind a certain fairy, except it was brighter and spilled from my skin.

The Magick felt heady, seductive. Every fiber of my being wanted to experiment with spells and discover what I could do. I didn't, though, since I was a guest in Xantos's home and playing with Magick the moment you set foot inside someone's home was beyond rude.

I slowly moved toward two chairs carved from a rich mahogany-colored wood that shone in the light from the candles and torches on the walls. Choosing the chair on my right, I sat and discovered it was padded and comfortable. Xantos watched me with an expression that seemed to be a mixture of amusement and seriousness.

"Why would you ever want to leave here for my realm?" I asked, still in shock. I could feel the Magick imbued in everything around me, even the air I breathed.

In Xantos's case, I suspected the answer would rank up there with 'deadly.'

Xantos chuckled at my question, though the amusement was fleeting. "You cannot perform any black Magick, especially necromancy, in this realm while you are pregnant."

That was rather unexpected, I thought, as I sat there silently.

When I didn't say anything for a few moments, he nodded slightly and continued speaking. "As you can see and feel, the Magick within this realm is far stronger than any you've ever encountered. Magick is as common as the air you breathe. It's part of everything. Priests are granted spells from the gods simply because of their beliefs and sworn oaths to their chosen deities. Magick items, depending on what they are, can be used by anyone—Magick user or not, Magickal being or human. Your spells will be stronger and more powerful within my realm. Black Magick, especially necromancy, can adversely affect your unborn child. It can, and will, turn her evil."

"That sucks," I said in a huff. Blushing, I glanced away from the dark elf. I held out a hand and shook it, causing the Magick to dance and rain from my fingers. "It would be rather interesting to see what I could do here."

"While I would normally encourage such chaotic exploration, I cannot condone it for now," Xantos said, his voice and body language remorseful. "In the time it would take you to learn how to control the sudden, drastic increase in your Magick, there would be too much damage to you and your child."

"Pity," I said. "I have no doubt I could learn a great deal from you. Hopefully, there will be an opportunity after I've given birth?" The moment I said that another thought occurred to me. "Perhaps, in the meantime, you could teach me how to shield my thoughts from others, from beings such as my mother and Sterling."

Xantos gave me a cock-eyed smirk and declared, "Both of those wishes shall be granted."

For a brief moment, I wondered if this was an elaborate ruse to get me to visit him in his realm. Then I decided he had better methods for making that happen.

"Would you care for a refreshment?" asked Xantos. "A tour of my facilities is also an option."

"I would love a tour of your... facilities," I replied with a smile.

Arylla uncurled from her hiding spot around my neck and perched on my shoulder where she trilled at Xantos. Reaching up, I scratched her behind an ear.

"I hope my having Arylla with me won't be a problem."

"The little one may find some members of my menagerie a little unsettling," he replied. "But I have no objections to her being here. If I had, she wouldn't have been allowed through my portal."

I nodded thoughtfully. "Fair enough. Speaking of your menagerie, how is the little tykcri?"

The tykcri were rare, panther-like creatures with snow white fur and delicate onyx horns. Nick had been collecting rare, mythical creatures and selling them to the highest bidder. After he was stripped of his Magick, I intercepted the egg from which Arylla hatched. That, in turn, led to the discovery of Nick's illegal collection of creatures, which had included the tykcri. When I rescued the little cub, it attached itself to me until I asked Xantos to care for it.

"Far from little, actually." Xantos's orange eyes twinkled, and he held out his arm. "I sense we should start your tour in my menagerie, near the tykcri's nest."

I moved toward the ancient dark elf and accepted his arm gracefully. "I would love that."

Oddly, Arylla whistled softly at Xantos, her head tilted quizzically to the side. I found it interesting, since she rarely did that toward Sterling.

The moment we stepped outside Xantos's office, I felt like a tiny mouse in an enormous labyrinth. The sensation didn't have anything to do with the stone floor and walls around me, the wide, spacious hallway, or the décor on the walls.

It had everything to do with the Magick I could sense around me. Staring at the wall, I noticed glittering strands woven among the stone. They shifted constantly, revealing themselves in fleeting glimpses.

I glanced at Xantos and debated asking about them. The Magick, I was certain, belonged to him. Thinking back to my days as the Lady of Death, I smiled.

"Your office is in the center of your abode, isn't it?" I asked, trying to keep the sly tone from my voice.

"Yes, like a spider in the center of a web," Xantos replied. "My people have an affinity towards arachnids."

"I suspected as much," I said, suppressing a laugh. My gaze drifted to the walls, where the flickering strands danced as we walked. "This is the first time I've been able to see Magick so easily. I suspect that particular enchantment allows you to know what is happening within your walls, yes?"

"Precisely," he replied. "Magick is at the heart of everything in my realm. Because I am so connected to it, even the marginalized levels of Magick in your realm are easy for me to manipulate. I breathe Magickal energy more than air."

I nodded thoughtfully, then thought about what he said as we walked. The silence between us was companionable, and I found myself enjoying every moment spent in his presence. We moved from one hallway to the next. Each one was decorated differently, and I realized there was a subtle reason behind it.

It was easy to navigate the labyrinth by memorizing the decor of each corridor.

The Magick trailing from me swirled around us and vanished. I suspected Xantos was absorbing or capturing it. Since I was in no position to argue, I said nothing. It didn't help that the longer I was in his realm and the longer I was around him, the more I realized my attraction to him was growing.

He may have been a spider, but I was determined to not be his fly.

As Xantos led the way into the depths of his vast estate, I was quite surprised we encountered no one else. I could hear and sense others around us, but apparently, when the master of this lair was escorting a guest, he was to be left alone. Not that I could complain. I had once demanded the same of my servants and guards.

I could tell the moment we neared his menagerie. The décor on the stone walls shifted from art and weaponry to carvings of enchanting flora and fauna.

There was an underlying scent of rich dirt and animal musk. The hallway grew wider, and I noticed a distinct change in my host. He seemed eager, yet relaxed, as though he were entering a domain he cherished and loved.

I wasn't surprised since I had seen him interact with the baby tykcri.

The doors were placed at odd intervals, which differed from those I'd seen on the walk here. They were also larger, which made me wonder what moved through these corridors. Xantos led me to a door that was elaborately decorated with finely carved images of felines—breeds that I could name and many I could not. Whoever had done the carving had breathed life into the images, for they were quite realistic. Each creature's habitat was depicted on the door, but they were melded together seamlessly.

I reached out and ran my hand over the image of the tykcri. The creature stared out at us, draped on the branch of an ancient tree. I couldn't tell if the tykcri was resting or preparing to pounce, but I could easily envision its tail twitching lazily. It was only when I stared at the tail that I noticed the artist had included other creatures in the design—a lizard crawled beneath the tykcri and insects dotted the air.

A low chuckle came from Xantos, and I felt myself blushing. "It's a captivating door," I said, trying to explain my fascination with the art.

"Is that what the humans call a pun?" Xantos asked. "It's one of many unique pieces I had made for the estate."

Uncertain about what to say, I merely smiled and shrugged. "I'm looking forward to seeing any other pieces you're willing to show me."

Xantos smirked.

The door opened without a sound. Apparently, he didn't like to open anything with his hands. That thought took my mind a few places it really shouldn't have. It didn't help that I suspected Xantos could easily read my thoughts, and I didn't know what he would do with them. Anything else I might have said or thought vanished the moment I stepped over the threshold.

It was like stepping into an enchanted forest. I looked behind me, and the door was still there, as was the stone wall. In front of me and on all sides, though, was a forest like I'd never seen. Some of the trees looked familiar, but most were not from my world. The trunks were different shades of brown, and the leaves were shapes I'd never seen. The greens were more vibrant and shinier.

I inhaled deeply, relishing the richness of the earth along with the fragrant flowers. I could smell the animal musk and hear their movements, but so far, all I could see was a path among the trees and bushes that grew within the vast cavern.

I wasn't sure how I knew it was a cavern. I suspected it was because I had started to realize that the phrase "drunk on power" could be a literal thing. Here, I could feel so much of what was around me and feel the energy being created by each part while it flowed and filled spaces. It reminded me of when I experimented with the talisman and had grown heady from the abundance of power I'd manipulated. On that occasion, I could sense the spaces in every room where I lived.

Xantos studied me while I remained still and relaxed at the edge of this enchanted forest. After a few moments, we moved forward along the path. He walked slower than he had in the hallways, and I thought, again, that this must be a place he enjoyed. Perhaps one he even loved.

No. I was not going to think about what it would be like to be loved by him. That way led to danger and possible death. Definitely danger, which was something I had once thrived upon. Silently, I admitted that I wouldn't object to the physical meaning of the word.

"Are all the creatures depicted on the door in here?" I asked softly, determined to distract myself.

"I have more than one door," he answered slyly. "But to answer your question, yes, they are."

I blinked a few times and bit my lip before replying. "I'm sure you do." *As do I.* The thought came unbidden, and I didn't voice it. Instead, I said, "Is there an entire ecosystem in here, complete with prey for the predators?"

Xantos retained the sly smile as he answered my question. "Not a complete ecosystem. That would be too difficult to control and maintain. No, I have keepers who feed the creatures that dwell within this part of my menagerie."

Before I could say anything else or allow my mind to continue on its errant path toward the gutter, we entered a clearing the size of a football field. I heard the sound of running water to our right. Having a constant source of clean water for the denizens of this habitat was logical, I thought.

Xantos didn't have to speak before a full-grown tykcri bounded over from the edge of the clearing nearest us. It raced across the short distance and pounced on me. For a moment, I wondered if I was about to become dinner. Then I realized this tykcri was the baby I had given Xantos.

How I knew that I had no clue. Somehow, though, I did, which was a refreshing thought as I landed on my rear. The tykcri began nuzzling me and purring loudly. He even licked me with his rough tongue.

Arylla screeched and flew into the air, where she scolded me as I rubbed the tykcri and tried to escape its affections. After a few moments of snuggling and rubbing, the creature licked me one last time before taking a few steps back. Looking over its shoulder toward the tree line, it yowled before purring again and moving forward to lean against me. I draped my arm around its neck.

A few moments later, a second tykcri emerged from the trees. The new arrival, smaller than the one who was trying to flop into my lap, padded daintily over to Xantos. The second tykcri's features were identical to those of the larger one.

She had the same snow-white fur and obsidian-black horns positioned delicately before her ears. The scorpion-like stinger at the end of her tail was curled around her feet as she sat, sphinxlike, beside Xantos. Looking down at the male tykcri, which was halfway on my lap, I grinned. My friend had grown up rather quickly and found himself a lady-love.

"I see what you mean about him not being so little," I said as I ran my fingers through his fur, which was far softer and thicker than I would have imagined. Looking at the tykcri female who watched me with a somewhat disdainful expression, I asked, "Are they as rare in your world as they are in mine?"

"They are," Xantos replied. His eyes twinkled with mischief and mirth. "The cubs are easy prey for the natural predators in this realm, and they provide valuable and rare components for specific spells and Magick items."

My fingers tightened in the tykcri's fur. I looked up and realized other felines were slowly emerging from the forest around us. I saw lynx and bobcats, as well as more fantastical creatures. Some looked like hellcats, for they had sleek bodies covered in black fur. Orange light flickered, giving the impression of sparks, as they stalked toward us.

My tykcri didn't move. Arylla chirped sharply a few times before gingerly perching on Xantos's shoulder. She kept looking at him warily and seemed ready to take flight at any moment.

I glanced toward Xantos, who didn't seem the least bit concerned, so I remained sitting on the ground. The felines padded closer. The tykcri on my lap raised his head and watched them, though he didn't move away from me. One by one, the others sniffed us before lying down. The sound of their purring filled the air.

Smiling, I let out a quiet sigh of relief. One of the sleek, black-furred cats curled up opposite the tykcri, leaning against me, its eyes closed serenely as I brushed a hand through its fur.

Xantos smirked. "It appears they like you."

Chapter Seventeen

Spending time with Xantos and his collection of creatures was an experience I would remember for the rest of my life. It was also one I was looking forward to repeating as often as possible. I could learn a great deal from Xantos and his realm. It would be interesting to see what would carry over to my realm.

As we were leaving his dragon enclosure, where I had been able to play with a couple of newly hatched wyvrns, a servant approached Xantos. Concern and fear were etched on his face.

"Master, there is a problem at the forge. Your presence will, unfortunately, be required." The servant spoke in a voice that wavered between respect and concern.

"Is it the same problem as before?" Xantos asked evenly. His manner was all business.

"Ah, not the same as last time," the servant answered. "But there has been such an error before. The same smith is responsible for this one."

"Thzrrzk?" The word made no sense to me, though Xantos said it quite articulately.

The servant nodded once, his features showing relief and a deep, somber gratitude. Xantos turned to me. "I apologize that business must intrude upon our time.

However, I had planned to show you the forge anyway. Shall we go?"

I tried to remain calm and collected, though I was fairly certain the delight and excitement I felt showed in my eyes, if not on my face. "It'd be an honor."

It took me a moment to realize that with the third step into the adjoining hallway, we had passed through a portal. The hallway we now walked in was nearly identical to the last one, but the temperature had risen by at least ten degrees.

"We are heading to my forge, which is, in the lexicon of your realm, a little under a mile away from where we were. Given your 'condition,' I thought I should shorten the walk," Xantos explained.

I was in so much trouble. I knew it. I had been rescued by one of the most powerful men I'd ever had the privilege of meeting. I was drunk on Magick, and it was still sprinkling off me like I was some fictional fairy. And now, he was being considerate. I already found Xantos highly attractive, and this was just making it worse. The sodding bastard knew it, too, if I read him correctly.

"That is very considerate of you," I said as I tried to ignore my theory that he was enjoying every single one of my thoughts. Time to change the topic. "I'm surprised the temperature is so warm here. Is that due to the size of your forge and the fact that it's underground?"

"I could answer your questions, but you will see for yourself. The forge is the source of the warmth you feel, but I will say nothing further," he teased. We walked on, and I could see a pair of massive stone doors ahead of us.

"Good thing I like heat." I couldn't keep the smile from my lips.

The temperature had risen even more, and I was sweating, which was something of a surprise, since I could usually walk around outside in ninety-degree weather and barely break a sweat. I brushed my hair from my face and realized it was damp. I wondered what the temperature was.

When we reached the doors, I could see ripples of heat leaking around the edges. Xantos touched me on the shoulder with his right hand and motioned me toward the entrance with his left. I felt as if I'd walked into an air-conditioned room. The ten-foot tall stone doors swung open at a measured pace, and I could see heat coming out in waves. I suspected the temperature had jumped at least twenty degrees, but I didn't feel it. Xantos urged me forward, and I walked through the doors with him.

Though Xantos didn't dawdle, he didn't rush, either. He was definitely master of his domain, which was evident from the few people we passed stopping and bowing to him. They were dressed in black uniforms with purple and silver trim. They were human or elves and all appeared healthy, though cowed. I suspected they were servants, since Xantos didn't strike me as the type who would own slaves. Slaves would revolt, servants typically would not.

I caught glimpses of rooms as we traveled the hallway. Some held raw materials, such as ores and metals. One had row upon row of shelves and cabinets, along with a table in the center covered in gemstones and gemologist tools. Another room held pieces of unfinished armor and unfinished weaponry. Several rooms were filled with tools typical of a forge, though they were far larger than those a human or elf would use. The contents of the rooms, as well as the source of the heat, piqued my curiosity.

Arylla ruffled her wings, then glided to my shoulders. Instead of curling around my neck or draping over my shoulder, she sidestepped until she was mostly hanging onto my back. She unfurled her wings until they stretched across my shoulders, her head snuggled beside mine. I felt her tail twitching from side to side in the middle of my back.

Xantos gave me a sidelong look before gently stroking Arylla's back. She raised her head and trilled at him before I felt her furl her wings. I was about to thank him when he turned back to the hallway before us. Something in his mannerism told me not to say anything, so I remained silent. I tried to figure out where we were, what was causing the shimmering heat around us, and why I had only seen male servants.

The first two questions were answered when I spotted veins of magma flowing in small rivulets down the wall. It took me a few moments to realize we were walking alongside a dike from an active underground volcano. My suspicions were confirmed when we stepped onto a ledge where rivers of magma flowed through a large pool of the molten rock. Also upon the ledge were large, bipedal creatures, blacksmiths who worked using the volcano's tremendous heat and lava, instead of a typical fire.

The enormous tools, made of stone and exotic metals like tungsten, made sense now. These smiths were easily nine or ten feet tall. Their features were rough, hewn from chunks of rock or quartz. The cartilage between the joints seemed to be made of lava. Their faces were smooth, and some had beards made of slate. All of them wore loincloths and nothing more.

"Fire giants," I breathed.

"Yes, actual fire giants, not the absurd version depicted in the legends of your realm," Xantos replied. "They work with the hottest fire, and thus can make the strongest weapons, armor, and tools. Unfortunately, they are also nefarious womanizers."

"So that part of legend is accurate," I replied, not sure what else to say.

"This will not take long," Xantos declared, and walked over to a smith who was standing alone.

He was slate gray, and his beard looked like it was made of small pebbles that had been scattered across a hill. Guarding him from a distance were a pair of smiths, who looked to be made of obsidian and pale quartz, respectively. They had no beards. There was no mistaking their aggressive poses and the way they held their large hammers at their sides. Clearly, they wanted to pound the slate fire giant into rubble.

My eyes drifted to the workstations and anvils. The anvils were incredibly large, and I briefly wondered if I had dropped into a live action cartoon. Would I see a coyote walking in with a box of dynamite or an absurd invention, next? My attention was drawn to a station where two incomplete swords rested against the cooling bucket. The blades were obsidian, full tang, but both were clearly bent. The other stations were surrounded by perfect work.

"Thzrrzk, you're wasting my materials. What have you to say for yourself?" Xantos asked in a silken voice.

"Giving no excuses," the giant replied, his voice sounding like stones rubbing together. "Expect no mercy."

The giant sank to one knee before Xantos. Unexpectedly, Xantos patted him on one slab of his shoulder.

"You have been in my employ for centuries." Xantos's voice had not changed from the silken tone, and I was starting to distrust it. The giant rose, his movements slow and cautious, as Xantos continued. "I cannot ignore that this has happened once before. Some hundred years ago, you obsessed over a dwarven chef in my kitchens. You terrorized her with your obsessive adoration until her beard fell out. I had to replace her, and you spent so much time thinking about her that you ruined four orders. Those orders took four years to make, to say nothing of the wasted materials. Clients had to wait an additional year. Since I know

Shindrulah's beard is full and healthy, you must be obsessing over another female."

Until then, I hadn't realized a great many eyes were staring at me. But I couldn't ignore it now. After Xantos's last statement, I heard a loud rumble as a group of giants turned away from me. The pair I noticed earlier were now staring hard at Xantos and the problematic smith.

"Who is it this time?" Xantos queried, not taking his eyes off the giant.

Thzrrzk said nothing. The obsidian guard spoke up. "It is the one who cleans the menagerie."

"We will not suffer for his folly again," the pale quartz guard added.

The guilty smith started and glanced at the guards. Apparently, he hadn't expected anyone to rat him out. I was almost curious to know what happened to the guards the last time.

Almost.

"You see," Xantos said cheerfully, "simple rules, obedience, and earned loyalty lead to a happy life. Your fellow craftsmen understand this, yet you do not. Utter failure."

"Lord Xantos—" Thzrrzk began.

Whatever words were to follow failed to come out once he spotted me. He stood a bit taller, and his left hand moved not so conspicuously toward his loincloth.

Great. Rotten males were the same everywhere, no matter the realm or race.

There was a flash of blue right before Xantos unceremoniously punched the fire giant in the jaw. It was a flying uppercut enhanced by Xantos's Magick. The impact resounded with a bone jarring crunch, and fragments of the giant's beard flew off. Suddenly, some mad part of me wanted to see Xantos and Merlin in a bar fight. Okay, it was a naughty part, too.

Stupid pregnancy.

The fire giant dropped to his knees, dazed, his mouth askew. I couldn't say for certain, but I think the obsidian giant was smiling.

"Your complete lack of respect and self-discipline is an even greater failure," Xantos said in a bored voice. "One I have no intention of tolerating."

He flicked one finger at the giant, and Thzrrzk flew from the forge, into the magma. The giant sunk into the hot liquid with a confused look on his face. Or maybe I was simply imagining it; I really didn't know anything about the expressions of fire giants.

"How long will it take him to die? Or will he?" I asked.

"He will," the pale giant answered in a slow cadence. "It will take half a day."

"Okay, then," I replied, finding myself at a loss for clever words.

Xantos turned to me and smiled. "So, dinner? Or would you like to rest?"

No one mentioned all the things pregnancy would do to you, like upping your libido or placing your mind solidly in the gutter. Xantos wasn't helping, and he knew it, if the sly twinkle in his eyes was any indication.

Lifting my chin defiantly, I swallowed my misgivings and said, "A rest would be lovely."

* * *

The walk to my chambers was quiet and uneventful. Neither Xantos nor I spoke as he escorted me, my arm through his. Even Arylla didn't make a sound as we walked the hallways of his manor.

I wasn't certain what to expect, but what I was given was breathtaking.

The bedroom suite was majestic. The silver walls were adorned with filigree and mosaic design. The four-poster bed was dark grey, nearly black, made from a wood I had never encountered. Its soft patina gleamed in the candlelight from large candles set in sconces along the walls and small ones placed in candelabras sitting on dressers. A plush deep coverlet was folded back to reveal black sheets that would make silkworms jealous.

Water trickled from somewhere I couldn't see. The sound reminded me of a bubbling spring. I was still in awe of the Magick that continued to drop from my skin. It tingled as it flowed through me. It was making me reckless, more so than usual. Reckless and willing to court danger.

Or, in this case, sleep with it.

I glanced right, a tightness building in my nether regions. Xantos stood in the closed doorway, a small smirk on his firm lips. His orange eyes bore into me. I shivered under his scrutiny. My abdomen tightened, and a flash of heat seeped through my body. He may not have known exactly what I felt, but his smug expression said he understood.

"You're a gentleman," I said.

Amusement grew in his eyes even though they narrowed a fraction. "When I wish it."

I waved a hand dismissively. Magick sparkled in the air around me. I ignored the glittering trail as it spiraled to the floor.

"You're a gentleman, and I have it on very good authority that a gentleman does not tell a lady 'no.' Is that true?" I met the docelfar's gaze evenly, a smile forming on my lips.

"That depends on what the request is," he replied, the smirk growing.

He was going to make me say it. Or perhaps take the first step. Regardless, I didn't care. Cowardice was never a word used to describe me.

I crossed the short distance between us and stopped a hair short of being nose-to-nose with the elder elf. A torrent of heat engulfed me, enough to warm the entire suite, if not the mansion. I slid my left hand through the silky strands of his silver hair, trying not to be distracted by the softness. I reached around his neck until I cupped the back of his head. I pressed my lips against his, ignoring the amusement in his eyes.

My, oh my, could Xantos kiss.

He didn't take control, but he didn't let me dominate either. Not that I minded. A shiver danced along my spine. I suspected his domination would come later. I looked forward to it.

When the kiss ended, I pulled back and looked into his eyes. I could still see amusement, but there was something else I couldn't decipher.

"Since I suppose you want me to ask, I will, in the formal fashion," I said. Given my rapidly beating pulse, I was surprised by the steadiness of my voice. "Will you stay the evening, Lord Xantos, for a night of mutual pleasure?" All was silent for a few moments before I added with a smile, "No regrets, no expectations, other than a night of mutual pleasure and debauchery."

"I suppose it would be rude to refuse such a request," he replied. He leaned closer until his lips brushed mine.

His kisses tasted of wine and Magick.

He pulled me closer, his hands trailing over my skin. Some part of my mind was aware I still wore clothing. At least, I had been. The air cooling my hot skin was a definite sign I was naked.

His strong hands skimmed along my skin, warmth following in their wake. My hands sought to remove his robes. Somehow, they managed to find a way through the soft folds to the hard body hidden within.

Xantos chuckled as he broke the kiss, leaving me breathless. His robes fell away, revealing smooth ebony skin and a well-toned body.

He was…incredible, slender as elves are, but darkly beautiful and sensual. His silver hair hung over him like a cloak, a shining contrast to his ebony skin. His orange eyes glittered with lust and the promise of a long, passion-filled night. He lifted a perfect, silvery brow.

My hands drifted over his skin, my eyes drinking in every inch of his body.

Every.

Inch.

My eyes didn't leave his as my fingers trailed along his faded scars. Some were jagged, others were smooth. He hadn't led a sheltered life. I touched each one.

Xantos grabbed my hands. I grinned and pressed against him, surprised by how well we fit together. He released my hands, swept me into his arms, and carried me to the bed. My lips found his collarbone. I nipped and bit playfully before scraping my teeth along his skin. He shivered, much to my pleasure.

He gently placed me on the bed. I pulled him down with me. The bed creaked as we turned to face each other. I trailed my fingertips along his well-toned chest, pausing long enough to caress each scar. I rose to my knees and kissed each silvery mark on his body.

Dinner could wait. Everything else, too.

Chapter Eighteen

Time was difficult to track in Xantos's realm. There was no clock in my room, so I had to rely on my internal clock, which was only partially working due to the influx of Magick I was experiencing.

Stretching languidly, I closed my eyes and thought back to the previous evening's debauchery with my ever-so-gracious host. Xantos was everything rumor said he was, and then some. Remembering everything, I opened my eyes and laughed softly.

I should have been sore. Possibly too sore to move, let alone walk. Yet here I was, rising from the incredibly comfortable bed to use the latrine and not the least bit sore. Or exhausted. Xantos was an extremely considerate lover.

Oddly, though, I was ravenous.

Exploring the bathroom, I discovered a medieval-style bathtub. It was the size of a hot tub and made of stone with water constantly flowing through it. The water was warm and comfortable. There was soap on one side that had a light floral scent.

As much as I was enjoying the lavishness of the bath, I didn't stay in as long as I would have liked. After I dried off with a luxuriously soft towel, I noticed a box sitting on the bench at the foot of my bed. Removing the lid, I discovered an exquisite gown.

Lifting the gown, I marveled at the soft, silken fabric that caught and held the light. It was black with a soft silver insert in the bodice.

On many occasions I had dressed myself in corsets, so it was easy to put the gown on. It fit like a glove. The bodice felt custom made, and the binding was easily maneuverable. The skirt had a train and an overlay, featuring a silver spider web design that shimmered with each step. Despite the amount of fabric, the gown was incredibly light and flowing, far more delicate than anything I'd ever worn, including the garments from my mother's realm.

The gown was accompanied by a pair of dainty slippers, which easily slid onto my feet, and a small black velvet bag. Opening the bag, I found a necklace. Dainty and delicate, it was silver with amethysts dripping down in a simple design. Since the necklace was obviously something Xantos wanted me to wear, I clasped it around my neck, then walked toward the door.

I hadn't taken two steps before Arylla began scolding me. Loudly. I stopped and looked at the little cloud dragon, whose scales were dark gray, shifting to black, with streaks of silver flashing intermittently. She was gripping my bigger-on-the-inside bag in her talons and glowering at me.

"I don't think he's going to harm me," I told her. When she didn't stop, I rolled my eyes and went to her.

As I took the bag and removed my hand scythes, I added, "Besides, it's not like I could best Xantos at anything." The elf was far too experienced. Not that I was complaining.

The moment I hung the scythes by my side, she stopped scolding me and perched on my shoulder. Shrugging, I opened the door to my suite and found a servant waiting expectantly.

"The Master requested that I escort you to his office, milady," the woman said in a dulcet tone. Her eyes remained fixed on the floor as she spoke. She turned and began walking swiftly down the hallway.

Closing the door behind me, I followed in silence. Magick still trailed from my skin, though it wasn't as brilliant or as constant. I wondered if Xantos had siphoned some of it off and collected it in a crystal or some other object. Smiling slightly, I realized I really didn't care. I would have done it had I been in his position. How could I complain about his acting as I would?

Our walk to Xantos's office was relatively short. The servant bowed as she held the door open, leaving me to cross the distance to Xantos's desk. Before I was halfway to the chairs, Xantos rose and met me in the center of the room. There was a smirk on his face, but the look in his eyes was indecipherable.

"I have requested that brunch be served," he stated without preamble.

Taking the proffered arm, I smiled mischievously. "I'd be delighted to have brunch with you. Thank you."

Xantos nodded, and we departed his office. I noticed his robes were black with delicate silver embroidery that was barely noticeable. I wondered why I was wearing an outfit that matched his. There was a reason for it, I was certain, but did I want to know? Sometimes, the less said, the better.

The hallways he led me down were narrower than the others. I realized we were in his personal domain. Decoration was sparse. The weaponry on the walls appeared far more ancient, and the paintings seemed to be of family members. The Magick here was thicker and reminded me strongly of him.

A servant stood before a doorway, ready to hold it open as we approached. Xantos led me into the room, pausing just over the threshold. I stopped and stared at the room. I'd never seen anything like it, let alone imagined anything as hauntingly beautiful.

The room was small, made almost entirely of black rock and colored crystals. Melon-sized crystals were set into the walls. They glowed with white, green, and blue light that illuminated the room, giving it a hauntingly ethereal appearance. The black rock walls rose to the ceiling twelve feet above us. They were festooned with small chips of white, yellow, and red crystals, giving it the appearance of the night sky.

A table carved from onyx, made for two people, sat in the center of room, flanked by two chairs made of intricately crossed beams of the same stone.

I held my breath in awe, then let it out slowly and turned my gaze to Xantos, who watched me with approval. He gestured toward the chairs, and when we were close, he pulled one out and seated me before taking the other.

"This is exquisite," I said softly, giving the room the respect it deserved.

A smile crossed Xantos's lips. "Thank you. I planned this room many, many centuries ago, when the materials were much easier to come by."

From the depths of his robe, he pulled a tiny, silver bell and rang it once. Servants flowed into the room carrying trays laden with food and beverages. They placed delicate cups before us, and a tray with a steaming teapot and a bowl of sugar cubes to the side. There was also a dainty container filled with cream. Small utensils rested on the tray next to the tea pot.

Another tray held a crystal pitcher, filled with fresh juice, and two tall glasses. Servants placed plates and silverware before Xantos and me, followed by trays of fruit and cheese. Like any good guest, I waited for my host to make the first move.

"Please, indulge," Xantos said as he began filling his plate with fruit and cheese. "There is nothing here that would harm you."

"I didn't think there would be," I replied, following his lead. The variety of exotic fruits and cheeses intrigued me, and I was eager to try them.

"Then why did you arm yourself?" he asked, his voice soft.

I recognized his tone for what it was: a warning. Offering Arylla a piece of red fruit, which she ate in a single chomp, I sighed. "Arylla refused to let me leave my room without them. I'm not entirely certain what she can do, and I have no desire to find out while I'm a guest in your home." Giving the dragonling a piece of cheese, I shrugged the shoulder she was not perched on. "I certainly don't think you would harm me, nor do I believe I would be harmed here."

"Nevertheless, you carry a weapon."

I searched for a reply. Xantos let me worry for several seconds before adding, "You would do well in my realm. One should always be prepared."

"Tempting," I admitted with a smile. "Very tempting. As for the weapons, I had little choice. I'm glad you aren't offended."

"I would rather be offended than find out you are nothing more than another sheep from your realm," he said. "But no, I am not offended."

"I'm very grateful you are not offended. I have seen what your wrath brings." Chuckling, I ate a piece of cheese followed by a piece of fruit. The tastes were exquisite as they melded together. My eyes met his, and my thoughts filled with images of the previous night. "And, no, I am not another sheep from my realm. Do you have any idea why my little companion believes I need to be armed in your domain?"

"Entering an unknown realm, where you may not be able to rely on Magick or your host for protection? If your companion hadn't wanted you armed, I think she would be looking for a new mistress."

My hand paused halfway to my mouth, and I stared at Xantos. His words were not reassuring, though he was not an all-knowing being who would keep me glued to his side. Eventually, I would be left to my own devices. His servants were mortal beings with their own thoughts. I had no idea what their motivations toward me might be.

"All good points," I said before eating the cheese and fruit on my fork. After I swallowed the delicacy, I added, "Even during my reign, in my castle, I did not depend entirely on my Magick."

"I am aware. How else would I know you prefer hand scythes?" he teased.

As my jaw dropped and warmth flooded my cheeks, he rang the bell again. Servants swept in to clear the dirty dishes and deliver covered platters.

A pair brought in a folding stand and placed it beside us. I was wondering how many platters they were going to bring when a half-giant brought in an enormous, covered tray. Another followed behind him. The second half-giant removed the lid to display an enormous crab claw. The servants removed the lids from the platters on the onyx table, and I could smell steamed vegetables and melted butter. The aromas mingled together in an exceedingly appetizing way.

The delivery of the food gave me time to gather my thoughts.

I waited until the servants had expertly cracked the giant crab claw, which was more than three feet in size, and extracted the meat, then left us before replying to his comment.

"How long have you been watching me?" I asked, almost afraid of the answer.

"As with many in your realm, you came to my attention centuries ago," he answered. "Or should I say the Lady of Death did?"

I knew I was blushing from my suddenly-warm face. "It was such a short reign, though. I suppose you continued watching me over the decades, hoping I would return to those days?"

"I watched you to see what would happen next," Xantos replied. "Not all the time, but enough to know when things became interesting again."

As he allowed the words to fade, he cut a portion of the crab meat and placed it on my plate before serving himself. His movements were fluid and precise.

The crab resembled a slice of perfectly cooked steak. At least an inch thick, it smelled divine. I considered my next words as I added vegetables to my plate.

"I think my biggest regret is not being more interesting sooner," I admitted. "My parents were very thorough when they forced me to end my reign."

"Belittling yourself is petty and annoying." Xantos said, his voice colder. "You've always been interesting. Your circumstances have not."

"How have I been interesting?" I asked incredulously, ignoring the cold tone. "I spent several centuries doing everything I could to stay out of the eyes and interest of the Council. I was terrified if I didn't, I'd be brought up on charges for what I did during my reign."

"I have lived for over two millennia, Catherine. I am much more familiar than you with what and who are truly interesting."

He smirked, and I suddenly felt like a mouse the cat wanted to devour. Unfortunately, that thought conjured images of the previous night, which were not helpful.

Thankfully, he continued, "You are powerful, skilled, intelligent, and beautiful. Being of interest is something that simply is, with you."

I felt the blush creep from my face to the tips of my ears. It wasn't the first time I'd blushed that much, but it wasn't a common occurrence.

"Ahem," I said, trying to get my brain to form words again. "I can't deny that my days as the Lady of Death weren't boring or dull."

They had been the exact opposite, and I was quickly realizing I missed those days. For that matter, I was starting to miss my talisman. Gods only knew what it could do in this realm.

"And you are not without interest no matter what style of living you choose," he replied in his silken tone.

Uh oh. I knew that voice.

"What have I done to warrant that tone?" I asked cautiously. Arylla wasn't reacting badly, though I could feel her crouching on my shoulder.

Xantos smiled. "Nothing unusual. Just being yourself. Please, eat."

"As you wish," I said with a smirk.

A companionable silence filled the room while we ate. Everything I tasted was richer than anything I'd had from any other realm. It also took less to fill me; a fact that didn't seem lost on Xantos.

If he was trying to entice me into visiting more often, he was succeeding.

I knew Sterling wouldn't approve, and my mother would probably want to destroy him, but they didn't govern my actions. I was a few hundred years past that age.

"You know some of my secrets," Xantos began. "Please, tell me about your talisman."

Oh, hell. He knew the truth. If not all of it, the most important pieces.

Sighing heavily, I leaned back in my chair, hands folded on the table before me. Silver light danced along my knuckles and fingers. Nervous energy taking form.

"I sincerely hope my parents cannot scry me here," I stated honestly. "There are only three other beings who know the truth behind the talisman; they know I created it as a birthday gift to myself upon my first century of life."

"No one sees into or enters my domicile without my knowledge," Xantos said plainly. "Most of the areas are protected from portals or scrying by my spells. I do not take well to intruders."

As I absorbed this, I continued to eat slowly, attempting to put off speaking.

He continued, "Why did you make the talisman?" Xantos inquired. "To see if you could, perhaps?"

"Partly to see if I could; mostly because I had captured a powerful demon and wanted to capture the Magick from his death." My eyes met his, and a slight smile pulled at my lips. "He was sent to assassinate me, and I didn't want to waste his death. Maekyl suggested making an amulet, an artifact. Between him and Trix, and Jade assisting with the ritual, I created the talisman."

It had been far more complicated than I made it sound, but it had been worth it.

"When faced with an enormous power source, you harnessed it, rather than finding a way to flee from it or destroy it," Xantos said. Then he did something I didn't expect. He laughed. "Your ambition is something I appreciate. The lack of greed is what tempers that ambition into wisdom." He clapped three times, which startled me as I realized it was applause. My blushing reached critical mass.

"It actually was a bit foolish," I stuttered. "I had no idea what the talisman could do. In fact, I didn't even consider that things could have gone horribly wrong."

I had placed a lot of trust and faith in Trix and Maekyl, not to mention my ability to perform the ritual flawlessly. At the time, I hadn't thought I would fail. Even now, I rarely allowed the fear of failure to stop me when I wanted to do something.

"Failure is something that happens, not something that is planned for," Xantos said. "What did you plan to do with the talisman? How did you plan to focus its power? Was the ability to morph objects into weapons an accident?"

"I had no intentions of any sort, aside from capturing the Magick generated by the demon's death." I shrugged and took a sip of cold mineral water. "The discovery that the talisman could create powerful, Magickally-enhanced weapons was pure accident. I had become drunk from releasing a surplus of Magick and decided to experiment. I was at the dinner table, so I grabbed a fork and tried to turn it into a trident. I'd never done it before, and instead of a simple trident, I created a full-sized Magickal one with the ability to freeze whomever I attacked with it."

Xantos's smile was wide. He nodded in approval. "What else could it enhance?" he asked in his calm, cultured voice.

"The talisman would augment any offensive spell I cast," I replied. Pausing, I smiled as I met his brilliant, orange eyes. "This is actually very refreshing. Aside from Maekyl, who can be an annoyingly smug git, you're the only other being with whom I've been able to have this sort of conversation."

"There is little surprise that Sterling, Merlin, has not opened up enough to talk with you," Xantos said, pushing his plate away. "A pity, since his understanding of Magick and the true laws of the dimensions is considerable."

"The true laws?" I asked, leaning toward him. My mind was whirring. Bits and pieces of knowledge and untruths were finally falling into place. "Let me guess, the laws put into place by the Council are rules Merlin decreed?"

If that were the case, I hadn't broken any true laws when I created the amulet. The Inquisition had begun when I reigned, and they began trying to keep Magick secret. Even so, it was potent and frequently used in the open. Since my rule was renowned among the mortals, mostly because of my lavish parties and orgies, and my penchant for killing those who tried to attack me, the knowledge of my Magickal abilities had been a carefully hidden secret among my peasants.

Providing protection, food, and homes went a long way toward obtaining loyalty.

"Energy cannot be destroyed, only changed." Xantos began, his voice formal, almost instructive. "Matter, distance, and energy are interchangeable, but all spells come with a cost. You never change your time stream. Attempting to do so only puts you in an alternate dimension where the changes you made were already done. The more destruction that is caused, the more life is created to maintain the balance."

It was actually rather scientific if you thought of Magick in those terms. Physics and chemistry were a large part of Magick, and they were subjects I'd studied. "Yet, time passes differently in the fae and human realms." I paused, taking a moment to consider. "Is that because time moves differently, and not because of any spell?"

"Correct. Time spells are nothing more than stepping outside of its influence for brief periods or riding it into other places in the multiverse." Xantos smiled at my widening eyes. "I have been well aware of other dimensions and universes for more than a millennium."

"Then you're aware that the veils between them are thinning," I said. Too late to take it back now.

"For some time, now, yes," Xantos replied. "There is little that can be done. The veils will strengthen later, but this pattern cannot be changed."

That wasn't ominous. Time to change the topic. Again.

"What have you learned about my talisman? I know it isn't complete and won't be until I get it back."

"Before or after it was broken into three pieces?" He countered.

"How did you—" I broke off my question, since I suspected I already knew the answer. "Let me guess—Maekyl told you?"

"Along with a great many other things," he assured me. "He still won't tell me how the talisman was put together or why you tore it apart. I can surmise why you kept the third piece a secret—to ensure the talisman will only be at optimum power when you decree it."

Leaning back in the chair, I studied Xantos. Silence grew as I considered my options. "Only Jade, Trix, Maekyl, and I knew about the birth of the talisman. Maekyl would have met a rather hot end by way of a volcano if he answered how it was made and why it was broken." There was no point in lying about it. I trusted Xantos only so far, but my trust was growing the longer I knew him. The jerk. "I broke it apart, erroneously believing that would destroy it, because I had to end my reign. It was either that or face charges before the Council. If someone hadn't found the pieces and put them together, I probably would still be refusing to reassemble it."

"The longer you live, the more you will see that allowing any leverage is going to end in someone forcing your hand," Xantos said. "You should have kept it, claimed it was destroyed, and hidden it away." He smirked and added, "If anyone came for the talisman, you could have destroyed them with it."

"I assure you, once I reclaim my talisman, it will not be leaving me again," I told him. "It was forged in fire and flame with my blood. It is mine." It also had a name, but I didn't mention that to him. He had given me a warning, even if he hadn't explicitly said it.

"Since whoever has the first two pieces has used some of its power, I take it the third piece is only required to unlock the most potent abilities?" Xantos asked. He absently gestured in the air to his left. One of the servants quickly appeared to clear our dishes.

"Yes," I said, keeping my answer simple.

The third piece contained the majority of the blood I'd used to create the talisman. Some had been infused into the gem used to capture the demon, but more had been used to create the rest of the talisman. Since blood was not something you wanted others to have access to, even days, weeks, or centuries after it had been spilled, I'd kept that piece to myself.

Standing up, Xantos nodded in satisfaction. "What would you like to do today?"

"If it isn't an imposition, I'd like to learn how to shield my thoughts from everyone," I said cautiously. "You are one of the most powerful beings I know. If I can shield my thoughts from you, I should be able to shield them from everyone else, including my mother and Merlin." Or so I hoped.

"I have a solitary chamber for such practice," he confided. "Join me, and we will go there."

Standing, I slid my arm through his, a smile on my face. "It would be my pleasure."

Chapter Nineteen

I spent most of the day learning to shield my thoughts from Xantos. Thankfully, I already had the basic skills for creating mental shields. Those skills just needed improvement.

Despite having the privilege of studying any tome in Xantos's considerable library, I decided to do some light reading.

My gracious host had excused himself to tend to personal business and left me to read quietly. Though he had been reluctant to leave me alone, I had reassured him I could easily find my way to his office or my chambers, and I wasn't helpless.

Looking up from the leather-bound tome on dragons, which included a large section on cloud dragons, I watched Arylla circle above me.

The room resembled a chapel that had been converted into a reading room. Enormous soft pillows and fur blankets filled the area where the altar would have been. Chairs of various sorts were placed around the room, a table beside each. Crystals adorned the walls, giving off the perfect amount of light. I deliberately ignored the carvings in the floor and walls. It would have been too tempting to give into the desire to do Magick if I gave them too much thought.

Necromancy and death Magick left a mark, and this room wasn't innocent. Not only that, but some of the carvings also resembled religious markings, and I had no desire to attract the interest of any deity of this realm.

I had curled up on an antique chaise lounge. Carved from wood as dark as onyx, with shades of gray in the grain, it was upholstered with soft, deep purple fabric that reminded me of velvet. I leaned back against the silver pillows, and my eyes grew heavy and drifted shut. Perfecting my mental wards had been more tiring than I'd thought.

I felt the book sliding from my hands seconds before it fell to the floor with a resounding thud. The noise echoed through the room, causing me to jump. Shaking my head, I stood and stretched. When I looked up to call to Arylla, I frowned. She was hovering directly above me, looking toward the doors.

Instinct is difficult to ignore. The doors flew open and three tall, bipedal beasts, with obviously malicious intent, piled into the room. They were followed by another being in a dark, hooded robe.

The beasts were similar to the ogres from my realm with their gray-green skin, the tusks that protruded from their lower jaws, and their thick, armored bodies. Upon entering the room, they hurled two shaped, stone spears at me. As the spears flew, I reacted instinctively and cast a spell to shield Arylla and me from them.

Normally, such a spell would have produced a translucent barrier of energy between four and six feet in diameter and as dense as two inches of tungsten. It would have been more than enough to deflect any ranged attack short of an anti-tank projectile or its Magickal equivalent. This time, however, the space in front of Arylla and me looked as though it had been filled with gelatin made with brackish water.

Details were distorted, but the spears were severely bent and suspended in the writhing energy. The expanding clouds of red and gray-green on the other side were all that was left of the attacking ogres. The hooded figure was spared, but its arms were thrust forward, dull green light emitting from its hands.

"Try and get a spell or anything else through this," I muttered as I tried to dissipate the overblown shield.

To my horror, doing so proved difficult. The amount of energy in the spell was far more than I had intended, and it would not dissipate or redirect quickly. A few flashes of light bounced harmlessly against the slowly fading shield.

I mentally ran through my options. Arylla snapped and hissed at the robed figure. The unknown assailant's head snapped to the side as though something down the hall had drawn its attention. The figure thrust its arms toward the ceiling. I felt a pulse of energy despite the distance and remaining shield energy between us.

The hooded figure was using the joined pieces of my talisman. Its energy and power were enhancing the spells it was casting. I could feel at least two spells forming.

A blazing portal of orange light consumed the hooded figure as Xantos appeared in the doorway.

His face was taut with anger. He looked at me, then bellowed, "Cast no spells!"

He whipped his left arm out toward me, and the remaining shield energy flew away as if it were vapor moved by a strong breeze.

I opened my mouth, but Arylla screeched in a way I hadn't heard before. She flew toward the portal as a brown wyvern stepped through the orange light.

The newly arrived dragon might have been another color in life, but this one was an animated corpse that had died so long ago that decay and mold had changed the luster of its scales. Strips of flesh hung from it and flapped behind as it raced toward me.

Arylla swooped in to bite the undead wyvern's pale eyes but was swatted away with a hard swing from the creature's jaws. I pulled my scythes free and stepped toward my newest attacker.

Moving with grace and confidence, I buried the left scythe blade in its jaws. The long, sharp blade pierced the undead creature and came out the other side. Turning, I buried the other scythe in the side of the wyvern's skull. I easily pulled the left blade free as my body spun against the wyvern's, then swung it down and decapitated the beast.

The wyvern's severed head fell to the floor as I moved out of the way of the rest of its body. The Magick that had given the poor creature a semi-life was gone, ended by the obsidian weapons and beheading.

The corpse landed in a heap against the chair I had been sitting in.

"Prettily done," Xantos said, standing at my shoulder. His face was still taut, and I could feel anger burning off him in waves. His words, though, were pleasantly said, and I saw no malice toward me in his eyes.

"I see why you advised me not to cast any spells here." My voice was unsteady, and my body quickly let me know I had pushed it too far. The fatigue and throbbing pain were likely from trying to get rid of the spell, rather than from casting it or from exerting my body to slay the undead wyvern.

"What did you try to cast?"

"Shield spell," I replied, suddenly wanting a blanket and a huge mug of hot chocolate. "When the doors opened, I acted on instinct."

Xantos nodded. "I apologize for my delay in coming. When I felt the portal opening, I was near the surface world, tending to a business exchange. When I tried to teleport to this door, my way was blocked by interfering energy. The being used the joined pieces of your talisman, I surmise?"

I nodded shakily. He wrapped a supporting arm around me and continued, "The closest I could get was one hundred cubits from here."

"It's fine," I replied. I knew that he had moved at considerable speed to get here as quickly as he did.

Xantos bent to pick up Arylla. She was not moving, but I could see her tiny chest rising and falling.

"She's only been stunned," he assured me.

The warmth of strong Magick surrounded me just before Xantos teleported us to my chambers. He helped me to the bed and laid Arylla beside me. After placing my scythes just below the pillow where the small dragon lay, Xantos smiled then nodded before leaving. I took the hint. Closing my eyes, I slipped into sleep.

Chapter Twenty

Arylla was still curled up beside me when I woke up. My first thought was to check on my little hatchling companion. Having met adult dragons, I knew she had a long life ahead of her and a lot of growing to do. She wasn't as fragile as a bird, but she wasn't as hardy as a juvenile or adult dragon, either.

My second thought was to find whoever had my talisman and liquidate them. I had to return to my realm, which was a pity since I was thoroughly enjoying being Xantos's guest. It was really up to him, however, when I could return.

The only way to answer that question was to find my gracious host and ask him. Since I didn't need to change clothes, I collected my scythes, attached them at my hips, and scooped Arylla up into my arms before leaving my suite.

I opened the door and paused at the threshold, blinking a few times at the guards positioned outside my room. I shouldn't have been surprised. Someone had tried to attack me in his domain, and though they had failed, it was still an affront to him. As I stepped into the hallway, I noticed two elves who didn't seem to be wearing armor or carrying weapons. I suspected they were Magick users. They remained silent, so I gave them a perfunctory nod and headed for their lord's office. They fell into step around me.

I may not have trusted them, but I did trust Xantos, at least enough to believe he would keep me safe from his people.

The servants I passed in the hallways paused to bow or curtsy to me. None spoke or met my eyes. I highly doubted it was because I was a guest. There was more to their subservience, and I couldn't figure it out. Not that it really mattered. It kept my mind off the fact that someone was using my talisman and had tried to attack me in Xantos's domain. Whoever it was had balls, I had to give them that.

As I approached Xantos's office, the door opened before me. I couldn't keep the smile from my face as I entered the room. The guards, not surprisingly, remained outside. Xantos, Arylla, and I were the only ones in the room.

"Have I mentioned I absolutely love your office?" I asked as I crossed to the chairs in front of Xantos's desk.

"I consider it my sanctuary and the briefest glimpse into my true soul," Xantos replied. "Now, as to the attack against you. I have traced the spell to your mother's realm. Into the room you were staying, to be precise. The caster used the remnants of the portal I opened to create a new one."

"My guess would be the talisman is drawn to me," I said as I settled into one of the chairs. "There isn't a single person in my mother's realm, aside from my mother, who could open a portal. The caster must have used my talisman."

That rankled me. I was fairly certain in another century of life, and with more Magickal training, I could open a portal. As it were, I would need to use the talisman to do so.

Okay, it was mostly the fact that someone else was using my talisman. Sharing had never been something I did well.

"The caster probably doesn't realize they could not have made the portal or found you without it." Xantos's tone was jovial. "Power in the hands of those who are not used to it tends to blind them to what is actually happening."

"Does that type of situation amuse you as much as it seems to?" I asked.

"To quote an adversary of mine, 'Give the fools what they want if you desire to see them fall the farthest.' I've discovered that to be a most accurate truth," Xantos replied. "So yes, it always amuses me that sentient races share that same weakness. Especially humans and dwarves."

"I can't argue," I said thoughtfully. "The attack does strengthen my need to find the talisman; however, I have no desire to return to my mother's realm. Do you think I could lure the caster into the human realm?"

"If the talisman is drawn to you, it's certain that whoever possesses it will find you in whatever realm you occupy," Xantos said. The joviality in his voice had been replaced with a more business-like tone. "Can the talisman be used against you in the realm in which it was created?"

"No weapon created with the talisman can harm me. If the bullets Nick used were created with the talisman, that still holds true," I replied as I absentmindedly stroked Arylla.

"Then your realm is where you need to be," Xantos declared.

"When am I to return?" I asked, trying to keep the disappointment from my voice.

"I leave that up to you," Xantos replied. "My suggestion is that you leave soon, however. I, a small contingent of my private guards, or both, will come with you to your realm for protection."

"Pity. I was hoping for another night of debauchery with you," I said with a smile. "As tempting as it is to accept your gracious offer to personally protect me, I can't accept it in good conscience. I don't know how long this will take, and it would be inconsiderate of me to expect you to ignore your business for an extended length of time."

The fact that he and Merlin were adversaries, and Merlin didn't like him didn't help. Xantos, I was fairly certain, would be a proper guest if Merlin behaved and was equally respectful, but I couldn't count on Merlin being respectful toward Xantos for longer than five minutes.

"Then the guards shall accompany you. No argument will change that," he said. His orange eyes glinted, and his posture warned me that he would park the guards in my living room if I protested. Then he smirked. "As for your request, it would be improper to refuse a lady."

No matter what anyone said, I would always consider Xantos a gracious host and gentleman.

Chapter Twenty-One

As I stood in Xantos's office the next morning, I couldn't help but be sad I had to leave. The gown I wore was another work of art. It was made of black silk woven with purple thread. Silver runes trimmed the hem, sleeves, and neckline. My scythes were attached at my hips, and the Magickal bag he'd given me hung from my arm as though it were an empty purse. The clothing, alone, was reason to stay, but the true reason was my host. There was a great deal to learn and explore in Xantos's realm, and two days weren't nearly enough to scratch the surface.

"Is the crystal you gifted me still the best way to contact you?" I asked, trying to keep my feelings from coloring my words. "I'd rather not rely on Maekyl to send you messages."

"Until you have practiced enough to scry to my realm, the crystal is your best method. If I wish to speak with you, it will be through the crystal."

I met his eyes with mine. "Thank you, for everything." My lips curved into a mischievous grin as I added, "I'll try not to keep your guards too long."

"From what I have observed, it doesn't take trouble long to find you," Xantos countered. "My guards are yours for as long as you wish."

I couldn't help but laugh at the accuracy at his statement. "I will keep you updated on how things progress." Though I knew he would be watching me, it would be polite to do so. Besides, it was an excuse to talk to him. "Perhaps, when this situation is resolved, I can return for a longer stay?"

"That can be arranged, Lady of Death."

A good bit of warmth crept up my neck to my face. The moniker had never felt like a true title in all the centuries I'd held it, but he made it true when he said it. Now I was determined to reclaim the title and keep it, one way or another.

The smirk didn't vanish as he gestured slightly. I heard the door open, but didn't turn around, not until his eyes looked past me.

Turning, I studied the five guards who entered the room. Three were male, and two were female. All five were elves who wore identical uniforms consisting of leather jerkins dyed a deep purple over black shirts and sleek, black breeches. Each one wore a symbol of a black hammer on their left breast. This was the first time I'd seen guards wearing the black hammer.

"Each of these guards can contact me," Xantos explained. "They are instructed to do so at specific intervals and when events escalate. Let them do what they are trained to do."

I noticed that the guards were armed and armored. Turning my attention to Xantos, I asked, "What are they trained to do?"

"Guard. Eliminate. Report." The five voices spoke in unison.

"They are individuals. No doubt you could come to know them well, should they be at your side for long," Xantos said. "They take to their duties more diligently than most, which includes acting as the many heads of a hydra, protecting the heart of the body. For now, that body is yours."

"I presume they are skilled in the ways of Magick as well as fighting?" I asked cautiously. "Is there anything else I should know about them or their assignment?"

"They have sworn their lives to protect yours," Xantos replied.

As I stood there, staring at Xantos, uncertain if he was joking, he gestured, and a portal opened to my side. With an unwavering smile, I said, "Until later, Xantos."

"Until then, Lady of Death," Xantos replied with a rare smile that met his eyes.

Without hesitation, I stepped through the portal and into the living room of my home. The five guards followed behind me, and I watched the portal close without a sound after the last guard stepped through. I dropped my Magickal bag on a table as I turned toward two of my oldest friends and Maekyl.

Trix hadn't changed her preferred human form from the last time I saw her. She looked like a svelte, beautiful, dark-skinned African American. Her onyx hair, a few shades darker than her unblemished skin, was no longer the waist length I remembered from my reign. It fell just above her shoulders and was sculpted to compliment her heart-shaped face and model-perfect features. It could almost have been described as "feathery." Maekyl spoke before I could utter a word. "Ah, how sweet, you're wearing Mistress Robes."

"I am not—" I said after a few seconds. Talk about a charming welcome home.

"That's the finery he always puts on his mistresses," Maekyl stated cheerfully. He pivoted his head, currently sitting on Ahndray, to face Jade. "When is Sterling checking in again?"

"Shut up," I snapped, really not liking where this conversation was going.

My annoying, undead skull continued in his faux sugary tone. "And you're accompanied by the usual contingent of guards he sends with his mistresses, no less."

"I am not-" I began, except Maekyl cut me off before I could finish the sentence.

"That's not a contingent of guards?"

Dropping him into a volcano never sounded so good. "Yes, but—"

Maekyl cut me off again, saying dramatically, "Have they 'sworn their lives to protect yours?'"

There was no way I could keep the blush from my face. The jerk. He had to have been eavesdropping on Xantos and me.

"Are you sure you haven't fornicated with him? I'm certain I can smell him from over here," he drawled in an overly curious tone.

"You don't have a nose," I snarled.

"No, but I do," Trix said slyly. I turned my glower on her. I had been happy to see her, and I would have still been excited, if she hadn't joined in on the tormenting.

"As do I," Jade added far too cheerfully. Her smile grew wider as she leaned toward, me, sniffing. "Step closer, my dove."

"Really? All three of you are ganging up on me?" I yelled at them, starling Arylla out of her doze. The dragonling squawked once before ruffling her wings in indignation and trilling sharply at the trio.

Trix snorted, the laughter in her eyes not evident in her voice as she spoke. "Those guards are quite good. They haven't slipped yet."

Jade nodded. "Although, if that one frowns any harder, he's going to soil his armor."

As I glowered at the trio, Maekyl began clacking his teeth together in a perfect imitation of a wind-up chattering skull. I had once thought those toys were fun, until Maekyl made the noise, and I realized it was his way of laughing. It never failed to grate on my nerves.

Turning, I stormed away from them. Arylla whistled sharply, an ear-piercing sound.

Trix's laughter was as warm and inviting as it had ever been. I heard her ask, "Did you teach her that, Maekyl?"

I didn't hear the answer, since I was halfway to my bedroom, the guards following on my heels. Perhaps they didn't think I'd be safe in my own house, which only substantiated Maekyl's claim. The louse. Did he honestly think I was going to admit that I'd enjoyed two nights of debauchery with Xantos? Besides, two nights did not make me Xantos's mistress, especially since there were no emotional strings attached.

I enjoyed his company and found him highly attractive, but that didn't mean I wanted to be his mistress. That would require more attachment and giving him more power over me than I wanted to.

Oh, gods. Was I convincing myself it wasn't true? Damn that undead dragon.

I quickly removed the luxurious gown and placed it gently on the bed before stomping into my bathroom. I did not need my two best friends and a troublemaking undead dragon tormenting me about who I spent my time with or what I did with them.

"Cat? Can you hear me? There's five guards in front of your door, so my voice might be a bit muffled." Jade's voice carried easily into my bathroom, even if it was softened a bit by the distance.

"Very funny," I yelled back. "If you're here to torment me more, consider it done and go away."

"Come on, open the door!" Jade called back. "Or, at least, tell your protectors to let me in."

Huh. That was unexpected. I wouldn't have thought they would keep Jade out. Or maybe she was exaggerating.

I pulled on a robe, wrapped it around me, and tied the belt. Opening my bedroom door, I found my guards standing in the doorway with Jade in front of them.

No one said anything for a few seconds.

"Come in," I grumbled.

With those words, the guards separated, giving my best friend just enough room to slip through. I shut the door once she was inside.

"So... did you?" Jade asked slyly.

"Yes," I replied, trying not to growl at her.

She nodded. "Figured you would. You've always been attracted to powerful beings and had a penchant for bad boys." Her demeanor changed from teasing to serious as she sat on the edge of my bed. "Tell me what happened from the time Xantos helped you leave your mother's realm, and I'll tell you what I know."

"There isn't a lot to tell," I replied, settling onto the bed next to her. She turned to face me as I continued, "Xantos opened the portal, and I became a guest in his realm. He showed me parts of his vast estate, including the forge where his obsidian weapons are crafted and his menageries."

"That can't be all," Jade said. "What did he want in exchange for showing you around?"

"Information about my talisman," I said. Arylla chirped before daintily crossing to Jade and curling up in her lap. "He wanted to know how I made it and what it could do. It's the same information every person who's ever heard about it wants to know."

"Did you tell him?"

I raised a brow. "I don't think I had much choice, do you?" Jade snorted and shook her head as she stroked Arylla. I nodded and continued, "So, I answered his questions. He, in turn, helped me develop shields to prevent Merlin from reading my thoughts after I accept the position of Speaker of the Council."

"Smart move," Jade said. She tipped her head to the side. "You're still leaving something out."

"I'm not leaving it out, I just haven't gotten to it yet," I retorted loftily. My tone grew somber as I explained, "I was also attacked by whoever has my talisman."

"Don't tell me all the details now. Trix will want to hear them, too," Jade said thoughtfully. "Why did Xantos let you return here with his personal guards, instead of keeping you squirreled away at his place?"

"Because neither the talisman, nor the weapons made from it, can harm me in this realm," I replied. "The guards were a compromise. It was either them, Xantos, or both. Since I doubt Merlin could keep from starting a war with Xantos, I thought it best to stick with the guards for now."

"Good call," Jade said with a smirk. "Your mom has banished your baby's daddy from her realm until further notice. Your father, I might add, is trying to keep your mother from destroying anything and everything that irks her. Needless to say, he kept her from storming Xantos's abode the moment she realized he helped you escape."

Uh oh. "Um, how pissed is she?" I asked nervously.

"Very," Jade replied. "Anyone even remotely associated with her realm, especially me, is supposed to contact her the moment you return." Jade's smile grew wider. "I can't wait to see her reaction when she sees your 'sworn protectors.'"

"I'm sure," I retorted. My life was becoming more interesting. Maybe I should have taken Xantos up on his offer of partnership and training. Bring on World War Three, baby! "What about Merlin? Do you know how weird it is calling Sterling by that name? Or how crazy it is that I'm having his child?"

"Speaking of the unborn," Jade began, "what did Xantos have to say about that?"

"Nothing, really. Only that doing necromancy in his realm would turn her to evil," I replied. No sooner had the words escaped my lips than my mouth dropped open. "Oh, no. Hell no. There is no way he could already know the gender." I paused as I stared at Jade for a few heartbeats before adding, "Is there?"

Jade shrugged. "I guess it's possible. He's lived longer than anyone I know, aside from Merlin. So, it's definitely possible he knows a spell that would reveal the gender. Or something about his realm could allow him to know. It's Xantos. Anything is possible."

"Yeah, we'll just go with 'it's Xantos,' and leave it at that," I replied, trying to wrap my mind around the fact I was having a daughter. "So, to change to a safer topic, you were about to tell me about Merlin and what's been happening here?

"You mother, obviously, was thoroughly pissed when you left her realm," Jade said with a smirk. "Your father kept her from storming Xantos's castle, as well as destroying her realm. He hopes her temper will keep the idiots there in line for a while. I left shortly after you did, since there was no real need to stay, and Cildur has taken the mantle of spymaster general for the time being. Trix, I might add, is in contact with him and approves of him. Merlin has been contacting us every four hours, or so, asking if we've heard anything from you."

"How long was I gone?" I asked, interrupting her.

"From this realm? A week," she replied. At my stunned expression, she laughed. "Did you forget that time moves faster in this realm? Or the old myths and tales? Is pregnancy brain already affecting you?"

"No, no, and no," I retorted. "I don't know how long I was gone, since I haven't looked at my phone or a clock since returning."

"Okay, I'll give you that," Jade said with a laugh. "Anyway, Merlin knows you were with Xantos. Your mother told him. He is rather unhappy, to put it mildly, that Xantos helped you escape your mother's realm."

"Honestly, Jade? I'm more concerned about someone using my talisman than I am about any personal spat Merlin might have with me, my mother, or Xantos. And that goes for my mother, as well," I stated, rising from my bed. "Mom is worried about her grandchild and me. Merlin is angry because Mom banished him, and I went to Xantos for help. Me? I just want my talisman back before whoever is using it realizes it is actually trying to kill them, so the demon's spirit can escape."

"Did you mention that to Xantos?" Jade asked slyly.

"Absolutely not," I replied evenly. "Though I'd lay bets he suspects as much. I did tell him I used a demon to create the talisman. Xantos knows more about creating Magickal artifacts than Merlin, if what I witnessed in his realm is any indication. Not to mention the things he and Maekyl have said about the items they've created."

"So, what are you going to do now?" Jade asked as she placed Arylla gently on my bed.

"I'm going to take a long, hot shower, dress in my most comfortable clothes, then I'm going to catch up with Trix. I need to find out how the bloody hells someone managed to put my talisman back together. Minus my piece, of course."

Jade nodded and stood. "I'll let the two dragons know you'll be down shortly." Pausing at the door, her hand on the doorknob, she asked, "Maekyl thinks you're going to reclaim your title. Is that true?"

"It's a strong possibility," I replied. "At the very least, I'm going to reclaim my talisman."

"All hail the Lady of Death," Jade murmured as she left my bedroom.

Chuckling, I went into my bathroom and turned on my shower. It would certainly be interesting to see if others were as enthusiastic about that prospect.

Chapter Twenty-Two

I made an executive decision after I showered and dressed in a cute, comfortable dress. Instead of cooking for everyone, including the elves who were my assigned protectors, I decided we were going to Fellhaven. Minus Maekyl, of course.

Since Jade had a large Suburban SUV, with plenty of room for all of us, we took her car. There really isn't anything like carpooling with a shadow dragon, a low giant, and five armed and armored elves. The radio played as we drove. No one wanted to say anything with a group of Xantos's personal guards sitting next to them who would inform him of anything that was said.

It was a slow night at my favorite tavern. The parking lot surrounding Fellhaven was less than half full. I sighed, relieved that there would only be a few people there to witness my entourage.

I was also thankful we wouldn't garner any weird looks from Fellhaven's clientele or staff. The hostess greeted Jade and me by name before escorting us to one of the VIP rooms.

The guards stood in a protective circle around our table, facing out. Even though they were as stolid as Beefeaters guarding the British royal house, it seemed as though they were just the slightest bit relaxed. I was frustrated, because I wasn't sure why, and I didn't feel comfortable asking them.

The door opened, and Jen walked in with Mark a step behind her. "Good to see you back. It's been pretty dull around here." She winked and grinned. "We were wondering about your guards."

"You're familiar with them?" Trix asked, a single brow raised.

"Oh, yes," Jen replied, the grin still on her face. "Good to see you again, Zarkull."

"Let's see," Mark said, pointing at the guards as he rattled off their names. "Zarkull, Krysdos, Alaria, Shyrrik and Wyrren. Yep, the gang's all here! Oversized tray of vegan potstickers and jalapeño poppers coming up."

I caught the slightest nods and smiles from the guards as Mark strode toward the kitchens.

"A distinct honor to see you and your partner again, milady," one of the guards—I presumed Zarkull—said to Jen before bowing slightly.

She returned the bow, and there was mischief in her eyes as she spoke again, "It has been too long since you and your crew graced us with your presence. I'll make sure your drinks arrive soon and no riffraff enter without our knowledge." She paused, before adding impishly, "May your current assignment be less difficult than previous ones."

"Posh. Where is the fun in that?" Zarkull chided, despite the playfulness in his voice.

Jen laughed. "I'll remember you said that! If you have any requests, please let us know."

She then turned her attention to my companions and me. "We've added a few protections since your last visit, Cat. Several of your friends may wish to speak to you, now that you've returned. There are many rumors swirling around about you."

"There always have been," Jade said.

"How do you know Xantos's personal guards?" Trix asked. "I highly doubt the ancient docelfar sends his guards to protect just anyone, let alone beings in this realm."

"We were introduced just over two decades ago, I think?" Jen said, tilting her head to the side thoughtfully. She shrugged. There was a definite smirk on Zarkull's lips, though the elf remained silent. "Xantos sometimes brings them when he dines here. On other occasions, he allows them to visit without orders. At least none that I know of."

The guards snickered. Jade and I exchanged shrugs, while Trix remained her usual expressionless self. Zarkull nodded, the smirk still fixed in place.

"Who is your curious friend?" Jen asked, still smiling. She was at ease and not the least bit worried.

"This is Trix," I replied. "She's an old friend."

Jen studied the shadow dragon, who met her gaze easily. "The shadow dragon," she said, thoughtfully. "I'm certain you know Fellhaven's rules. It's a pleasure to finally meet another of Cat's Court."

Trix nodded pleasantly, understanding showing in her features, as she smiled. "I'm aware of the rules of your esteemed establishment, and I will adhere to them." She paused, before asking, "Catherine's Court? Is that a new moniker? Or simply a part of one of the lesser known tales?"

"It's actually how her godfather refers to those who were once her advisers," Jen replied. "Not to everyone, mind you, but since we cater to the majority of those in the Magickal, supernatural, and preternatural communities, he found it beneficial to keep us advised, especially since Cat's attack. It's rather difficult to put the proper protections in place if you don't know what you're up against."

There were a few moments of silence before Jen nodded. "If that's all the questions, I'll get back to work. I'll send in your usual drinks," she said nodding to Jade and me. "What would you like, Trix?"

"A local hard cider," Trix replied with a smirk.

"I'll send in one of the favorites," Jen said.

With that, she turned and walked out, leaving us to ourselves. None of the guards moved, but they seemed to relax even more. For some reason, they trusted Jen and Mark and their protections, whatever they might be. Perhaps they'd seen said protections in action.

"With Maekyl's and Tony's help, I have been able to create a rather well-informed spy network," Trix said. "It seems Maekyl is sly. He's kept in touch with some of our former compatriots who have made their livelihoods as mercenaries. Very successful mercs, at that. A few have even 'retired' from working for some of this world's governments."

"Naughty is a very mild word for anything Maekyl does," I muttered. Glancing at Jade, I narrowed my eyes. My best friend was staring at the table's centerpiece and avoiding looking at me. "It appears you knew what he was up to."

She finally looked at me. "No, but I suspected it after I received a message telling me where you were living. It was unsigned, but the wording was familiar, and I knew Maekyl despised the end of your reign. It wasn't difficult to put two and two together, as humans often say."

"Fair enough," I said with a sigh. "I did keep my head in the sand for a long time. I wouldn't be surprised if you told me he had conspired with someone and arranged to have had the amulet stolen."

"Maekyl has always been sly, conniving, and duplicitous. It is part of why he and Xantos were such adversaries before your father imprisoned him in the skull," Trix said with a smirk. "That he has been able to keep a sleeper cell of spies in place is actually very beneficial to us. That you, Catherine, have made friends with all manner of fae and Magickal beings is also helpful."

"Why is that?" I asked, leaning forward. "What have you discovered?"

"Your little gremlin friend, Viriato, is appealing to you to hand over your now-deceased ex-beau's estate to someone of his choosing. Word is also spreading that you're going to be the Speaker of the Council," Trix replied, the amusement in her eyes not evident in her voice.

Jade added, "Viriato showed up looking for you. Maekyl knew he was a frequent source of information, so he was allowed into the house. He'd heard about the attack on you and delivered some useful information, then dropped his little bomb. He was actually really cute when he requested we pass along the information to you."

Well, damn. "Does everyone know I've been asked to be the Speaker?" Jade and Trix nodded. "Isn't that lovely. What about the information he provided?"

"He gave us the address of the person Nick was conversing with," Trix replied smugly. "Jade and I discussed it and decided to wait for you to come home before investigating the domicile."

I looked to Jade for further details, since I doubted Trix was current with the latest technology. She didn't disappoint me.

"It seems that Viriato is trying to make amends for not telling you about Nick's illegal trafficking in Magickal creatures. Once he heard what Nick did, he went through his former master's emails and tracked down the so-called priestess's location. He said it took a while because she was using software that hid her location." She paused and color rose in her cheeks. "He said my eyes were starting to glaze over with the techno mumbo jumbo, so he wouldn't bore me with details. Instead he gave me the address and wished us happy hunting."

I laughed. "Okay. I'll see what I can do for the gremlins. They've lived at that estate since before I knew Nick, so I think it's only fair they get a say about who moves in."

Before anyone could say anything else, the door opened. Jen and Mark's second oldest son entered the room with his mother trailing behind him. She was carrying two trays of beverages and her son had menus. She placed one of the trays on a table near us before handing us our drinks.

"I'll leave Hunter to take care of you," Jen said before disappearing from the room.

Hunter was in his early teens and all arms and legs. He wasn't homely; he just hadn't grown into his frame. In a couple more years, he was going to be a handsome young man. I didn't envy his parents.

"Thanks, Hunter," I said, taking a menu. "I imagine you're looking forward to summer vacation."

Hunter laughed. "Yeah, though that means more work here. At least I'll be able to start saving for a car."

"Oh, gods," Jade teased. "Does that mean you're almost old enough to get your license?"

"Yeah, next year I'll be able to get my learner's permit," he replied cheerfully. "I'm still trying to talk Mom and Dad into letting me get a car for my sixteenth birthday."

Jade turned to me with a serious expression, though her voice and eyes betrayed her merriment. "You'll have to make me a protection charm before then. Might want to make something for his parents, too. Maybe an anti-anxiety charm?"

"Oh, ha ha, very funny," Hunter retorted, though he was still grinning. Jade laughed. "I'll be back in a few, unless you know what you'd like?" He turned to Zarkull and added, "Dad said he'd be here with your tray in about five minutes."

Zarkull nodded, and Hunter returned it before looking expectantly back at us.

"How about a large sampler tray to start with?" I asked, looking at Jade and Trix, who nodded.

"Sounds good," Hunter replied. "I'll be back shortly for the rest of your order."

"Thanks, Hunter," Jade and I said together. We looked at each other and grinned.

Once he left, Trix tipped her head to the side and studied me for a few moments. I ignored her as I began looking over the menu.

"Why, precisely, did you decide to hide in this area of the state? Staunton is a rather charming town that has a church on nearly every corner. What in all the heavens and hells brought you to this place? Waynesboro, I might add, is almost the same. Only without as many churches, I believe. It's rather quaint and far too docile for you, Lady."

"That was exactly why," I replied with a smirk. "Let me tell you how I tried to be uninteresting for the past several centuries, from the time I ended my reign until I was hired by Merlin to find the Eye of Amon."

"I am all ears," Trix replied.

Since I already knew what I wanted, I began telling the shadow dragon about my life. Trix was riveted by my tale, and so was Jade.

Maybe my life wasn't as boring as I thought.

Chapter Twenty-Three

O nce upon a time, I had been accustomed to dining with guards. That was a few centuries ago in a castle. Locations and eras truly do make a difference.

The guards were on their third round of local craft beer and their second helping of poppers and veggies. Our entrees had been delivered, and we were enjoying the food and each other's company, when the door opened.

This time, however, I felt a distinct shift in the guards' postures. They went from slightly relaxed to rigid and wary.

I turned to find Jen at the door. She wasn't the reason for my guards' change in behavior; Merlin was.

"I would have thought you would be happier to see me," I commented, my fork of loaded mashed potatoes halfway to my mouth. "You look absolutely grim."

"I worried what condition I would find you in!" Merlin said loudly. "You disappear, I have no way of getting information about what happened for days, then I find out you've been abducted by Xantos, of all beings!" He took a deep breath and was more composed when he continued. "Obviously, he was a good host, as he sent a guard detail to watch over you. But I did not know what I would find when I got here."

"I was not abducted by Xantos," I said as I lowered my fork. Zarkull frowned, and there was no missing the guards' irritation at the slight toward their employer. "He graciously offered me a chance to leave my mother's realm, and I accepted it. He was a wonderful host. It isn't my fault you were banished from my mother's realm, leaving you unable to track what I was doing."

"I'm actually surprised he isn't demanding to know why you still have the guards. It really wouldn't be that difficult for me to eat them," Trix said conversationally. I caught her winking at Jade, so I didn't think she was serious.

"If Xantos extended such an offer, it would be poor manners to refuse," Merlin said to Trix. He was, however, moving slowly toward me, the guards watching every step.

"At least they both believe in being polite, when it suits them," Jade said sotto voce.

"They are 'old fashioned,'" Trix quipped.

I couldn't help laughing. There was still tension in the room, but it was lessened by their joking.

"We do have a lot to discuss," I said.

Jade smirked at Merlin. "So, do we call you Merlin or Sterling? And aren't you the least bit curious about why she returned?"

Trix leaned forward. "Perhaps he's already aware of Xantos's discovery? Maybe that's why he's here?"

"I answer to both, however I have come to prefer Sterling. There are fewer connotations and negative beliefs connected to that name," he replied, holding her gaze. His body was far from relaxed.

"I don't believe he's going to answer your question, Trix," Jade commented.

"I do believe you're right," Trix agreed.

I bit back my laughter and cut off their antics. "Enough, you two. There will be plenty of time to torment him later."

"Yes," Trix said with a smirk. "When you aren't around."

I noticed a malicious sparkle in her eyes when I glanced at her.

"They do have valid questions. Why don't you join us and talk?" I asked, glancing at my guards. "Please let him through, Zarkull."

Sterling stepped forward with his usual confident stride. He glanced at the guards individually, his eyes assessing each one. The guards moved just enough to let him pass, bodies ready for action at the slightest provocation. It was a brief, but fun, pissing contest, and I smiled until Sterling sat down across from me.

"Now that you're seated, please answer Trix's questions," I said pleasantly.

"What has Xantos discovered? That someone from The Royal Fae's Court is responsible for the attacks, and they are covering their tracks quite efficiently?" Sterling asked with deliberate slowness.

Trix snorted as we looked uneasily at each other. Then we looked back at Sterling.

"Is that all you're aware of?" I asked, trying to sound casual.

"Was there something else should I be aware of?" he countered. "The presence of Xantos's best personal guards speaks volumes about things that I do not feel are of any concern to me or our child. Do you want me to continue?" He looked at me as he said the final sentence, but it felt like he was asking, or perhaps challenging, all three of us.

Trix giggled. It was a girlish sound one would not expect from such a being. "For once, you are wrong, Merlin. Xantos would not send his personal guards, especially this troupe, simply to babysit her. They are here because he believes she will need the added protection of a force that knows how to fight and protect against a powerful Magick user."

"He never sends guards to babysit," Sterling countered, his eyebrows furrowing. "That is a romantic misconception entertained by the willfully ignorant. They are always sent to protect in case of malicious intent. This time it is not a simple consequence of his playboy behavior or successful ploy to usurp a relationship for his own gain." As he let that sink in, he added, "I welcome their presence and prowess as protectors. Should I send Xantos a fruit basket?"

One of the guards snickered.

"You could try," I replied with a shrug. Glancing at my two companions, I sighed. "Might as well be open about this, I suppose. The reason for the guards is this—someone located two of the pieces of the talisman I used during my Lady of Death days. This unknown person is using my talisman to try to kill me. Since it cannot be used against me in this realm, Xantos sent me back here."

"Thank you," Sterling replied. He smiled before asking, "The last piece is still secure?"

My jaw dropped slightly. It took me a moment to realize he knew I had kept a piece.

"Yes, it is," I replied slowly. "How much do you know about my talisman? Mom and Dad told me the truth, that you approached them and allowed them to put an end to my rule."

"As the being trying to regulate Magick and avoid war with the Mundane, I am very aware of powerful Magick. It matters not if it is within a person, object, or place." Sterling tilted his head slightly to the left as he asked, "Did you think I would mistake the piece beneath your basement floor for something else in the room or, perhaps, Maekyl?"

I shrugged. "I was doing my best to ignore it, actually. Now that someone has put two of the pieces together, however, it's become impossible to ignore." I paused a moment and met his gaze. "I sincerely hope you don't have a problem with my reclaiming the talisman."

"Curious," Trix interrupted. "If I didn't know better, I'd suspect you already knew who created the talisman, Merlin. I know no one at this table has spoken to you about its creation and Maekyl would rather see you chasing rumors than speaking the truth, so I have to question why you aren't more surprised by Catherine's words."

There was absolutely no missing the wincing every time Trix called him 'Merlin.' He did not, however, show any other reaction. It was rather amusing, and I knew Trix did it to antagonize him. Considering there were few people she liked, and he was not one of them, it wasn't surprising.

"It's called deduction, little shadow. But that object and the Eye of Amon were never the issue," Sterling countered.

Time gives you the ability to think about your actions. It also allows you to watch the world around you and witness the rise and fall of civilizations and rulers. I'd spent a good deal of time trying to figure out why I'd been forced to put an early end to my rule.

If it wasn't the power from my talisman or the Eye of Amon, it was something else. Or perhaps, a few something elses.

"It was during the era of never-ending witch hunts," I said thoughtfully. "There was little suspicion about my being a sorceress. Everyone in the villages I ruled knew I used Magick. It wouldn't have been long before the witch hunt reached my lands."

Wouldn't that have been interesting? There would have been no hiding the truth about Magick.

Jade started before nodding. "You never were good at keeping Magick secret during those days."

I shrugged. "I've gotten better over the centuries."

Everyone laughed, and Sterling seemed to relax. The smile he gave me was definitely softer and far warmer than any I'd received so far. We did have a lot to discuss, but that would come later, preferably when there were no guards listening.

The lull was temporary.

Jen came back into the room wearing an expression I had rarely seen on her face. Her forehead was furrowed, but her eyes were wide. Her lips were in a tight thin line. Her gaze locked on me.

"Heads up, Cat," Jen's voice was calm, but unhappy. "Your Mom just came through the VIP entrance. I don't think she's here for Mark's drinks or the food."

Words formed in my mouth as I stood. I vaguely noticed Sterling and Trix looking at me with concern. Jade was already on her feet. Then, just like that, Mother burst into the room, followed by three of her courtiers.

"Jumping from one realm to another, or is it beds?" Mother asked loudly. Her voice did not convey happiness to see me. "At least you're intact and in a safe place for the moment!"

Jen spun smartly around to face my mom. Her hands fell to her sides and curled into claws. Magick and anger pulsed from her in steady waves.

"A safe place that you, your worshipfulness, have just violated," Jen corrected my mom in an icy voice. Sparks flew from her blue eyes.

I noticed that Xantos's guards were in defensive positions, covering my mother and her minions. One of the minions was Miri.

"I am the Queen of Fae," Mother began, her body stiff and regal. "As an honored guest of this establishment, I am given use of the VIP portal."

Jen opened and closed the curled hands at her sides. The power I sensed was growing.

I suddenly had a lot of questions for the hostess.

"I am aware of your identity, especially since I gave you the key spell for the VIP entrance." Jen's words were no warmer, although she said them through a smile. "But no one walks inside these walls as if they own them, save me and mine. And you should remember that anyone who enters the private rooms uninvited is considered hostile. It's a rule you have counted on more than once."

Mom didn't allow herself to be outwardly affected by Jen's words or behavior. She went on as though a waiter had explained a desired food wasn't part of the menu.

"This is my daughter who was taken from my realm days ago." Mother looked at me briefly as she spoke. "Her well-being and that of her unborn child are more important than any civilities at an eating establishment." Mom casually gestured at Jen's hands. "You would do well to get control of your hands, lest you raise them in a way you'll regret."

Smoke burst behind Mom and her minions. Mark loomed over them. It may have been an illusion, but I swear some of the smoke was coming from his back in the shape of thick, bat-like wings. His eyes, normally a warm brown with laugh lines surrounding them, were black, glinting slits.

I suddenly had more questions.

"You'd be better off if she raises her hands." His friendly voice was absent. A hard, nearly insane growl had taken its place. "I will slaughter your little pets and ask you how you'd like them prepared before I feed them to you."

"I believe, Mother, you've been out maneuvered," I said, trying to sound pleasant and reasonable.

Although I'm not certain if it was everything sinking in or one of us speaking, Mother finally stopped acting like she was in charge. Blinking, she glanced at me, then behind her, at the guards, and finally at Jen.

"I have allowed my personal concerns to overstep propriety. You and yours have always treated me and mine with proper respect," Mom said. "Such an oversight will not occur again."

Slowly dropping her hands to her sides, palms out, Mom looked back and forth between Fellhaven's owners.

"Prettily said," Jen muttered, seemingly unfazed.

"But properly implied," Mark growled.

He stood straighter, and the area around him seemed to grow brighter. The smoke was gone. When Jen didn't change her stance, he raised a single eyebrow at her. Finally, she relaxed and stretched her arms out, the palms of her hands facing Mom in a non-threatening way.

Turning toward me, Mom asked, "May we join you?"

Glancing at my guards, a thought occurred to me. "You may, Mom, but not your entourage."

Mom nodded and gestured past Mark, toward the single door.

"You may wait at the bar," she instructed. "Or you may return home."

The other fae slowly made their way past Mark and exited. Miri was smiling. Maybe she was like Jen and enjoyed his methods. Perhaps she was amused at seeing my mother stopped in her tracks. Regardless, she left with the rest. I bet she'd go to the bar.

"The usual double Black Rose to drink?" Mark asked my mother when her minions were gone.

Mom nodded. "Thank you. Some of those lovely stuffed mushrooms as well, if you will."

Jen added, "Mark and Chef Sierra whipped up some of the chawanmushi you are fond of tonight."

"Oh, my," Mom replied and smiled brightly. She looked at Mark and said, "A large bowl of that, instead, please."

Mark put the rectangular glasses he usually wore back on the bridge of his nose. I hadn't noticed he wasn't wearing them. Damn pregnancy.

He smiled and said to my mom, "As you like. It'll be up in a few minutes."

After Mark left, Jen came over to me. "Anything else you need, just say so." Then she asked confidentially, "Do I need to poison any of the entourage at the bar?"

Laughing, I shook my head. "As tempting as it might be, I'd best not accept that offer." Pausing, I glanced at my mother before adding, "I would appreciate it if you kept a close watch on Miri, the last one who left. And thank you for everything you and Mark have done."

Jen grinned benevolently. "Always. I will be in later to see how everything is going."

As she walked away, I realized I'd forgotten something. I called after her, "When you have a chance, I have some questions."

Jen laughed. Before she went through the door, she called back to me, "I bet you do."

Zarkull and the rest of his crew didn't seem thrilled, but they allowed my mother to join us at the table. She didn't look happy, but she didn't look as pissed either.

"For the record, Mom, I was not taken from your realm. I left freely. If you had not forbidden my leaving, I would not have had to seek assistance from Xantos who, I might add, has graciously given me the protection of his best personal guards." If I had to repeat this story one more time, I was going to smite the person who asked. It was an amusing thought that helped keep my temper in check. "Let me answer the most pressing questions. I'm fine. The baby is fine. I'm safer here than in any other realm, including yours. Someone found two of the three parts of my talisman, and it's been restored to a degree. Any other questions?"

"Explain that," my mother demanded as she took a cautious seat between me and Sterling. Her eyes darted to the guards before returning to me. "I do not trust that elf. He's an interfering megalomaniac who doesn't do anything without an ulterior motive." Her eyes narrowed as she added, "You and power are two things I prefer not to see together."

"I understand your concern," Sterling said gently. "But let her fill in the gaps."

"Thanks, dear," I muttered. Jade snickered, and I caught a smirk on Trix's face. Sighing, I ate a bite of food and took my time chewing and swallowing. "The talisman is mine, Mom. It always has been. It wasn't something from Maekyl's stash or an item I found." There was no need to say it hadn't come from Trix. Shadow dragons did not give up their hoards. "I made the talisman, Mom, shortly before you and Dad came to tell me to end my reign. The last piece is still hidden where no one but me can get to it."

There was a long silence. Finally, Mom said with a grumble, "Your father is going to be insufferable. He won that bet."

"He is a very poor winner," Sterling confided.

Jade and Trix laughed. I couldn't help but join in, especially since Mom and Sterling weren't exaggerating. We all knew what my dad could be like when he won a bet.

Mom turned to Sterling. "It seems you were right about wanting us to stop her. If she created that talisman at such a young age, there is no telling what she could or would have done." She reached over and touched his hand. "It will take some time for me to accept your intimacy with Catherine, but I can't fault you for it."

Covering her hand with his free one, Sterling said, "Thank you."

"Now," Mom said, turning back to me, "tell me all that has happened."

Glancing at Jade and Trix before turning back to my mother, I told the tale with them adding details and comments. It felt good to talk to my mother again.

Chapter Twenty-Four

Lunch with my mother ended far too quickly. She departed for her realm, taking her courtiers with her and leaving us to our whims.

My whim was to find my talisman before something horrible happened, like the wielder dying and the demon escaping.

Since I had Sterling and the guards, Jade returned to her business, taking Trix with her.

I didn't doubt Trix had her own agenda that didn't entail selling jewelry and blown glass items to mundanes. Since I trusted the dragon, I didn't question her. She was an adult and could take care of herself.

That left Sterling and me to locate the abode of the so-called priestess. Thankfully, we had a GPS, which I used to find directions to the location of the computer she'd used.

When we stepped outside, we found five black, 1970s Harley Davidson Ironhead Sportster Choppers lined up in a row. Each of my guards went to one, climbed on, and started it. By the time we got into Sterling's Stingray, they had surrounded us.

Giggling at the odd image of elves on Harley's, I entered the address in the GPS.

"They aren't quite as intimidating as red-eyed mounts," Sterling commented as he pulled out of the parking lot. Laughing, I had to agree as I watched them easily keep pace with us.

* * *

The questions were piling up, and I was determined to get answers, but those would have to wait until after we investigated the apartment, which was located on the west side of Staunton.

The apartment complex consisted of tall brick buildings with stone and metal staircases. Toys, chairs and flowerpots with half-dead plants were scattered around the complex. I spotted several misery demons trotting around or sprawled outside doorways.

Finding the appropriate building wasn't difficult. Since there was no designated visitor parking, we parked in a random spot, then walked up a cement staircase to the second floor of the building.

Each floor had three apartments on both sides of the stairwell. The apartment we wanted was in the middle on the left side. We knocked and waited a few moments for a response. Three of my guards positioned themselves outside the building and along the stairwell. Two posted themselves outside the apartment.

Hearing no response, I unlocked the door with a touch of Magick. I could have used lock picks, but Magick was easier and quicker and would leave no visible marks. Sterling grumbled, but I ignored him as I opened the door and stepped into the apartment.

Moving to the side, I heard a crunch. I looked down and saw that I had crushed a handful of stale, orange potato chips. Sterling followed behind me, allowing the door to shut quietly.

I really did not want to move from where I was standing for fear of what else I might step on. Or in.

Empty snack containers littered the floor of the small apartment. To my right was a small dining room and kitchen, to the left was the living room. A closed door led into what I suspected was the bedroom. There was a filthy flat screen TV that looked like it was at least five years old and had never been cleaned. A La-Z-Boy recliner was situated in front of the TV with a wooden tray table beside it.

The table was covered with dried liquids and food. There were cans and discarded plates on the floor under and around the table. There was no sofa, but there were folding chairs filled with empty soda cans, discarded snack containers, and dirty dishes.

The air was stale and musty. I suspected things were growing in the corners.

Behind the recliner, I could see an old gaming system that looked like an Xbox 360. It was difficult to tell, though, due to the dirt and dried grease coating the console.

As I turned back toward Sterling, I couldn't miss the stacks of dishes piled up in the kitchen.

"It's worse on this side," Sterling said, his face filled with disgust. "I wouldn't advise coming closer."

"Yeah, I think I'll pass," I replied, trying to ignore the stench of rotting food and who knew what else.

Turning, I opened the door to reveal the bedroom. I waited for Sterling to join me, and we moved into the room. To our left was a bathroom with a walk-in shower. I didn't want to think about what was growing in there. The bathmat was covered in black spots.

Shuddering, I turned back to examine the room. The bed wasn't made. The sheets were dull, but not because of the color of the fabric. A stereo system sat on a dresser beside the bed. It was slightly cleaner, but not by much.

The one thing in the entire apartment that was spotless was the latest version of a MacBook sitting on top of a large card table. A clean, leather office chair was positioned in front of it. Boxes were stacked neatly beneath the table.

On one side of the MacBook were stacks of tarot cards. On the other side were little velvet bags and bowls. One bowl, upon closer inspection, held reiki stones carved with runes. The other bowl and the bags were filled with unmarked gemstones.

"One of these things is not like the others. One of these things doesn't belong," I joked, trying to ignore the growing queasiness in my stomach.

Who would have thought I couldn't handle the smell of garbage? I was fine with the foul odors produced when a body dies or is badly burned, but not the stench of stale air and rotting food.

"Are you well, Cat?" Sterling asked, his hand gently rubbing my shoulder.

Before I could reply, we heard the door open. We moved into the bedroom doorway and saw a man in his early twenties, drinking a slushie that was half red and half blue. He paused to stare at us.

We looked at each other for a few heartbeats before he asked in a mellow, drawn-out voice, "Who are you? What are you doing here?"

"Oh, fuck this," I muttered.

Moving my hands subtly, I wove a spell to soundproof the apartment. That led into my second spell, one that would force him to truthfully answer our questions. Once we were done, I could easily manipulate his memory so he wouldn't remember our being in his apartment.

I didn't want him reporting our intrusion to anyone, least of all his keeper.

Sterling grumbled again. I suspected we would have a 'discussion' later. That was fine. He would have to learn to live with my methods sooner or later.

"Who are you?" I asked once the guy's eyes glazed over.

"John Franklin," he replied. "Everyone calls me Johnnie. Who are you?"

"Inspectors," Sterling replied smoothly. "Do you live here, John?"

"Yeah, this is my place," John replied before taking a slurp of his slushie.

Giving him a pleasant smile, or as much of one as I could manage through my growing nausea, I asked, "Is highelfpriestess667@gmail.com your email address?"

"Sorta? I'm paid to answer emails for that address," he replied between loud slurps.

"What else do you do?" I asked. The sooner we got answers, the sooner we could leave.

"I send and receive packages, make special decks of tarot cards, and fill bags with gemstones. When I've got enough to fill a box, I call the store and let Genevieve know. She comes and gets them." As John took another drink, I bit my cheek to keep from snapping at him. He'd pronounced 'tarot' like 'carrot.' At least he pronounced her name correctly, though I suspect it was because the woman had bashed it into his thick skull.

"What about the apartment?" Sterling asked.

"Everything is paid for by the boss, the high elf priestess. I emailed one of those online psychic people, and she replied to me. So, instead of being tossed into the street because my no-good, poser friends didn't understand me, I got this sweet apartment." There was actually some spark in his words, and my curiosity was piqued.

"Go on," I encouraged. "Everything is paid for? Does the priestess contact you directly?"

"Nah, not after that first email. Everything comes from a call, email, or text, and it's always from Genevieve," John replied. His voice was dull again, and he'd returned to slurping his drink.

"You say your friends were going to throw you into the streets?" Sterling asked.

"Yeah, my pals said I had to pay a hundred a month for my part of rent and stuff. I couldn't get a job, and they said if I didn't start paying, I'd have to leave." His yellow teeth and blue tongue were visible behind his grin. "But look at me now! Don't have to pay anything, and all I have to do is make a couple dozen stacks of those cards and fill bags with rocks. I don't have to worry anymore. Pretty sweet, man."

I looked around the trashed apartment before turning back to John. "Yeah. Lovely. What's the name of the store?"

"Summers Sage. It's located in Fishersville." Johnnie blinked and continued to suck down his frozen drink.

"Thanks, John. We'll be going now." I made a few subtle gestures with my hand, and his eyes closed slightly. "You won't remember anyone being here, anything missing, or any questions asked. Continue on about your day, as usual."

Stepping back into the bedroom, I swiped a stack of tarot cards and departed. Sterling followed at my heels.

"The truth spell will wear off, and he won't remember anything," I said as I hurried down the stairs. "That doesn't mean I want to stick around, though."

Sterling chuckled. "I am well aware of the spell and your abilities," he said. "Is your memory being affected by your delicate condition?"

Since he was beside me, I backhanded him good-naturedly on the chest. "Very funny. I just wanted to make sure you weren't going to be a hard-ass about what I did."

Sterling kissed me on the cheek.

"Only when you break too many rules," he said.

"I'll try to keep my rule breaking to a minimum," I quipped as we got in his car. The guards climbed on their motorcycles. Ignoring Zarkull and his crew, I handed Sterling the stack of tarot cards. "Speaking of rule breaking, tell me what you think of these."

"Printed overseas, where labor is considerably underpaid, on second-hand, heavy cardstock," Sterling observed. "They're not Magick or remarkable, even by mundane standards. There are many cards that are incorrect. The art isn't common for the Western Hemisphere, so it could be mistaken as exotic or mystical by the uninformed. In short, it's shiny junk."

Rolling my eyes, I grabbed the top card and ran my hand over it. The silver inlay on the cup shifted slightly, revealing a haze.

"They are wrong in this realm, certainly. And useless to anyone who doesn't understand how to use them," I replied. "But haven't you seen these in Mom's realm? They're popular among those who have little Magickal ability. Everyone else sees them as 'parlor tricks.'"

Sterling blushed a little. "No. Even before we became involved, I rarely traveled to the fae kingdom or the realm it dwells in."

"I suspect anyone, here, with Magickal ability or high on dragon's blood, could use them," I continued. Smirking, I couldn't help but needle him a little. "I'm surprised you didn't visit Mom more, all things considered."

Maybe, just maybe, it was a good thing I was going to accept the position on the Council. Sterling's lack of travel beyond this realm explained a lot about Xantos's attitude toward him. Admittedly, though, I didn't know everything that was going on around me.

During my reign, though? I knew exactly what was happening among my Magickal and non-Magickal subjects. And not just those in my castle. If you dwelled within my domain, my spies watched and studied you.

It was part of why I didn't reside in my mother's realm for extended periods. My mother would give me power, and I knew what I would do with it.

Fae were masterful spies and assassins, and with Trix at my side, I would have a network that would make my mother's look like child's play.

"There is plenty to keep me busy in this realm," Sterling replied soberly.

"You should learn to take vacations," I said as I finished searching for the address of Summers Sage. I put it into the GPS and waited until it gave directions before changing the topic. "You know, Mom is right. We do have a lot to figure out. Especially about us."

Sterling glanced at me as he drove. "Is now really an appropriate time for this discussion?"

Shrugging, I replied, "At least you can't pop out when you don't like the direction it's going." At his frown, I laughed. "I'm joking. I don't believe you would walk away from a conversation simply because you don't like it." At least, I didn't think he would, but people could be unpredictable. "Let's start with a simple question. Why didn't you tell me you were Merlin?"

"There's such a stigma attached to the name. I didn't want that stigma to color your opinion of me."

There was silence as I considered what he said. "It would have been nice if you had told me, rather than hearing it from my mother," I said quietly. "No offense, but it is hard to equate the Merlin of myth and legend with who you are today. And when I officially accept the role of Speaker of the Council, someone would have had to tell me."

"It is actually protocol for all members of the Council to give their original or best-known names at the Ceremony of Titles." Sterling relayed this in a weary voice. "Sometimes it matters, sometimes it makes no difference to the one being brought into the fold."

"Secrets can be the downfall of those destined for greatness." I let that sink in for a moment before chuckling. "I would rather have learned it from you, but I can understand why you were reluctant to say anything. Just imagine what our child will think when she finds out."

"I'll let you handle it," he said with a sad smile. "My experiences with revealing my true name have been bad. They tend to be rather..." he trailed off, sadness filling his eyes.

"Disastrous?" I suggested. "So I've heard. Perhaps the fact that I'm not a human and have Magickal abilities will make a difference."

"Perhaps," Sterling replied, though he didn't sound optimistic.

"So, what about us?" I suddenly felt like a teenager as I stumbled over the words. Maybe I could blame it on the pregnancy and hormones? "How do you feel toward me? About me?"

"I am dangerously in love with you," Sterling admitted. His voice was brighter, though, and he smiled. "I could easily become obsessed, so I hold myself back. While I have not had the rumored number of lovers or the child-bearing harem, I have had a few failed relationships in my time. And the offspring have, for the most part, been spectacular disasters. One son came close to being all a parent could hope for, but he was destroyed by his sister and their bastard child."

My heart did flips. Not about his failed relationships and problem children, but at his declaration of love. I could feel my face soften, and I practically melted into the seat of his car. I might have blinked away a few tears.

"Oh," I finally managed to whisper. My smile couldn't get any bigger. "I love you, too. Far more than what's safe for anyone." I reached over and placed my hand on his thigh. "Our daughter will not be like Morgana. She may have a few troublemakers for role models, but none that would allow her to turn against us."

Or, at the very least, me. Maekyl, Trix, and Jade were loyal to a fault, and none of them would want to see my heart broken by my having to kill my child.

"She may be worse than you," Sterling said, though the smile didn't fade.

I laughed. "If so, you might end up visiting Mom's realm more often!"

Sterling glanced at me, blinked, then burst out laughing. After a few seconds, I joined in. The conversation turned to more mundane topics as he followed the GPS to our destination.

* * *

Our destination was located in Fishersville, which was one of the expansive rural areas that separated Waynesboro from Staunton. Parts were built up with businesses and schools, but for the most part, it was rural.

Summers Sage was a two-story house in one of the residential areas just off Route 250, near the county library. Dragon heads topped the corner posts of the wrought iron fence surrounding the house.

The yard was a work of art, presumably requiring daily lawn care from a local company. Elaborate marble water fountains bubbled and gurgled merrily, while birds bathed in extravagantly carved baths. Steppingstones with Elder Futhark symbols carved into them created a path to the front door. Medium-sized gazing balls lined the path, each one shined to mirror-like perfection.

Sterling and I got out of his car, and Zarkull and his crew got off their bikes. They all wore grim expressions and moved with deliberate steps. I took a second look at the house and wondered what was bothering them.

"Zarkull?" I asked. "Is something wrong?"

The leader of my guards stared at the house for a few moments before making a slight gesture to the others. Alaria moved opposite Zarkull as the other three flanked us. Zarkull and Alaria vanished from our sight between blinks. I could hear Sterling grinding his teeth. Glancing over my shoulder, I discovered that the other three had vanished, as well as the motorcycles.

Damn! I knew they were good. I now had to up my esteem a few more notches, and it was already pretty high. Shrugging, I took the lead and stepped onto the stone path.

So far, everything felt normal, though I could sense some Magick pulsing somewhere. It wasn't strong, but it was there. That made sense, though. After all, whoever was behind the fae tarot cards had them delivered to this address.

Sterling moved in front of me as we neared the door. If he wanted to take the brunt of an attack, that was fine. I preferred to pick my arguments with him, and this wasn't one I wanted to start.

He climbed the single step to the porch and opened the front door. A long moment of silence ensued before Sterling gestured for me to join him.

Through the open door, I saw a polished wooden staircase. The short hallway beside it led to a dining area and a single door to the left, just past the one we were looking through. I didn't see beings of any kind.

The moment we entered, two of my guards reappeared and moved past us to check the left-hand door. Silently, they swung the door open and darted inside. Within a few seconds, the pair emerged, shaking their heads to indicate no one was in the room. Sterling gestured for them to move ahead of us. As they crept down the hallway, I noticed that each guard had a long dagger in one hand and a dark wooden wand in the other. I wondered what they could do against someone with a firearm before they signaled for us to join them.

The dining area was actually the end space of a kitchen that was large enough to run a small restaurant. The stainless-steel equipment included the brands preferred by the network cooking channels. Everything was clean and in its proper place. A trio of stairs led down into a lounge area. Both rooms had seventy-inch televisions.

A half dozen wooden chairs sat around a circular mahogany table in the dining area. The antique set was in great condition. The furniture, like the floors and kitchen, shone.

Everything we saw, even the long leather couch in the lounge, had been meticulously cleaned and kept in perfect condition. Shelves of books ran the entire length of the lounge's back wall, and although some volumes appeared to be quite old and frayed, none were dusty or neglected.

The guard that stayed behind when we first entered was now standing outside the closed front door. I turned to the two who accompanied Sterling and me and asked, "What was the room you looked into?"

"Office space," said Alaria. "Desk, paper files, all the gadgets you humans rely upon so heavily."

My guess was that we would find a computer, printer, some form of phone and even a calculator in that room. The computer and files might prove informative once the house was secured.

"Where are the others?" I asked.

"They have finished checking the exterior and taken up positions to watch for approaching beings," Alaria explained.

"Thank you, Alaria," Sterling said. The woman nodded. In the next instant, she had silently bounded up half the stairs leading to the second floor.

While we waited for her and Zarkull to finish checking the second floor, I peered into the office. An antique mahogany desk, which took up half the room, held a stack of ledgers, an open laptop, a large printer and scanner combo, and half the contents of any office superstore's supply aisle. The chair was a modern contraption, complete with stereo speakers and massage options.

In the far west corner of the room, almost hidden by the desk, were two stacks. One was a stack of pre-paid postage boxes of various sizes, though most were the right size to ship a full deck of tarot cards, legitimate or otherwise. The other stack contained large storage boxes, stacked three high. The top one was open, so I went around the desk and peeked in. It was filled with decks of tarot cards held together by rubber bands. Handwritten sticky notes were attached to each, giving a name and address. These must be the decks her minion put together. His handwriting was neater than I expected.

Sterling stepped into the office, smiled, and told me the second floor was ready for us to search.

The second floor could have functioned as either a lair or coven house, since the three bedrooms, full bath, and second floor living room provided ample space. The master bedroom had its own bath, so Genevieve or a coven leader could bathe in private, with the top wards or witches in the smaller two bedrooms.

The living room resembled a tarot reading room from popular fiction, complete with candles, dangling sashes, crystal prisms hung to make the sparse light dance in multiple colors on the walls, and a round table with a crystal ball. The oddest thing was how much Asian influence could be found along the walls. For every cheap looking prop from a gypsy movie set, there was an expensive piece of jade or a bamboo figurine, and there was at least one authentic vase from an early Japanese dynasty. Sterling said nothing as we examined the rooms. I was about to ask him if anything had intrigued him, when Zarkull called out to us. He was standing next to a small closet door next to the master bedroom. We hadn't bothered to look in there.

"You missed the one interesting find on this floor," the guard said impishly. He swung the door open so we could see inside.

The closet door was a sham. The front, which faced the hallway and stairwell, had been covered with inch-thick boards of finished maple to match the floors. But the actual door was made of ghostwood, and we could see a metal grid woven into it.

"Someone nailed tungsten to the ghostwood," Zarkull said, as if he was answering my unspoken question. In his realm, tungsten deadened Magick, much the same as Xantos's obsidian weapons did. In my realm, it drastically diminished it.

He stepped aside, and we could see that the door hid a small set of steps that climbed up and turned sharply to the right. I could now feel Magick from the petite doorway.

"Let's see what's up there," Sterling suggested.

"After you," I said, gesturing to Zarkull. "The ghostwood explains why we didn't feel any Magick until now."

"You're familiar with it?" Zarkull and Sterling asked at the same time.

The guard glanced over his shoulder, and the two men exchanged grins. I was tempted to pinch myself to make sure I wasn't dreaming.

"Yes," I replied. "Mother has several small houses built of ghostwood for those who are addled by illness, Magick, or potions. They are kept there until they're healed or until a final decision can be made about their disposition."

For all my mother's fury and strictness, she was compassionate toward the ill or injured. She gave them every chance to be saved before choosing death. It made her unique in the fae realm. Most rulers preferred to kill anyone who could lay waste to a kingdom instead of giving them a chance to be healed. She wasn't soft, mind you, but she was fair and just.

"How does the wood work in the fae realm?" Zarkull asked curiously.

I grinned. "Those who are crazed are kept in ghostwood houses, so any spell that is cast is contained. The wood dampens Magick and either absorbs it or causes it to rebound within the house. There is nothing of great worth in the houses, and food is typically delivered on a set schedule. They aren't exactly prisons, but they aren't luxury homes, either."

Zarkull made a thoughtful sound but didn't comment. Sterling appeared to be deep in thought, so I left him alone. I was trying to sift through the various Magicks that were permeating the narrow staircase. All of it felt familiar, and I could all but taste the Magick from my talisman as it wove its way through the other Magicks.

I really wanted my talisman back, preferably before the demon managed to convince the current user to do something catastrophically stupid.

Or broke free. I still wasn't certain which would be worse.

The staircase ended in a large room that was vastly different from all the others.

It was more like what I expected when we first entered the house. Whoever owned this house had taken advantage of the angled roof. The sides and floor formed a triangle, and the room stretched the entire length of the house. It might have been an attic space, except that there was no excessive heat, and it was furnished.

My eyes quickly swept the room, absorbing everything in it. Bookcases lined each side, built to fit the angled ceiling perfectly. The shelves to our right were filled with books. I recognized some of the more popular spellbooks used by wizards and sorcerers. Some I had even used during my youth. Others were ancient, and I narrowed my eyes upon reading some of their titles. The bookcase on the opposite wall was filled with spell components and utensils used for mixing ingredients. There was a commonality between everything, and it wasn't one I enjoyed discovering.

Someone had been naughty and extremely sneaky. One might even say devious.

I moved further into the room, ignoring the enormous circle on the floor. The runes and sigils indicated it was a base used for spell casting or summoning. It could be easily altered for any particular spell. I didn't bother with such things because I had been taught not to rely on such crutches. They often led to laziness or sloppiness, and I'd seen what happens to lazy or sloppy spell casters. The end result is never pretty.

Glancing behind us, I noticed a small altar on a corner shelf to our far right. It wasn't the work of an amateur. There was a reverence in how it was set up, a purpose in its placement, and an understanding of an altar's true purpose.

All of this was interesting, but not nearly as interesting as what was on the far wall. The portal which spanned almost the entire wall shifted in a rainbow of colors. It was currently inactive, but I knew the Magick that came through it intimately.

"Who's going with me to my mother's realm?" I asked no one in particular.

Chapter Twenty-Five

The answer was rather evident. None of the guards or Sterling were going to allow me to leave without them. So, after everyone assembled in the secret room, I touched the portal, much to the dislike of my guards. There wasn't any choice, really. Only another fae from my mother's realm could activate the portal so all of us could pass through it safely.

The Magick from my talisman was thick, and it slid against my skin. The untold promise of unlimited power was a temptation few could pass up. As we stood within the luxurious chambers of someone I knew well, I could taste the Magick left by the use of my incomplete talisman. I could tell the five guards felt it too.

Sterling was watching me, an indecipherable expression on his face. "How is it no one felt this?"

"Handmaidens are given complete privacy, if they desire it. Even servants aren't allowed inside certain chambers if the person doesn't wish it," I explained. Frustration grew as I stalked around the room, my right hand outstretched as I sought the Magickal pulse of my talisman. "It isn't here. Damn it. My talisman is not here!"

"Only our lord's chambers are allowed such privacy," Shyrrik said. She was going through a dresser, distaste evident in her expression. "Granting others such privacy allows for treachery such as this."

"You won't hear any argument from me," I replied as I moved to the elaborately carved writing desk.

There are some things modern fiction got right, and one is that if a spell is cast, someone more powerful than the spellcaster can block or overpower it. In my mother's realm, no one was more powerful than my mother, except perhaps Xantos or Merlin. There are exceptions to every rule.

I was far more powerful than any of my mother's handmaidens. Even if their Magick was augmented by a stolen talisman.

I rolled the desk top back, revealing little pigeonholes filled with stacks of envelopes, papers, and writing implements. There were even wax and a stamp for her use. I glanced through the papers before turning to the drawers. There were folders and papers bound together neatly, and it didn't take more than a few minutes to pull out the incriminating evidence.

Letters detailing Trix's travels were accompanied by sketches and photos. Neatly written notes and comments were attached to the letters, photos, and sketches. There was also a large, detailed drawing of my talisman. It wasn't entirely accurate, but it was close enough for someone who had spent decades searching for the pieces. The most important piece was missing from the drawing, a detail I was relieved to discover.

"Princess?" Krysdos said quizzically behind me. He had a journal in his hands and was looking at me strangely.

I shrugged. "In my mother's realm, yes, I am a princess. My mother is queen."

"Whoever wrote this wishes to take your place as heir to this realm," Krysdos stated, nonplussed by my statement.

"I imagine she does," I acknowledged. I gathered up the damning papers. "Let's find Mom. I'm certain she'll be interested to know about this potential coup."

"You know who is behind this?" Zarkull asked.

I nodded. "Yes. Her name is Miriria Lathos. Her Magickal skill isn't noteworthy, though apparently she doesn't need it when she's being clever."

With that, I strode from her chambers, Sterling at my side and my guards in a protective formation around us.

"She has confederates," Wyrren stated. "For someone planning a coup, she kept meticulous notes about it."

I held out a hand, palm up. Without a word, I summoned a mirror, and said the name of my mother's Captain of the Guards. "Aerynir, I need you to secure Miriria's chambers immediately, by my order."

His image did not appear in the mirror, though his deep voice was clear as he replied, "It will be done, Your Highness."

"I want you to personally ensure nothing within her chambers is touched until I, my father, or my mother has had the chance to thoroughly investigate them."

"Yes, princess," he replied. "It will be done."

I wasn't certain if I was angrier that Miri had plotted this under our noses or because she'd found my talisman, reattached two of the pieces, and used it. Either way, I wanted retribution in the form of her head on a platter.

Preferably, literally.

My mother's court was in full session when we stormed through the doors, though I'm not sure it counts as storming through the doors if the guards open them for you. Then again, with five armed guards daring anyone to move close to Sterling and me, maybe it did count. My mother's features darkened as she rose from her throne. My father descended the steps and met me at the bottom of the dais.

None of us bowed before my parents, something no one would miss. The guards didn't stop my dad from approaching me. Worry was evident in his eyes.

"Where is Miriria Lathos?" I asked. It was more of a demand, but who was going to quibble?

"Your Majesty," an elderly man called. It wasn't anyone I recognized. Judging from the formal attire, I suspected he was from an outlying duchy or from another kingdom. "Certainly, this is a breach of conduct! None of these beings are your guards, and they barged in in full armor, complete with weapons!"

I looked at him closely as he spoke, taking time to memorize his smooth Celtic features and white hair. He wasn't a youth, judging by the lines on his face and the way he held himself. The luster of his hair was fading. He had little Magick, or it was also fading, which sometimes happened when fae entered their elder years.

"I am her daughter," I commented, curious to hear what else this idiot would say in front of my mother.

"All the more reason you should follow the queen's rules!" he retorted forcefully. "To come into Court and demand a fellow fae is beyond insolent!"

My father's expression turned from worry to fury. I looked up at my mother who was glaring at the fool.

"I think we have found Confederate Number One," I murmured to Sterling.

"Perhaps," Sterling replied in an equally soft tone. His eyes swept the room, and I wondered what he was thinking.

My mother's voice drew my attention back to the argument. "Contrary to popular belief, Crown Princess Catherine is allowed the guards she chooses. They are her guards, to protect her as they see fit, in the manner they and she deem appropriate." My mother paused; her gaze leveled at the sputtering elder. "She has yet to show insolence or disloyalty to her father, myself, or the realm."

A hush settled over the room. There wasn't even a shuffle of feet or a rustle of clothing. Sterling smiled proudly. But that wasn't as weird as seeing the warmth in his eyes as he watched my mother.

Good thing I didn't find the age thing creepy or weird. Otherwise, I think I'd run away from everyone and everything.

"Why do you seek Miri, Catherine?" my father prodded.

I handed him the stack of papers I was carrying. "I believe treason is a good reason, don't you?"

An interesting ripple ran through the gathered subjects. I noticed Cildur in the crowd, and he quickly slipped through the fae with an ease I had envied during our youth.

"Your evidence?" Dad asked calmly.

"Yes. Krysdos has a journal with further evidence," I stated.

"Very well. The Queen and I will look over this. Join us in her study, along with your entourage," Dad replied.

"Is that it?" the elder demanded in a surprisingly shrill voice. "She comes storming in here, demanding one of your subjects, claiming she committed treason, and that's all you have to say?"

With each word, his voice rose in pitch until it started to hurt my ears.

"Mother?" I asked plaintively. "May I?" I even attempted to use the puppy-dog-eyes and pout.

"Please do." Mother said briskly. She stared at the elder, her expression flat but her eyes blazing. "Better he suffers your retort than mine."

My right arm lashed out toward the elder. He started to shriek, but my spell snapped his jaws and teeth together. A tiny point of white-hot heat appeared at the left corner of his lips. Moving swiftly, the smoldering dot of Magick traveled the length of his mouth, sealing it shut. The elder tore at his face with his fingers, finally collapsing to his knees. The silence within the court became heavy and palpable.

"Lest anyone forget, this is my daughter, and she is held to a higher standard than this Court or any other," Mother bellowed. "She has shown mercy to an insolent. I would have kept his tongue as a souvenir."

As the silence grew, Mother descended the steps and led us from the room. My guards moved closer to Sterling and me, but it wasn't entirely necessary, since Mother's subjects were quickly moving away from us.

Once outside the throne room, Wyrren glanced at me before turning his attention to the empty hallways. "I have fewer questions, now, about why our lord enjoys your company, though I am curious as to why you showed that cur mercy."

I shrugged. "As tempting as it was to kill him, death is often forgotten. A walking reminder of what I can do, with my mother's blessing, is not so easily forgotten."

"Lord Xantos has done similar when he deems it useful," Alaria murmured. "There are many walking around missing appendages. They do not make the same mistakes twice, and those who witness his wrath, rarely cross him for fear of what he will do to them."

"Maybe that's why he and Mom clash so much," I muttered.

Father coughed, and Sterling snorted. Glancing at Sterling, I saw him trying to hide a grin. The guards had blank faces, and I couldn't tell what shone in their eyes. Mother's back had grown stiffer, and I could hear her gritting her teeth.

Thankfully, she opened the door to the family room before anyone could say anything else. The moment we were inside the room, the guards fanned out against the walls, leaving Sterling and me to face my parents.

"Xantos and I clash, as you put it, because we don't agree on a great many things," she stated primly. Father snickered, causing her to sigh heavily. "Though, I suppose we are similar in many ways."

"That's as much of an admission as you will ever get from your mother," Dad said cheerfully. "Now, about this business with Miri. Is it she who located your talisman?"

"Yes," I replied. "She is also part of a group that is plotting against Mom." I held my hand out, and Krysdos moved away from his position long enough to give me the journal he'd procured in her chambers. Once the book was in my hand, he returned to his position against the wall. I gave the journal to my mother. "I suspect the elder who spoke against me is one of her cohorts."

"Any idea what they are plotting?" Dad asked.

"No; I could only guess."

Mom stopped skimming through the journal. Looking up, she turned her attention to Sterling. "You have more experience than anyone here. What do you think?"

"There are few reasons for anyone to plot or act against a governing power," Sterling said. "The people who do so think someone else will give them what they want—what the current boss won't or can't give them."

"That sounds like a single reason," Dad commented dryly, but he winked at Sterling.

There had to be something more to this, especially since Miri had gone to extreme lengths to hunt down the pieces to my talisman.

"The elder's Magick was fading. Everyone could see that," I said thoughtfully. "Miri has never been strong in Magick, not when we were growing up, and not now."

"The tarot cards we found," Sterling began. "You said they were seen as 'crutches' in this realm. That they are popular among those with little Magickal talent. Miri would be familiar enough with them to design her own sets or find reasonable facsimiles."

"And mundane fans of those would give her praise," I added, "feeding her ego."

"How are those with negligible Magickal skills treated, your majesty?" Shyrrik asked.

"They are given the same rights and privileges as anyone else," Mother replied.

"But they are rarely placed in positions of power, aside from being handmaidens," Father interjected.

Mother looked sharply at him. "Challenges are still a way of life here. I don't encourage them, but we are fae. If someone with little Magickal ability is given a position of power, they are quickly challenged. It is rare they survive." She sighed and shook her head. "It isn't that I don't think they are capable; it's that I don't wish to see any more of my people die because they cannot protect themselves from their fellow fae."

"Being a fae queen doesn't automatically give you power?" Wyrren asked.

My parents looked at him in confusion.

"No," I answered. "It would be like a novice in your realm taking over Xantos's throne. They may be able to tap into the web at his estate, but would they have his innate power?"

"Unless the heir he chooses has as much power as he does and the knowledge to rule a vast empire, the heir would be under constant attack by those who desire his throne," Zarkull replied.

"Exactly," I said. That made everything fall into place, and I could see the full picture. "My talisman is believed to be a source of immense power. Miri has only the legends to go by, so she doesn't understand the truth behind it. She thinks the talisman will allow her to possess the power to rule."

"Until it destroys her," Sterling said slowly.

"We really do not want that to happen," I replied. "That would be bad on an epic level."

"Catherine, what did you do?" my mother asked cautiously.

"It involved a demon, a ceremony, and the creation of the talisman," I answered, trying not to sound smug, though it was decidedly difficult to keep from smiling as I said it.

"So, you captured a demon in the talisman. Please explain why it won't destroy you if it will destroy her," my mom demanded.

Great. She was going into über protective mode again.

"Because I created it, Mom," I replied. "It has to obey me. It's probably part of why Miri keeps finding me—the talisman is drawn to me."

"You always did like to bind things to yourself," Dad commented. "Why would an artifact of power be any different?"

I had the good grace to blush as I giggled. Mother snorted, but there was a smile pulling at the corners of her lips.

"Fine, fine," she grumbled. "I'm torn between being proud and concerned that our daughter was able to create a legendary artifact at such a young age and keep it hidden for so long."

My father was studying me closely, and there was something in his expression that made me nervous. "As soon as everyone realizes you've regained the talisman, you will have more enemies than you do from being with Sterling."

"Let them come," I said confidently. Lifting my head, I met my father's gaze. "I ruled before, and my domain grew because humans thrived beneath me. My growing power was enough to warrant sending a demon to assassinate me. Only a fool would believe my power would wane over the decades."

"I hope you know what you're doing," my dad said.

"She always comes out on top," my mother said with a resigned sigh. "I have my doubts about Xantos, Catherine, but I trust you."

"Where's Miri, Mother?" I asked quietly.

"She returned to her family's estate in the outer lands," she replied as she snapped the journal shut. "I think it best if only a small group goes in search of Miriria."

"Who do you want to take, Viv?" my dad asked.

We turned to her as she considered the question. A grim smile formed on her lips as she drew a breath and let it out.

"You will stay, my love." At my father's frown, she brushed a kiss across his lips. "I have to go with Catherine. Sterling will be going with us, as will Catherine's appointed guards. You must stay here and do what you do best."

"As you wish," he finally said. "Who else will you be taking?"

"My personal guards, as well as my chancellor, Ashalla," Mother replied. Crossing to a painting, she touched it, breaking the illusion of a forest glade. "Captain Aerynir."

There was a three-second pause before the captain of the castle guards appeared in the mirror. His dark auburn hair was braided away from his face and fell over his shoulder. His features were sharp, and he'd gained a scar just above his left eyebrow in the past year. His eyes, though, were the brilliant blue as a clear summer sky.

"Your Majesties," he said in greeting. "Mirira's chambers have been secured, and none have been granted entrance. Those who have approached have been assigned a shadow."

Mother's eyes slid to me, and a single brow rose. I smiled sweetly, batted my eyes, and didn't look away. She shook her head, and when she turned back to Aerynir, I did the same.

"Excellent," Mother said, accepting his actions as though she had ordered them herself. "I will be departing for the Lathos barony. I will be taking only my personal guards. Ensure that Captain Evandra and her people are properly equipped. The king will be staying here."

"What of the princess, Your Majesty?" he questioned. "Will she be staying or going with you?"

"My daughter is safely guarded. I am not surprised she evaded your guards during her most recent visit," Mother reassured him.

"How soon will you be leaving?" he asked, relief in his voice.

"As soon as my guards have been equipped," Mother said.

"They will be ready within thirty minutes," he replied. As he reached for the mirror, he began calling orders to his underlings.

I had to give credit where it was due—Aerynir was efficient and damned good as his job.

Mother restored the illusion of the forest glade and turned to us. "I think thirty minutes is plenty of time to tell Cildur what is happening. I'd hate for your appointed spy to not be on top of everything going on."

Exactly thirty minutes later, my mother opened a portal to the gates of Lathos Manor. It wasn't a castle, but it wasn't a small abode, either. It reminded me of the plantation houses in the Deep South of the United States. It was sprawling and designed to appear grandiose.

The gates were shining silver, with sharpened spears on top. The family crest covered three-fourths of the gates. Guards patrolled the grounds, though the moment they noticed the queen and her assemblage, they opened the gates.

I could almost hear the spines of the guards holding the gates open for us snapping as they stood straighter. The other guards immediately froze and bowed deeply to their sovereign queen. One guard disappeared through the front doors, probably to announce our arrival to the duchess.

The door opened to reveal a stately woman with pale blonde hair pulled back into a simple chignon. Her gown was elegant and modest from the square-cut bodice, to the snug, long sleeves, to the skirt that swept the floor as she walked. Even the color was a modest dark green with simple black trim.

Everything about the woman screamed strict, old school elegance and grace. Her back was straight, and she didn't look particularly thrilled to see us. She was a force to look at, and I could sense that she controlled no small amount of power.

As we neared, she curtsied low before us. When my mother asked her to rise, she rose slowly, her eyes sweeping over us before returning to my mother.

"Your Majesty, this is a pleasant, if unexpected, surprise," the baroness said in a strong, smooth voice. "Please come in and be welcome."

She moved back from the door and beckoned for us to enter. My mother nodded, and we moved forward. The moment we passed over the threshold, I noticed the foyer's polished marble floor. The walls were a dark, polished wood, and a large tapestry covered one wall. The tapestry depicted the history of the realm and featured an embroidered image of my mother and father and a baby, which I presumed was me.

"Thank you for your gracious welcome," Chancellor Ashalla said once we were inside.

The Chancellor was a few decades younger than my mother and had held the position for as long as my mother had been queen, or close to it. She wore the robes of an adviser as though they were armor. Her raven hair was braided in multiple strands, then pinned in delicate loops that didn't quite brush her shoulders.

"Now," the baroness invited, "tell me what brings you to my humble home."

Chancellor Ashalla glanced at Mother, who nodded. "We are here to seek an audience with your granddaughter, Miriria. Items of question were discovered in her chambers. Her Majesty, Queen Viviane, and Crown Princess Catherine wish to speak with her about them."

The baroness's face seemed to slowly collapse in upon itself. Once my eyes adjusted to the lines that appeared, I realized she was scowling with a frown that rivaled my parents'.

"That ungrateful child has not, to my knowledge, returned to her home recently." The baroness spoke in the same pleasant, cultured voice. It was rather eerie coming from the scornful face. She gestured with her left arm. A guard bowed and quickly exited the chamber.

"I'm sending a guard to her room. If she is there, the guard will fetch her for you."

"Thank you, Baroness Silthea," the chancellor said with a pleasant smile.

The tap dancing was getting rather annoying. Sterling squeezed my arm in warning. I never did take warnings well.

"Baroness," I said in my best courtesan tone. When the woman looked at me, I continued, despite the narrow-eyed gaze of the chancellor. "Your words make me curious. You call her ungrateful. Why is that, if I may be bold enough to ask?"

"Miri has always been greedy and unappreciative of what she has." This time the anger and disappointment came through in her voice. "It was never enough that she had ten score of whatever the barony's children did. Her envy and greed grew as she approached adulthood. She always wanted to live above her station. She has an entire wardrobe she only wears in her room when she thinks no one is watching. Miri demanded duplicates of any outfit worn by the other courtesans, along with imitations of the finery worn by you and your mother. There is a silly crown that she's worn since childhood, locked in a box under her bed."

"So, she's had delusions of grandeur her entire life," I quipped. "That certainly explains a great deal."

Ashalla's eyes narrowed, and I was exceedingly thankful looks could not maim or kill. My mother wore her queenly Court expression no one could read. I knew I was breaking all sorts of protocols and royal rules by speaking, but I truly didn't care. We needed answers, and we weren't going to get them by playing polite, political games.

"What idiocy did she attempt this time?" the baroness asked.

"Lady Miriria is the voice and face of a group that is plotting against the throne," Ashalla stated before I could say anything.

"Chancellor Ashalla is being polite," I interjected. "Miri has spent decades searching for the Talisman of Death and has managed to put the parts she found together. She has been using it and humans to try and kill me. We recently found evidence that proves her actions are part of a grander scheme to overthrow the king and queen."

"While I do not disbelieve your claim," the baroness said cautiously, "I would want to see the evidence before taking action."

Mother handed the woman Miri's journal. We waited in silence as Baroness Silthea flipped through the pages. The guard returned just as the baroness was closing the journal.

"As you can see, Baroness Silthea, your granddaughter is guilty," Mother finally said. She touched my wrist gently before turning to the approaching guard. "Is Lady Miriria here?"

The guard bowed low. "Your Royal Highness, the Lady Miriria is not in her chambers. I questioned her servants and the other guards, but none have seen her at the estate."

"Thank you," Baroness Silthea said to the guard. He rose and drifted silently into the background. The baroness turned to us, gravity evident in her movements, as she returned the journal to my mother. "I thank you for your frankness. There is no question about my granddaughter's guilt." She paused as though she were searching for the proper words before continuing, "May I make one request?"

My mother nodded. The baroness turned her gaze to me. Surprised, I nodded as well. It wasn't my place to agree to anyone's request, least of all that of the baroness regarding Miri.

"Do not make a spectacle of Miriria's execution. I will need time to choose an heir from one of her half-siblings' children. Apparently, their accusations that she arranged her parents' deaths were not without merit," Baroness Silthea said in a solemn voice. "Her duplicitousness and cunning were not as grand as she believed they were, otherwise, she would not have been foolish enough to write everything down in a journal."

"Perhaps she should have been an actor," Sterling said. "It sounds as though she craves an audience."

"She was always like that, even during our youth," I said. "She always wanted to be the center of attention."

"I doubt any audience would have been large enough to fill the hole in her chest," the baroness said. "Do what must be done, my ladies. Please leave me to begin my duties in this shameful event."

"Of course," Chancellor Ashalla said.

The baroness curtsied, rose, then strode away. Her guard fell into step beside her.

My mother nodded to Ashalla, who conjured a portal. The captain of Mother's guards entered first, followed by my mother. My guards formed around me and Sterling, and we followed behind her.

Once we were back inside the palace, mother dismissed the chancellor and her guards.

"That went better than expected," I said. "Though we still don't know where Miri went."

Mother sighed, then looked past me.

"Merlin?" she asked cautiously. "What do you think?"

Sterling smiled briefly at Mom. He nodded, then voiced his thoughts.

"It is unlikely, but not impossible, she remains in this realm. With the power of the talisman, she could easily skip to another. We know she has been to your daughter's realm, and that of Xantos. She could flee to yet another realm, but her behavior suggests she is prone to impulsive actions fueled by that which is already familiar to her." He steepled his fingers in front of his face and took a breath. "We should search the three realms. If the search proves futile, there is little to do but wait. In time, she will come for Catherine. The two parts of the talisman Miri wears are drawn to the third. All the parts are drawn to Catherine." He smiled at me, then at my mother. "No, I am not suggesting we use our dear Cat as bait."

After a few moments of silence, Mother nodded.

"I shall command the search, here. I trust that Xantos will be willing to do so in his realm." She looked at Sterling. "Will you take your realm?"

"I shall work in tandem with your beloved to completely search the human realm," Sterling declared.

"Well, then, we all have a job to do," Mother said.

Except for me, I thought.

Chapter Twenty-Six

Two days later I was sitting at the bar in Fellhaven ignoring the night's band as they were setting up. It wasn't the Beast, so ignoring them was easy.

It probably didn't hurt that I was on my fourth drink. I was also nibbling on an appetizer platter to keep up the appearance that I wasn't an alcoholic.

"It's been two days, and no one has located that traitorous bitch," I grumbled to Mark. The bar wasn't full yet, and I had chosen the corner-most barstool. "I've kept in touch with Xantos, who has been searching his realm. If she's there, he can't find her. Mother can't find her. Sterling and Dad haven't located her here, and nothing I've tried has helped me locate my talisman." I knew I was whining, but I really hated the current situation.

"Nothing, eh?" Mark replied. He leaned over the bar and narrowed his eyes. "Funny, I neither see nor smell the last piece of the talisman on you. So, I don't think you've tried everything." He stood back and smiled. "As for the rest, you didn't think finding her would be easy, did you? I know you're exhausted and pregnant. If you weren't fae-born I would have cut you off three drinks ago, but I didn't think either of those conditions would lower your intelligence. Think like the Lady of Death, not the Girlfriend of Merlin."

"Excuse me?" I snapped.

Mark smiled broadly.

"That's better!" he exclaimed delightedly. "You aren't one to let other people do all the work, unless they have a skill you don't." He took a drink shaker from under the bar and began filling it with ice. "Start thinking like the investigator you are and the ruthless bitch you've been. Or take up a new hobby while you wait for your adversary to make her move."

"You built a bar just so you could dole out advice without consequences, didn't you?" I asked, trying not to snicker and smack my forehead at his reminder.

"I tried doing it the way angels and docs with couches do," Mark said as he poured ingredients into the shaker. "Humans tend to listen better when they're mellow and mildly tipsy."

He began shaking the beverage over one shoulder and winked at me.

"I never know when to take your tales seriously," I said, trying not to giggle.

"No worries. I do it intentionally," Mark replied. Just as he finished pouring whatever concoction he'd made, one of the servers came up to the bar.

"Hey, boss? Miss Belemont is asking for-"

Mark pushed the finished beverage toward the server.

"Oh!" the server said, clearly startled. "Uh, thanks! I will get this to her right away!"

Nodding, Mark said, "Good man" to the server, who grabbed the drink and dashed off.

"He must be fairly new," I observed.

Mark smiled and looked back at me.

"Nah, Rick usually works in the kitchen," he explained. "He asked for more hours. Probably wants to buy another guitar." He chuckled before continuing, "One of the regular servers had to call in, so he's covering the shift."

I nodded.

"Any advice about my day job?" I asked.

"Beings are still coming in here, asking about your services," Mark confided. He stepped over to one of the touch screen tablets and began typing in an order. "Jen and I tell people you haven't closed up shop and aren't going to. We say that you're currently overbooked. Some have suggested that something or somebody man your office, and we agree that would be a smart move."

"Tired of dealing with my would-be clientele?" I asked in a pleasant voice.

"Not at all. Those folks drink like fish when they come in, and it's not the cheap stuff!" Mark replied happily. "It's just something to consider. Your schedule isn't going to slow down." He waggled one finger toward my barely swollen belly. "And if you plan to keep the office open, you won't be able to do it alone."

"Yeah, okay, maybe," I grudgingly agreed.

He had a point, even if I didn't like admitting it. I picked up a deep-fried mozzarella stick and munched on it, much to Mark's amusement.

Pointing a half-eaten mozzarella stick at Mark, I asked, "Any idea where I can place a 'help wanted' ad for non-human types?"

"Sure. Right here," Mark replied. "Word of mouth is still the best way. Give me a list of what you're looking for, and the staff and I will get it out to the clientele. Jen will weed out the less trustworthy."

"Give me a few minutes, and I'll email you the details," I said, fishing my phone out of my pocket. Mark nodded before drifting away to tend to other patrons.

I popped the last bit of my mozzarella stick into my mouth and wiped my fingers on a napkin before pulling up my email. It took a minute for me to figure out what I needed.

As I was tapping away, the band began tuning their instruments and doing sound checks. I couldn't help wishing it was Mark's cousin, the Beast, and his band. Then again, I knew if it was, my dear friend, Clair, would be here. She and the Beast had hit it off, and she'd enjoyed a spectacular night with him.

I really needed to call her and ask how she was doing.

As I was enjoying my appetizers and working on the email to Mark, I noticed the local werewolf Alpha and the Master of the local vampire cabal approaching the bar.

Roland Kaufman and Alesio Salvatori weren't enemies, but they weren't best friends, either. They kept peace between their groups and had managed to forge a friendship of sorts.

Since they were approaching me at the same time, I saved my email and put my phone down.

"How goes it, Lady?" Roland asked. "Mind if we join you?"

"It goes," I replied. Gesturing toward the empty bar stools, I added, "Please do. How are you two doing?"

The guys took seats on either side of me. I knew this was a defensive position, but it wasn't a concern. Taking them down simultaneously wasn't on my agenda, even if it was in my bag of tricks.

"Same old, same old," both men said simultaneously.

They shared a grin before the smiles faded and somber expressions took their places.

"There are a lot of rumors floating around," Roland began, "which lead to a lot of questions and speculations."

"We are here to ask you, in person, about them on behalf of our respective peoples and other concerned beings," added Alesio.

I always did enjoy hearing the gossip about me. It made it so much easier to encourage or discourage certain tales and stories. Not to mention generating fear, though I wasn't in the fearmongering business anymore, unlike several centuries ago when I sat upon a throne of bones.

"What rumors have you heard that you wish me to address?" I asked, a smile forming on my lips.

"For starters," Roland began, caution evident in his words, "are you and Sterling an item? You've been seen together an awful lot, and it's no secret your mom showed up, here, pretty pissed about something."

"Very much like a parent whose child is dating someone unsavory," Alesio added. "I dread to think about the explosion that would have occurred had you not been here when she arrived."

I coughed to cover a laugh. "Mother wasn't too happy about a family matter. As for Sterling and me, yes, we are a couple." I lifted a brow. "Certainly, that isn't the juiciest rumor about us?"

Alesio chuckled. "Are you referring to the rumors surrounding your possible pregnancy? Or the ones about the child's father—is it Sterling's or Xantos's child?"

I stared at Alesio before bursting out laughing. Once I was able to breathe again, I addressed those rumors. "You found me out. I am pregnant, and it is Sterling's child. No, I am not planning a wedding, nor will I be asking either of you to be my maid of honor, though I suspect you both would look absolutely darling in gowns of my choice. I'm thinking poufy and lavender."

There was no way I could threaten them with pink. I abhorred that color.

"I dunno, man," Alesio said cheerfully. "Roland and his gang would look tight in lavender."

"Get staked, douche nugget," Roland growled.

"Now, children, you can settle the argument about who would look best in pretty gowns later," I said cheerfully. "Or were those the only rumors you wanted to discuss? If so, I am rather disappointed."

Roland snorted. He sounded very much like a dog, and I had to bite my cheek to keep from laughing.

"There was talk about you becoming a member of the Council before the Speaker died," Roland said. He leaned against the bar, motioning for Mark. "Word has it that you've been moved up the ladder and are now the top candidate for that position."

"And?" I prompted as I selected an onion ring and bit into it.

"And are you?" Alesio retorted.

"Am I the top candidate for replacing the Speaker? Yes. Will I accept the position when it's offered? Yes." I paused to consider everything before continuing. "In fact, I suspect the Council is already aware that I will take the position of Speaker."

"We, Alesio and I, were placing our bets that you'd take the post," Roland stated smugly.

"Though, what we are wondering, is if or how things will change within the Council," Alesio interjected.

"You believe I'll change the dynamic of the Council?" I asked. They both nodded. "Before I answer that question, answer this—how much do you know about the Council and its workings?"

"We have both been at Council trials and requested meetings," Roland replied. "Obviously, the Speaker is the mouthpiece, speaking for whoever is in charge. The other Council members chime in, but they don't have the final say."

"That's fairly accurate." I took a sip of my drink, giving myself time to think. "The Council is usually the last resort. It's called to order for hearings and trials for major indiscretions and crimes. If anything changes, it will be that approaching the Council will be far easier and will have fewer life-threatening results."

"You're saying that, if you're the Speaker, someone can come to you with a complaint, and you won't immediately demand punishment?" Roland scoffed.

I shrugged as I tossed back the last fourth of my drink. "You haven't paid close attention to my history, youngster."

Alesio barked a single laugh. "She was always fair. She just didn't want anyone coming to her for trivial bullshit that could be resolved with compromise and a pint of beer."

Roland shook his head and remained silent. Mark appeared with drinks for all of us.

"You're definitely going to need assistance with your business if you're taking on the role of Speaker," Mark commented. He smirked at me before moving away again.

"What sort of assistance do you need?" Roland asked curiously. He took a long pull from the bottle of craft beer Mark had set in front of him.

"It seems the demands for my services are growing while the time I have to sift through the requests, let alone take jobs, is decreasing." I sipped from the tall glass filled with an iced, green beverage. The tang of apple and alcohol bit my taste buds deliciously. It wasn't an appletini, not exactly, but whatever it was, it was good. "For simplicity's sake, the job requires someone knowledgeable about our kind and the business I do, who has basic secretarial skills. Being organized is also required."

Roland tipped his head to the side. "You deal in Magickal antiquities and artifacts, right?"

I nodded, curious where this was going.

"I may not be as old as the mosquito over there, but I can tell a real antique from a fake. I'm also good at figuring out who's legit and who's a fraud."

I held my hand up, palm toward Alesio. The vampire master didn't say anything, but I could tell he really wanted to. "How knowledgeable are you about Magickal artifacts?"

"Pretty knowledgeable. I know the legends and rumors about most of the major items out there. As for the rest? My mom is one of the old school witches. She has a lot of journals and papers about Magickal items and whatnot. If I run into anything I can't identify, I can go through her tomes."

"Or ask the old battle ax," Alesio muttered darkly.

There had to be an interesting story there, but it was for a later time.

"They haven't asked the question that's been wagging their tongues since that douchebag ex-boyfriend of yours was turned to slime," Mark quipped as he passed by us.

"There have been rumors that the talisman you once used has been put back into play," Alesio hedged.

"And you're wondering if it has, and if I'm planning to take it back from whoever is currently using it," I concluded.

From their expressions, I'd hit the nail on the head.

"To be fair, that's been a frequent question around here, especially after you went to your mom's realm," Mark interjected. "People also want to know where the talisman came from, why you ended your reign, and other things."

"And I'll bet you've been busier than ever," I teased. He winked at me, causing me to laugh. "Thought so. Gossips love having someplace to gather, and if that place has amazing food and beverages, it's all the better."

"So, what are you doing about your talisman? I would think the Lady of Death wouldn't be happy knowing someone else is using it," Roland said.

"The talisman is mine, even if someone else is in temporary possession of it," I replied. There was no use lying about it. "I'll be reclaiming it, and this time, it will be staying with me."

"Thinking of reigning again, Lady?" Roland asked quietly.

"I ruled once, during a bygone era. That time has passed," I answered nebulously.

"Power is still power," Alesio said thoughtfully. "You're going to have an awful lot. The talisman, the position as Speaker. Hell, even being Sterling's girlfriend. A lot of people will wonder if you're going to take over the Council and rule us all."

"Now you're just being silly." I took a long drink. "I'm not going to take over the Council or become anything like that giant eye in a tower from Tolkien's novels."

"Says the once and future Lady of Death," quipped Mark as he set a curious batch of appetizers nearby.

The appetizers included half a dozen sealed straws accompanied by near-raw strips of beef and pork and a generous portion of onion rings with a light pink dipping sauce. Roland grabbed the small plate that Mark offered, took several strips of meat and rings, then poured half the sauce over both. He began wolfing down the food as he passed the remaining appetizers to Alesio.

The vampire smiled at the platter. Throwing his head back, he emptied his drink and slammed the empty glass on the bar. He delicately took one sealed straw and a strip of meat.

"Hey, bartender, I'm going to—" Alesio began, as Mark placed a fresh beverage beside his empty glass. "And that's why we come here."

He bit into the straw and sucked gingerly before taking a bite of meat. He moaned in delight.

There was no way I was going to ask Mark where he got sealed straws filled with blood. Even I had my limits.

"More mozz sticks, Cat?" Mark asked. "Or shall I whip up some veggie ramen?"

"Veggie ramen sounds delicious," I said. I hadn't realized how much I'd missed his food.

Talking with Mark had allowed me to relax and almost forget the guards who were watching me and everyone else. Maybe they'd decided that Alesio and Roland were okay. Either that, or they were poised to end their lives at any wrong twitch.

"It'll be up in a few," Mark replied. "Meantime, I'll leave y'all alone to figure out his work schedule and pay." He winked at Roland and walked away.

Chuckling, I grabbed the last onion ring on my tray. "The schedule is open for discussion. I only open the office for appointments. Mostly, I do my emails and paperwork at home. I check the mail at least twice a week." I munched on the onion ring so he could consider my offer. "Is this going to be your main job or a second job?"

"Being the leader of my pack is what I do. My day job is whatever I find," Roland said as he twirled an onion ring around one finger. "So, if I'm in, I'm yours unless the pack is in need. Fair?"

"Very. You're their leader. This position doesn't have a strict schedule, so you have the ability to come and go as needed." I contemplated him. "You aren't known for slacking or welching on a deal. So, unless you have another job, this would be your main income."

"More or less," he replied flippantly.

"I'm certain you have investments and such, but that doesn't count. The salary is forty grand a year, paid weekly." I took another sip of my beverage and waited for him to decide.

Roland nodded. "I can live with that. I should be able to man your office on banker's hours, except the nights before and after the full moon." He paused for a moment before asking, "Am I on the books or is this under the table? I'm only asking because I suck at keeping track of taxes. If you don't have a bookkeeper, I can bring in the pack's bean counter. She's got plenty of time now that her cubs are older."

"It's all aboveboard. I have a CPA who handles everything for me. Saves me from headaches, and she makes sure nothing is questioned," I replied with a smile. "As for the nights you specified, that's perfectly doable."

"When do I start?" Roland asked, a very wolfish grin on his face.

I returned the grin. "I'll have the paperwork for you Monday, along with a key."

"Works for me," he replied cheerfully. "You staying for the band?"

"Yeah," I answered. "You guys sticking around?"

Both men answered affirmatively, and we settled in to watch the performance. Mark brought my veggie ramen, and I enjoyed a pleasant meal with them.

The band was good, not that I expected Mark and Jen to invite a bad band into their establishment. We enjoyed their set and chatted amiably during the intermission. It was a pleasant and relaxing night out.

As the band was packing up just after midnight, I stood and stretched.

"Leaving so soon?" Mark joked.

"Yeah, I thought I might get in some light reading before bedtime," I returned with a grin.

Mark laughed as Alesio moved to stand beside Roland.

"Mind if we walk out with you?" the vampire asked.

"Not at all," I replied, sliding my purse strap over my shoulder. "I'd enjoy the company."

Mark snickered but waved as he moved to the other side of the bar.

As I moved toward the door with Roland and Alesio, my trusted guards fell into their self-designated positions around us. Jen held the door open, and we bid her good night as we left.

The parking lot was lit better than most, and I suspected that had to do with an incident in which a patron was attacked. I looked up at the moon. It was between half full and a crescent, and it was shrinking. The stars glittered against the blue-black sky that was their canvas.

There were still a handful of vehicles in the lot, aside from my guards' motorcycles, my car, and Roland's vehicle. I didn't know what Alesio drove.

Maybe he flew in every night or had another way of popping in and out of the area. I didn't ask.

Roland paused and drew a deep breath, and I swear it was like watching a hound scenting a rabbit. His nose didn't quiver, but it was close, and I could see his eyes shifting from human to wolf.

Alesio and Roland growled at the same time. Alesio's eyes turned to vampire-red, and his lips peeled back in a snarl, revealing his fangs.

Since no one was playing Ballroom Blitz, I decided things were about to get really interesting.

"Stay behind us." Roland said in a low timber, a definite growl in his voice. My guards suddenly fanned out into a circle six feet in diameter, surrounding Alesio, Roland and me, and drew their weapons.

"Where's the fun in that?" I muttered.

This would definitely teach me not to go anywhere without weapons, though I would need to figure out how to conceal my hand scythes.

I wasn't completely without weapons, though. I had a vast arsenal of Magick at my fingertips that included offensive and defensive spells. My mother hadn't raised a fool, and I'd been in my fair share of spell battles.

A brood of faerie dragons swooped in from the darkness. They were adults, between five and six feet long, with gold, silver and bronze scales. The lack of other colors marked them as females, and they looked pissed.

The eight flying hellions stayed in a loose group but broke apart just enough to attack my guards, Alesio and Roland. They were dazzlingly fast, and this initial strike was a strafing run. They swooped down but stayed out of range of our weapons. As the brood shot past, two expelled lightning bolts from their mouths, and the rest vomited clouds of shimmering glitter.

"What the furry Hell?" Roland said as he frantically tried to shake the glitter off. I glanced around to see who had been hit with the lightning. Alesio was on fire, and Zarkull was on one knee, trying to regain his composure. The black scorch mark across his chest plate was still smoking.

Whipping off his leather trench, Roland began putting out the fire that was spreading over Alesio. While he worked to cover the vampire, the glitter was falling off his body.

"Idiot!" Alesio spat at the erratically moving Roland, "You're covered in sleeping dust! Quit shaking it all over me!"

"What? Aw, man!" exclaimed Roland as he abandoned his smoldering friend and thrashed about, shaking his head like a dog, his hands brushing his beard and chest. His movements were becoming more sluggish. I could see his legs starting to give way as though he had gotten sloppy drunk in Fellhaven.

"Do you believe this dog?" I heard Alesio say as I turned around, assessing the situation and looking for a second attack from the small dragons or a yet-unseen attacker.

The male guards were passing out. The women were still lucid and looking around, readying for the next assault.

The faerie dragons flew in from different directions. Hissing the proper incantation, I flung my hands toward the sky. A huge spider web flowed from both my palms.

The webbing ensnared five of the dragons. They crashed to the parking lot with satisfying crunching sounds. Two of the remaining dragons swooped toward the women guards, one vomiting more glitter, the other spewing more lightning.

Both women were ready. Alaria curled into a fetal ball, so most of the sleep dust passed over her. However, the dust coated Roland again, and he swore profusely at the renewed coating of glitter.

Shyrrik threw her spear at the lightning bolt. It wasn't a powerful throw, but the spear intercepted the lightning and channeled it to the ground. She dashed forward and grabbed the hot spear before it fell flat. She then turned and chucked it at the dragon that tried to fry her. The spear sailed through the air and struck the dragon just under her left wing. She screeched and careened into the blacktop.

Alesio, covered in severe burns, leapt inhumanly high into the air and latched onto the last dragon. A split second after wrapping his limbs around her, he sank his fangs into the long, scaly neck. The dragon struggled as she crashed just beyond the parking lot.

"Damned fae and their pets!" Roland roared drunkenly. I caught a glimpse of him falling to his knees, still trying to rid himself of the sleeping dust, just before the fireball flew at my face.

I reached out with my right hand, sending energy to dispel the fireball. Instead of vanishing, it transmogrified into water, which splashed to the ground and soaked half my entourage and my boots.

I wondered for a split second if my pregnancy had affected my casting or if the caster's spell had been too powerful for me to completely dissipate. Then I focused on the next spell coming at me.

A bright bolt of blue heat zipped at me. Moving my hands like the arms of a clock, I formed a convex shield of energy. The heat pounded against my shield, followed its curve, then lost cohesion and drifted safely away from my compatriots and me.

"It seems you can take the heat," a female voice yelled. The voice was shrill, almost hysterical. The owner was coming closer. Unfortunately, she wasn't Miri.

Coming toward me was the leader of Miri's entourage, a "yes-woman" who stayed just behind her mistress until needed. She normally stood and walked with her head down, and her voice was rarely heard by all but a few. I only felt a little shame at not immediately recalling her name.

"Where is your mistress?" I demanded. "Too afraid to do her own dirty work?"

Alesio walked up beside me. Zurkel had finally gotten to his feet and positioned himself just ahead of my right side.

"Damned fae and their pets." Roland repeated in a weary voice from somewhere behind me, just before I heard a heavy thump against the blacktop.

"She has far greater things to worry about!" the woman screamed. "The minor matter of embarrassing the heir to a worn throne is nothing to she who works to be a goddess and ruler of our people!" She waved a wand, and I could sense the power from my talisman sparking from it. "I, her faithful maid, chosen to be her right hand, have the power to assert her will!"

"Ah, Maudnait," I addressed her, after finally remembering her name. "Miri gave you a wand hyped up with power and fed you words you ached to hear."

"Her will is for you to perish!" shrieked Maudnait, swinging the wand in my direction.

As I was bracing myself and readying counter spells, her wand exploded. Energy sparked in a wide corona as the top half landed in splinters on the parking lot's surface. The explosion had been caused by something from behind me. I did not want to risk looking back to see what had happened, until I realized that Maudnait was gawking, mouth hanging open. She kept looking back and forth between the shortened stick in her hand and something or someone behind me.

"Not on our turf, bitch." The booming voice gave me goosebumps. "Not ever. Tell your owner."

I decided it would be prudent to turn around.

The owners of Fellhaven stood about twenty yards behind me. Jen was standing stock still, her hands curled into claws at her hips. Greenish light swirled around them. The corpses of the slain faerie dragons were moving to her side, their eyes glowing in the same green. Mark held the large, ancient revolver I'd seen him occasionally wear in a holster while moving around the tavern. Wisps of smoke lazily flowed from the gun's barrel. Even more curious, Jen's ears seemed pointed, and a hint of large, leathery wings twitched behind Mark's back.

"Ummm... how did a mortal weapon destroy her wand?" I asked.

"Not entirely sure. Met a fellow who passes through many places. He gave me one of a pair of guns he carried. Said it was his final trip through New York," Mark replied while keeping his gaze on Maudnait. "All I really know is that it has yet to miss and wrecks everything it hits."

The undead dragons prowled past Fellhaven's owners. They walked uneasily, the damage to their bodies evident. They moved into formation around me.

"Better run, if you can," Jen advised Maudnait.

I turned slowly back toward the woman who had tried to kill me. As I was moving, I heard Mark say in a soft, playful voice, "My five friends can move faster than yours."

"Hush," Jen playfully snapped back. "The poor dears have had a rough night. Y'know, dying and all."

I wondered if I would ever figure those two out.

The "poor dears" moved past me and gained speed as they headed toward Maudnait. She finally seemed to realize her situation. She moved backward as she glanced at the approaching dragons and all of us.

"Enjoy your petty lives." Maudnait tried to sound indifferent, but her eyes were wide, and her steps backward were getting more rapid. "She Who Will Be the Power Supreme shall return at her leisure to smite you all!"

"Ugh. Who even talks like that?" Alesio complained. "Can we just kill her now?"

As I considered my answer, Maudnait stopped and clutched something beneath her tunic. Energy engulfed her, and she disappeared from sight.

"That could have gone better," Jen observed. "But, hey, now I have new pets."

I looked around and saw the small pack of undead faerie dragons sitting around her and her partner. Mark replaced the spent round from the revolver. Once he snapped the cylinder shut, he casually stuck the long barrel through his waistband.

"I don't know what you plan to do with the others," Jen continued, "but I have to make a nest for these darlings." She made a kissing sound, and the undead dragons began following her back toward the delivery entrance of the tavern.

"I'm surprised you aren't wearing the holster and belt," I said to Mark. "I'm also surprised to see your partner knows necromancy."

"Didn't want to take the time to strap up, so I just grabbed the big iron and some loose shells," he explained. "Xantos has been giving my lady lessons since before we opened the tavern. Heard you've gotten better at it as well." He looked around the parking lot. "What kind of help are you going to need to clean up this mess?"

"Just how long have you—" I began, then stopped, shaking my head to clear it. One day, I vowed, I was going to order everything on the menu and have these two answer questions until the food was gone. "I think we can manage." I said. "Thanks to both of you for the intervention."

Mark nodded and followed his wife and her new 'pets.'

"Ugh, my ears," Roland groaned. He was slowly getting to his feet. "Is it normal for faerie glitter to make your ears ring, or is it because I'm lucky enough to be a wolf?"

Alesio nodded toward Fellhaven.

"For those about to rock," the vampire said.

Roland winced. "Damn, the demon fired the hand cannon? No wonder my ears feel beaten." He tossed a sloppy salute at the tavern. "I pity whatever he was aiming at."

"Demon?" I asked sharply.

"If those two are ever mad at you, you'll see why we call Mark a demon," Alesio said as he helped Roland stand up.

I looked at my guards and processed Alesio's words. They were all standing, and Zurkell was gathering up the fragments of wand. The two female guards were freeing and herding the living faerie dragons.

"Shall we send these back to your mother's realm, Lady, or to our lord's menagerie?" Alaria asked.

"My mother's realm," I replied. "They're intelligent and usually sympathetic. We need to figure out why they were attacking before deciding their fate."

"Not normally trained for offense, then?" Alaria remarked. "They moved well during the attack."

I shrugged. She nodded, and I turned my attention to Zurkell. He walked up to me, holding the shattered bits of wood in one hand.

"There is still power in the remains," the lead guard observed. "It's barely there, but if you hurry—"

My hands were already out, reaching for the shards. Before the sixth piece of wrecked wand touched my bare skin, I knew the source of power used to charge the hawthorn wood. I had used it to forge and fortify dozens of objects in a very short period of time. My mind and body remembered the heady feeling that came from using the talisman. The essence of the demon's raw power was like a flavor your senses never tired of touching.

"Hey, dummy, why didn't you turn into your wolf form?" Alesio's harsh voice cut into my revelry. "You could have easily shrugged off the dust's sleep effect."

"Are you kidding? All that in my fur? I'd never get rid of it!" Roland countered angrily. "There's a reason glitter is called the herpes of the art world."

Unable to stop myself, I snorted. The two men looked at my smiling face.

"So, it doesn't look like the big bad boss is going to come and play," Alesio observed. "Is there anything else to do but wait? I hope the slivers in your hand, or the dragons hold a needed clue."

"There is something else," I said. "I'll let you know when it's done."

Chapter Twenty-Seven

The quiet of my house was ominous as I moved through the rooms, down the stairs, and into my basement. Arylla was curled around Maekyl's skull, eyes open and watching me. That only added to the creepiness, since Maekyl's eyes were glowing with almost fiendish delight. I recognized the twinkle in his eyes and again wondered if he had helped create the situation that led to this predicament.

Taking a few moments to cast a shield around the perimeter of the floor so nothing was broken or damaged by flying chips of concrete, I adjusted the bracers on my wrists. After assuring myself they were secure, I hefted the sledgehammer, testing the weight of the tool.

Lifting it above my head, I swung it down. The hammer cracked against the floor, the handle reverberating in my hands as chips of concrete flew. Arylla shrilled sharply and darted from the table to hide under a pillow on my sofa. Only the tip of her quivering tail could be seen.

Sighing, I checked the slight damage done to my floor. The extra strength from my bracers helped. There was a large dent in the concrete, but not the hole I needed. I brought the sledgehammer down again and again, until I had a hole just larger than the head of the sledgehammer with fissures spider-webbing out from the center.

"Please tell me you aren't planning to use that annoying thing and completely ruin your floor," Maekyl said. "There are far better methods of retrieval."

Smirking, I set the hammer down beside me and dusted my hands off. "Of course not. I was thinking I'd make the area explode."

Maekyl snorted and rolled his eyes. "Really, Catherine? That's the best retort you have?"

Shrugging, I smiled. "I was actually thinking lava, to be honest."

There is nothing quite as satisfying as watching my skull shudder. "That is low. Even for you."

From beneath the pillow, I heard what sounded suspiciously like laughter coming from my hatchling. The darkening glower on Maekyl's face confirmed my suspicions.

Chuckling, I turned my attention back to my task. Holding my hands out, palms downward, I channeled Magick and gradually warmed the floor. The heat was enough to cause me to break into a sweat, and the room grew decidedly warmer. That was fine, though. This would be a quick and easy retrieval once the floor melted.

It took ten minutes to melt the concrete, extract the lock box two inches below the melted area, and restore the floor to a semblance of normalcy. Cooling the room to a reasonable temperature took another five.

Sitting on the floor, I unlocked the box and lifted the chain from which the final piece of my amulet hung. The red garnet centered in the piece caught the low light in the room and glittered brilliantly. Even though it was only one piece of my talisman, I could feel the Magick of the demon. It was a slow, deep thrum than stayed steady and sedate.

Drawing a deep breath, I fastened the chain around my neck, relishing the coolness of the metal against my skin. I had to draw another deep breath and release it slowly, so I didn't remain fixated on the Magick.

It was addictive, and since it had been out of my grasp for several long centuries, I craved it like a junkie craved their next hit. The difference, now, was that I could control myself and the temptations it offered.

Mostly.

I hoped.

"You should have done that sooner," Maekyl commented. His tone was far too thoughtful for me to do anything other than narrow my eyes at him. "It would have saved you a lot of trouble. The demon's essence is linked to that piece by your blood. The other two pieces are compelled to find this one. Now that it's been unsealed, it won't take long for that trollop to discover where you are and to come looking for you." He paused. "You might want to call Jade and Trix to come assist your guards."

"Good plan," I said, pulling out my cell phone and dialing Jade's number.

I wasn't worried about weapons harming me. I was the talisman's maker. It couldn't harm me in this realm. That did not mean I wanted those who were sworn to protect me to be harmed.

"I need someone to handle whatever Miri brings with her, while I keep her attention on me," I muttered before my phone connected with Jade's.

* * *

An hour later, Sterling arrived via portal. Jade was sharpening weapons and comparing experiences with the guards. Trix was playing with Arylla. I was wearing the last piece of the talisman around my neck and my favorite robe.

"All taken care of?" I asked Sterling before kissing him.

"The faerie dragons are in your mother's stable, under the care of the kingdom's best dragon trainer," Sterling confirmed. "Your parents send their love and best wishes. They would have preferred to do so in person."

"I know." There was a little pang of regret in my voice. "But this needs to happen here, where Miri thinks she has an advantage. Besides, my parents would have tried to help, but for the sake of the kingdom, it needs to be personal."

"You'll need to explain that to me at some point," Sterling confessed. "Fae politics don't always make sense to me."

"If you didn't grow up with them, they never will," I said. "Even then, there are events that make little sense. They only happen because they're traditional and the only things anyone knows."

"Fae aren't known for changing their ways," Trix added. "They personify 'the old ways' in a manner few can comprehend."

Sterling grunted.

Watching Jade talking amiably with the guards made me think. Or maybe it was the piece of my talisman against my skin. I kissed Sterling again before moving toward Zarkull and his guards. Sterling might not agree, but I hoped he wouldn't argue with the logic behind my idea.

"What will you do once this is over?" I gestured toward the group, even though I addressed Zarkull.

"That depends on what our lord, Xantos, and you, decide, Lady," Zarkull responded. "We all agree that we enjoy being your guards and being in this realm. However, we are employed and compensated by Xantos, so his will is final."

"He did say I could keep you as long as I wanted." I couldn't help joking with him, especially since I was beyond thrilled to hear his words. "Perhaps I can convince him to allow me to hire you away from him."

There was a ripple of wide-eyed response from the guards. It seemed I had taken them by surprise.

"You would pay to gain our release from Xantos and keep us in your employ?" Zarkull asked. His voice had slowed, and the inquisitive lilt reminded me of a child making sure he'd been told he could have as many cookies as he wanted.

"If you would be willing to continue your jobs as my personal guards, I'd be more than willing to obtain your release from Xantos. Should you, at any time, decide to seek employment elsewhere or return to your homeland, I would only require you to find suitable replacements." I held up a hand to hold off any questions until I'd finished speaking. "Obviously, you would not be required to watch me twenty-four hours a day, seven days a week as you have been. As my personal guards, it would be up to you, or whoever you designate, to approve of any other guards I hire. We can discuss this in further detail at a later date, if you decide to accept my proposal."

"We will consider your offer," Zarkull said. All of the guards were smiling, which I took as a good sign.

One more task completed. I didn't think Xantos would have any objections, but he was very devious. I wasn't going to count anything as sure until all the details had been worked out.

"So, what's the plan?" Jade asked as she moved toward the bar. "How long do you think it'll be before Miri gives into the amulet and comes looking for you?"

Everyone's eyes turned to me. I absolutely loved being put on the spot. Magick was an exact science, after all, so I knew exactly when some insane, Magickal heretic would come after me.

"That's impossible to say. Miri is using the talisman without knowing what it does, but she's always been a stubborn idiot. She'll put off coming after me, thinking she's putting everything in place so she can pull off the perfect attack." Crossing to the bar area, I removed a few glasses and handed them to Jade, who held a bottle of my favorite whiskey. As she poured, I continued to talk. "I suspect she'll wait until sunset to attack again."

A smart person would attack before dawn before the enemy could regroup and prepare. Miri, though, was not smart, nor was she a warrior. I was taught warfare from an early age, participated in fae war games, and commanded armies as the Lady of Death. Though certain times of day and night added power to certain spells, you couldn't depend on that. Not if you wanted to win the battle and the war.

As far as I knew, Miri had never learned the art of war or taken part in any of the games Mother orchestrated. She had no true knowledge about how to win a war. That didn't make her stupid, but it did make her dangerous, especially to the innocents around her.

"What do you want to do?" Trix asked as she tossed Arylla into the air.

The little dragon glided down to her arm in a gentle spiral, a look of contentment on her face.

Yawning, I stretched languidly. "We rest. We've set wards and placed traps. We're as prepared as we can be for now. Tomorrow, we'll continue preparing for the approaching battle."

"We'll stay over, if you don't mind," Jade said as she handed out glasses of whiskey.

"Not at all," I replied.

Once everyone had a glass, we lifted them in salute before tossing them back. I slid my glass back to Jade, crossed to Sterling, and took his hand.

Looking back at the others, I bid them good night before departing my basement. They were adults and could argue over who got which room. Morning would come soon enough.

Chapter Twenty-Eight

The following day was spent preparing for Miri's inevitable attack. I delegated the task of fortifying the perimeter to Zarkull and his people, Trix, and Jade. Sterling and Maekyl remained with me in my basement. Despite the fact that Sterling didn't approve of my necromancy and black Magick skills, he couldn't deny I had a unique skill set few could match. There was one other spell I needed to master and doing so would keep my mind off the current situation.

By the time the sun started to set, I was getting antsy. Roland had joined the party, and according to him, Alesio was planning on coming too. Everyone acted like this was the event of the season, if not the year.

Didn't that make me feel all sorts of special?

"The betting pool on this fight is insane," Roland told me. "I haven't seen this kind of money flying around since the Sox went to the World Series in 2004."

"Lovely. What are my odds, according to the gambling community?"

"Huh? The bests are on when the fight will start!" Roland replied cheerfully. "You're favored for the win, but the mad money is on when she's gonna crack and come at you!"

"Ugh. I would have already lost my money," I complained. "Is it bad that I wish she came yesterday?"

"Nah. The waiting is the worst part," Roland reassured me. "Once the fight comes, and the blood gets pumping, there's no anticipation, just the battle."

"That's not always true for someone who isn't a wolf, but yes, that's how it usually goes," I said.

"She'll come when she comes," Roland replied. "At least you have a pantry and a deep freezer full of food. We get to avoid the delivery person as a Trojan horse cliché."

That made me laugh.

"I hope she isn't dumb enough to try any of those half-assed tropes." I walked to my freezer and dug around for a few minutes. I pulled out a box of my favorite ice cream bars. "Speaking of a fully-stocked freezer, want some ice cream?"

There was a collective "Oooo!" as the guards gathered around me.

I grabbed the boxes of chocolate-covered, peanut butter cup ice cream bars. I opened three boxes with scissors and handed one box to Zarkull one to Roland and kept the last one for myself.

I didn't mind sharing, not when I had six more boxes in my deep freezer and three others in my regular freezer.

I didn't have an addiction. I simply preferred buying in bulk, so I didn't have to replenish my supply frequently. Besides, they were on sale.

Apparently, I wasn't the only one who loved the ice cream bars. Within seconds, everyone was enjoying the cold treats.

Arylla flew over and settled on the counter where she began trilling at me. I paused long enough to place an unwrapped treat in a bowl for her to enjoy.

"You're spoiling her," Trix teased.

Looking pointedly at the ice cream bar in Trix's hand, I shrugged. "She asked nicely."

Trix snickered and took another bite from her bar.

THOOM.

We all heard the sound. Nothing shook in my house, nor was there any sound of something breaking or falling. I looked around and saw nearly identical expressions of mild confusion on everyone's faces, except for Trix's. She had a sour expression on her face.

"So much for enjoying a treat. I'll find out what that was," Trix grumbled.

THOOM.

Still nothing but that sound. Trix opened the blinds of my living room window and looked outside. She grunted before speaking.

"She's gotten ballsy or crazy," Trix observed, sounding amused. "She's throwing spells against your wards. She's out in the middle of the road with a squad of goons surrounding her."

"Where the mundanes can see her?" I asked. "That's several violations of the law, and the fun hasn't started."

"You sound like Sterling," said Jade.

I chose not to acknowledge her comment.

"Pardon my asking," Alaria interrupted, "but how many strikes will your wards withstand?" After a moment's thought, she added, "Didn't you feel the impact? I know your wards absorbed the energy, since we felt nothing in your adobe, but you seemed nonplussed with that—"

THOOM.

"—strike. You didn't seem to react to that one, either," she said.

"I barely feel anything from my wards, to be honest," I replied. "That is unusual. I thought her first attacks were too weak to do anything but make sound."

"She looks like she's putting a lot of effort into throwing them," Trix said while she continued to watch out the window. "If she holds your talisman any tighter to her chest, it's going to leave a permanent mark on her skin."

"She's relying on the talisman to power her spells," Sterling said as he entered the room. "Since the amulet was forged by you, the energy is being absorbed by your wards. Every attack strengthens your defenses."

He smiled as he relayed that last bit of information. Trix and Jade chuckled, along with most of the guards.

"What's making the explosive sounds?" Alaria asked.

"The absorption process is burning the air around the wards," Sterling explained. "The sound we're hearing is air flooding back into the empty space, much like thunder is caused by lightning."

"So," Jade interjected, "do we plan to let her continue her noisy, useless attacks until she grows bored and leaves?"

"That may take some time," Sterling said wearily. "From the bedroom window, you can see how excited she is. She's wild-eyed, standing there like an eager general wanting to give the order to charge. Even if the sound of the spells being absorbed wasn't garnering attention, her behavior and presence would. The twenty beings she brought with her are also quite a sight."

"I don't think walking out the front door and serving them a summons from the Council to answer for breaking Magickal laws will get us the results we need," I remarked.

The expression on Sterling's face was priceless. His lips were pursed, his brow was wrinkled, and every inch of his face silently scolded me as he tried not to acknowledge my dry humor. He was so cute when he did that.

"No, it would not," Sterling said in a monotone voice. Jade bit back a laugh.

"Should I invite her in?" Trix asked. She looked at me with a wicked grin.

Her suggestion sparked a thought in my mind, and it bloomed into a complete idea.

Two minutes and plenty of booms later, Trix opened my front door and yelled in a bored, faux drunk voice.

"Heeeyyyy, Miri, Miri, Miri, Miriria!" Trix threw in a giggle before continuing, "Did you have to bring your exes along? Front door's been open the whole time you've been making all that noise. Come on in before the rum punch and the good hors d'oeuvres are all gone!"

There was nothing but silence for several long moments.

"C'mon!" Trix said in a more aggressive tone. "Somebody's gonna call the cops on all y'all loitering around! Hoss your freight in here! Giddyap! Move 'em out!"

Sterling groaned into his hand. I bit my tongue to keep from laughing.

Trix stepped further outside and held the door open. She began pinwheeling her arm and continued to holler at our adversaries as if they were stubborn cattle. Slowly, one by one, Miriria and twenty mercs of various races walked cautiously into my front room. They were anxious, confused, and trying to make sense of what was happening. Except for Miri. She just looked angry, like the birthday girl whose party gets up-ended by people she didn't invite.

Sterling, Jade, Roland, the elven guards, and I were sitting or standing in my living area. We all held cocktails in martini glasses. Roland was also completely wolfed out.

And we all were wearing lingerie.

Teddies for the fellows, boxers and silk smoking jackets for the ladies.

"Sorry about the disturbance!" we could clearly hear Trix yelling to the neighbors. "I didn't want to get dressed and come outside either! Don't you hate it when the in-laws crash the orgy? Same here! Have a good night!"

Trix stepped in and closed the front door with a resounding thud.

"What in the Hell is this?!" Miri demanded. The mercs were trying to decide if they wanted to stare at us or their footwear.

Roland raised his martini glass and declared, "It's called a tactical diversion, sweetmeats!" He poured his drink down his open muzzle in a single gulp. His rows of sharp teeth gleamed. "Surprise!"

"You shouldn't have interrupted dessert," Trix said. Most of Miri's hirelings looked at her.

"Alesio!" Roland called out. Some of the hirelings turned toward him as he said, "Let's get this party rolling!"

None of our adversaries had looked up since entering my abode. Alesio was crouched against the ceiling. He pounced down, knocking the two largest mercs, a pair of ogres, face-first into my marble floor. Their skulls crunched from the impact.

That drew the attention of everyone, including Miri.

Trix took advantage of the distraction and shifted into a scaled-down version of her true shadow dragon form. She impaled two hirelings with the talons at the ends of her leathery wings, and she opened her mouth and spewed a thick black cloud at the remaining enemies. Roland took two steps forward, and just before he leapt into the fray, the illusion that Sterling and I had cast dissipated.

He had never been in lingerie. None of us had. But we had cast a spell to glamour the intruders. The werewolf, in all his furry, unclothed glory, disappeared into the darkness. Sounds of ripping flesh and screams immediately followed.

The rest of my party moved to encircle the blinded intruders. We were all wearing battle gear and armed to the teeth. In my pregnant state, form-fitting armor wasn't comfortable, so I wore a leather cloak with Elvin metal woven into the hide. Protection spells, written in silver thread, festooned the exterior. My portion of the amulet lay against my neck. The obsidian hand scythes I favored hung from loops at my waist.

White light exploded from the center of the opaque cloud. Miri held the incomplete amulet in her right hand and was using its power to burn away the dragon's breath. It took a moment for me to realize that everyone but her and me were blinded by the amulet's brilliance.

At my side, Sterling bent forward, his left hand covering his eyes. He hissed something I couldn't understand, and his right arm lashed out. The blinding light became fog, thick and white like a daydreamer's vision of heaven. Everyone's vision was obscured, but they were no longer debilitated. The dark elves and my comrades began to slowly move around. Sounds of clashing metal and tearing flesh emitted from the fog.

The fog began to dissipate, just before Miri changed it into a volatile gas. I didn't have time to warn my comrades before she ignited it.

The gas covered the space the fog had occupied, and that was a blessing and a curse. Because the pockets of fog were thinner, the flames had less fuel, and those beings lucky enough to be in those areas incurred less damage. Most were not, though, and the fog filled nearly every foot of my living room.

The flames didn't affect me. This realization was a cold comfort as people I cared about were savagely burned. Only the hirelings standing closest to Miri were protected by the sphere of energy she projected around her body.

I looked for Sterling and caught a glimpse of Roland, engulfed in flames. His bare body was visible beneath his cooking fur. His body was not human, but his howl of pain was recognizable as the man who had willingly come to aid me. I took a step toward him, preparing to flood my entire house to save him and the others who were in peril.

A large hand grabbed my left shoulder and spun me around. Jade, almost devoid of any human resemblance, stood before me. Her armor was glowing. The clothing underneath was smoldering. Her hill giant skin was ashy and filthy, but it withstood the heat. Her green eyes were hotter than the flames as they blazed at me.

"Sterling will handle the fire. We will hold the house," she bellowed over the cacophony. "End. That. Bitch."

I broke from my friend's grasp. It took two seconds for me to march through the bodies. By the time I stood less than an arm's length from the source of the misery and pain in my room, I had gained plenty of momentum.

I punched the pouty tart right in the mouth.

She made an odd yawping sound as she stumbled back two steps. Her lip split, and her blood drew a line down the center of her chin. I pressed in, swinging from my hips to add velocity to the follow-up punch. Miri's right eye began swelling the instant I drew my fist back from striking her.

Good and satisfying, but not enough. Not even close.

A roar of anger tore from my mouth as I landed another blow on her face and another. I spun as I delivered a back-handed punch to her temple with my right hand. I pulled one of my scythes from my belt with my left hand and sliced through Miri's right shoulder until the tip of the blade broke through the bone. She was pinned to my front door like a squirming fly.

But she was smiling.

The cut on her lip was already healed. Her swollen eye was returning to normal. Miri pushed back from my punctured door, inching the scythe blade deeper, but her expression showed no signs of discomfort or pain.

The damned amulet. It was healing her and feeding her brain pleasure to overcome the pain from the wound it couldn't heal until her body was free from my blade. The fragment against my neck was straining to break free from the chain, eager to touch its lost partners. I could see the two joined pieces pressing against the cloth of Miri's tunic. In my mind, I heard the trapped demon laughing. The bastard was having more fun now than he'd had in ages.

His distraction worked. When my focus cleared, Miri's hands were around my throat. Two of her hirelings, a pair of warrior fae, held my arms. The scythe I'd struck her with was shaking in my grip. One fae began putting pressure on my forearm and cut the flow of blood to my hand. A quick glance at my waist confirmed my suspicion that the other weapon had been taken from me. Neither full-blooded fae could have wielded my weapons without getting burned, but that wasn't their intent. They just wanted to disarm me.

This hadn't gone as planned. We thought we would have a tactical advantage, and that there would be no time for our enemies to treat their wounds. Miri was not physically strong or trained in combat. She had the wrong grip on my neck to choke me or lessen the flow of blood to my brain. But she was smiling, eyes wild and wide.

Blue energy leapt around my face. She was trying to cast a spell while her hands were on my throat. It amounted to little more than pretty lights. The amulet could not harm its maker. That didn't stop the demon inside from laughing harder. This was great sport to him. Miri's hate fed him, he gave her energy, she uselessly spent it trying to kill me, and that fed the demon all over again.

There was no way to gain a true advantage. My spells could only harm Miri's body, which the amulet would heal too quickly for the battle to turn in my favor. I didn't have enough power. Perhaps I could signal Sterling to cast a spell at the same time I did. Maybe that would provide enough power for me to get ahead of the partial amulet Miri wore.

Power, I suddenly realized. So much power. I knew what to do.

I released the scythe and croaked the needed words. A portal formed beneath Miri, her two fae warriors, and me. We fell together.

Aware of where we were traveling, I was prepared for the impact against the cold stone. I landed in a squat. Brimstone and sulfur filled my nostrils. Miri and her warriors looked quite confused as they scrambled to get upright. The tunnel we were in was carved out of stone, big enough for giants to shuttle through, and extremely hot.

The energy of Xantos's realm flooded through me, as though we were lovers who had been separated too long. Miri, who'd had little talent as a mage, likely felt a little tingle. The incomplete amulet glowed through the material over her torso. She and her guards stood.

I conjured pure fire that filled the passage we were in. The fire was as hot as the magma that flowed through the forge at the end of the tunnel beneath Xantos's manor.

Within seconds, the three beings were nothing but ash. The incomplete amulet fell with a clang into the soot that was once Miriria Lathos. I smiled fiercely at the remains.

As the amulet fell, Xantos appeared before me. His face and body language suggested he was not pleased. His scowl made me want to giggle. Instead, I smiled widely.

"You have made a mess." He stated the obvious in a droll tone. "In addition to entering my domain without my invitation or my permission."

I snorted and rolled my eyes.

"I needed to come to where I could use, to full advantage, the raw power this realm freely gives me," I explained, stepping closer to him. "Would you have preferred it if I had done this in your office?"

"No. Nor would we have had the opportunity for civilized conversation afterwards. I would have reacted to the invasion, not caring who was among the casualties."

"Oh, such sweet talk," I purred. "I would have believed you were threatening me, once upon a time."

I stopped where the two joined pieces had landed. My fragment, still hanging tightly from my neck, quivered and sang. The remaining pieces flew from the stone floor and joined the holdout.

The amulet was complete. The demon sighed with pleasure. My body tingled with renewed focus and control. Xantos's gaze narrowed.

"So, as suspected, the amulet will only be at full potential if you possess it," he said. His smirk was the sole indication of his approval. "I shall leave you to it. More promising interests await me."

"Not for much longer," I said. He raised an eyebrow.

"Don't take your eyes off my realm for long, Xantos," I warned. "It may become a great deal more interesting to you."

Xantos nodded a single time in acknowledgement. "Until the Lady returns."

I smiled. He might have had an inkling of what was coming.

Chapter Twenty-Nine

oments later, I stepped through my portal. Upon returning to my living room, or what had been my living room, I paused to take in the damage and casualties.

Every piece of furniture had been trashed. Standing lamps lay in pieces, but the overhead lights had survived the scuffle. Scorch marks trailed along my floor and walls. Blood, most of it red and drying, was splattered everywhere. Thankfully, none of my colleagues were among the corpses. Only Sterling seemed to have come out of the fight unharmed. Why was I not surprised?

He was tending Jade's wounds. Trix was sitting between Roland and Shyrrik, fussing over their bloody bandages. Alesio paced back and forth, holding a snifter of my best cognac. My guards stood or squatted by the windows. They were still doing their jobs, bless them. Sterling noticed me first.

"Oh, good, you're back. Ahndray won't stop knocking on the closet door to be let out," Sterling reported in a casual voice. His eyes were twinkling, and the smallest smile pulled at his lips. "Is there anything to clean up at Xantos's place?"

"Someone there has to have a broom," I replied. "If not, he can bill me for the maid service."

I walked into my kitchen and opened the door to the small pantry. My table promptly trotted out and stopped at the entryway to the living room. While I Magickally summoned a tea service, brandy, cognac, whiskey, and glasses, I thanked the gods that I had been sensible enough to move Ahndray before the confrontation. I could replace the other furniture, but not him.

Sufficiently supplied, Ahndray walked into the living room to offer refreshments. Sterling intercepted me at the entryway.

"You appear to have suffered no ill effects from the trip," he observed. "Even with the difference in time flow, you were only gone for a short while. Did you drop them off for Xantos to finish?"

As I explained, a touch of smugness crept into my voice. I did try to clamp down on it. I failed, but I tried.

"I vaporized them, the amulet pieces joined together, and I came back."

For a moment, Sterling looked unhappy with my explanation, then he smiled.

"I wish I could have seen Xantos's face when you left."

I returned the smile. "It was as priceless as you're imagining. Remind me to tell you about it when we run out of things to do together."

"I can wait that long," Sterling assured me. Then, he embraced me. Not too forcefully, but none too gently either. "Have you thought about what you'd like to name our child?"

"I have, but I'm not telling you," I teased.

Sterling laughed and led me into the living room.

Jade looked up the moment we entered the room. Roland was only a few seconds behind her. Alesio stopped his pacing.

"Long live the Lady of Death," Trix said, a wicked smile curling her lips. "I see the demon's content now that the talisman has returned to its proper owner."

Reaching up, I lifted the talisman from my chest, allowing it to gleam in the light. "He is, indeed," I murmured before tucking it under my shirt.

Arylla trilled and flew to me from wherever she'd been perched. Landing on my shoulder, she nuzzled my face before draping around my neck.

Everyone in the room was watching me as I scratched her under her chin.

"Sterling," I said. "Please arrange for me to be the Speaker."

"You're sure?" Jade asked, a sly twinkle in her eyes.

"Oh, yes," I replied, taking a glass from Ahndray. Lifting my glass in salute, I added, "To a new era."

Sterling didn't groan. Instead, he chuckled as he wrapped an arm around my waist. In the other hand, he held a glass that he clinked against mine. Everyone else raised their glasses before taking a drink. No one was surprised at my announcement, and they all wore pleased expressions.

Long live the Lady, indeed.

About the Author

Wife and a mother of five, J.F. Posthumus is an IT Tech with over a decade of experience. When she isn't arguing with computers and their inherent gremlins, or being mom to the four younger monsters (the eldest has flown the nest and is doing quite well on his own), she's crafting, writing, or doing some other sort of art. An avid gamer, she loves playing Dungeons & Dragons, and a variety of other board games with her family and friends. She's also a hopeless romantic, thanks to all the fairy tales she cut her eyeteeth on—they were what J.F. Posthumus learned to read before she discovered the Boxcar Children Mysteries. From there, she fell into the rabbit hole that's reading, where she discovered a love for mysteries, fantasy, and the occasional romance. Since writing was her favorite subject, she naturally incorporated her love of murder, mysteries, and fantasy into her works.

When she came up with the idea of a body being found at a local building, it was only natural to create a necromancer for the job. From there, Catherine's story unfolded, complete with monsters, magic, and a little bit of romance.